For my wonderful dog, Jess, who keeps me company when I write.

They act as though I'm no one, as though I don't even exist.

That's about to change.

I'll make them regret it.

But first I'll make them suffer.

CHAPTER ONE

I tilt my head to listen. Hold my breath. I'm sure I heard an odd sound coming from downstairs. But all is quiet. I'm in the house alone. Or at least I thought I was...

Leaving my bedroom, I pause on the landing, listening... Silence. And then, again, that same irregular sound making the hairs on the back of my neck stand up. Until I realise what it is... the scrape of claws on wood, followed by a low yowl.

'Frank! What are you doing?' I pull my old dressing gown around me and clatter down the creaky cottage stairs, hoping my ginger tomcat hasn't brought a mouse or a rabbit home. I really am not in the mood to deal with a dead rodent. And I'm even less in the mood to deal with a *half*-dead one. Blood and guts are not my forte, especially first thing in the morning.

In the kitchen, Frank is crouched by the back door, glaring down at the floor, his white-socked paw swiping at something, claws extending and retracting. He barely acknowledges me.

'What is it, Frank?'

With a certain amount of relief, I realise there's nothing untoward lying around the kitchen. Well, nothing that I can see so far. So what is it that has got my mischievous cat so worked up? I walk over to him and see that it's a piece of old paper sticking out of one of the floorboards. Frank gazes up at me and miaows, his green eyes softening for a moment. I scratch his head and stare at the triangle of paper, rising up like a shark's fin. Frank makes a sound deep in his throat and bashes at the paper with his paw once again. What is it, and how did it get there?

Intrigued, I tug it out with my fingers, dislodging a cloud of dust. The paper is thick and brittle with age. I realise it's actually a small envelope. From the look of it, it seems years old. I brush away some of the dust and see that the envelope is unopened. Still sealed. My curiosity piqued, I wonder what's inside. I turn it over and blink at the name written on the front in blue cursive script:

Lizzy Beresford

The letter is addressed to *me*! How strange…

Could it be from my boyfriend, Joe? Perhaps he wrote it months ago and it accidentally fell through a gap in the floorboards. But then how did it work its way up again? Could Frank have somehow got his paw down there and pulled it up? No, the gap is too narrow.

I stare at my name for a moment, at the blue swirling letters. Finally, I ease the envelope open and peer inside. I pull out a single sheet of faded writing paper folded in half. Straightening out the sheet, I stare at the words – there are only a few – which have been penned in the same unfamiliar handwriting:

Dearest Lizzy,
You're my only obsession

Weird. Is this some kind of love letter? Whatever it is, it has me spooked. And then I see something that troubles me further – in the top right-hand corner of the letter, someone has written the date:

26th July

That's… Yes. That's *today's* date. How can that be possible? The envelope looks as though it's been unopened for years, or at the very least months. Maybe it's just a coincidence. After all, there's no year written. But what are the odds of discovering a letter from the past on the exact same date that it was written? I grow hot. And then I shiver.

This is crazy. There must be a logical explanation. The back door has no letterbox, so it can't have been posted through. Either the letter worked its own way up through the floorboards, or... did someone come into the house and deliberately leave the note there? I drop the letter and jump to my feet, my heart thumping uncomfortably as the paper floats to the floor. Could someone have broken in this morning, or last night? Why would they do that? Do I have some creepy secret admirer? I glance out of the window. And try the back door – it's locked.

I wonder again if the letter could be from Joe. It's the least horrible explanation. But that doesn't explain the age of the envelope, or why Joe would tell me I'm his obsession. He's never said anything like that to me before. Maybe it's a practical joke. But it's not funny, and it's not Joe's style. He's a straightforward guy – flowers and chocolates on Valentine's Day, a card and a pressie on my birthday. Joe has never written me a letter or a note in his life – he hardly even uses texts. And besides, this is nothing like his messy writing. It's way too neat and beautiful.

I snatch up the letter and stuff it back into the envelope. Unsure what to do with it, I slide it into the side pocket of my handbag for now.

Checking the time on my phone, I realise I only have fifteen minutes before I need to leave for work. I suppose I should have some breakfast, but my hunger has evaporated, my head is buzzing, my hands trembling. Besides, I'm not even dressed yet. I always like to give myself plenty of time to get ready before work. Can't stand it when I have to rush around. Joe leaves for the garage at seven thirty, so I usually have a whole hour to myself. My quiet time. But now I'm going to have to hurry.

I run back upstairs. With my heart still pounding, I get dressed on autopilot, shrugging on a blue and white wrap dress, picking out a necklace and slipping on a pair of kitten-heel sandals. I'm lucky to own such nice clothes. One of the perks of being the manager of Georgio's – Malmesbury's most upmarket clothes and gift shop – is that I get a decent staff discount. But as I'm getting ready I can't seem to distract myself, all I can think about is that letter. Someone obviously put it there deliberately for me to find. Why would they do that?

I check myself in the wardrobe mirror; the dress suits my curvy figure, the china-blue pattern bringing out the blue of my eyes. I grab a hair tie from the dressing-table drawer and sweep up my thick, chestnut hair into a ponytail. That will have to do.

I make my way back downstairs and into the kitchen where Frank is walking around, his ears flat, tail twitching back and forth. He obviously feels as unsettled as I do. With my phone on speaker, I call Joe while spooning cat food into Frank's dish. As expected, my call goes straight to voicemail, so I leave a message:

'Hey, it's me. I found a weird letter at home. It's not from you, is it? It doesn't look like your writing, but I can't think who else could have put it there. Call me back when you get this. Love you.'

But I already know the letter isn't from Joe. Was it written by a secret admirer, or is someone playing a twisted kind of game, trying to get my attention? I don't know. But I can't shake the feeling that this is something far more sinister…

CHAPTER TWO

At Georgio's, Pippa and I are kneeling on the floor, a small electric fan angled towards us, redistributing hot, stale air as we unpack box after box of designer handbags. Her eyes are wide as I tell her about my strange and unsettling morning discovering the letter.

'Ooh, darling,' Pippa says in her plummy drawl. 'Sounds like some freak's got a giant-sized crush on you.'

Pippa Hargreaves is the poshest person I know. She lives locally in a crumbling stately home with her brother and parents who are an actual lord and lady – but extremely broke. I suspect her connection with all the royals in the area is why our boss, George, hired her to work at Georgio's because Pippa pulls in the wealthy customers – the hunting, shooting and fishing crowd, most of whom she went to school with. Her parents were only able to afford the exorbitant education fees by selling off land from their estate.

'Maybe it's a love letter from a customer,' she continues.

'Do you think so?' It's all I've been thinking about this morning – who could possibly have left me that letter?

'Could be,' Pippa says, pulling out a navy Radley handbag, sliding the strap over her shoulder and walking over to the mirror. 'What do you think?' she calls over, pouting at her reflection. She's attractive in a horsey way, with slightly protruding front teeth. But her skin is clear and her hair is shiny and blonde.

'Looks good,' I reply, thinking that for someone who claims to be broke, she has an awful lot of handbags.

'Hmm, it does, doesn't it,' Pippa muses, gazing at her reflection, turning this way and that. 'I might put it out the back and have a think about buying it.'

Pippa and I met at a local modern dance class when we were about ten years old. We always got on well, but never really socialised outside of dance events due to our vastly different backgrounds. Then, after leaving school, we were always bumping into one another at local parties, pubs and bars, and we became sort of friends – the overlapping part of a social Venn diagram.

'What about George?' Pippa calls from the stockroom.

'What about him?'

'You know,' she says, returning and kneeling down next to me. 'Our dear, darling boss, George. He's your landlord, too, isn't he? So he's got a key. Could have been him who left the letter.'

'George?' I straighten up, thinking about it. 'No. No way. And anyway, he's old enough to be my dad. He's married with kids.'

'Since when has that stopped anyone?' she drawls.

'Stopped anyone what?'

'Being a stalker?' She laughs.

'It's not funny, Pip. It's creepy.'

'What about Leon? We already know he definitely fancies you.'

She's talking about Leon Whittaker, who owns the wine bar up the road. 'Well, I hope it's not Leon,' I reply, 'because if it is, then that means he's asking for trouble.'

'True. Forget that. On second thoughts, there's no way it's Leon.'

I'm transported to last Christmas Eve when Leon Whittaker started chatting me up. Joe got angry with him for paying me so much attention when it was clear I was there with him, but Leon was cocky and refused to apologise. Punches were thrown, and Joe ended up knocking Leon unconscious. Joe was arrested. He pleaded guilty in court and received a fine and a twenty-six-week prison sentence, suspended for eighteen months. But we went through a few really stressful months, not knowing if he would end up behind bars. I wish I could forget the whole terrible episode.

I shake my head, trying to dislodge the memories. 'Seriously though, Pippa, it's weird, right? The letter sticking out of the floorboards.' I hand her the pricing gun but instead of actually using it, she lays it down on her lap.

'It is a bit spooky, darling,' she agrees. 'But maybe it really is just an innocent love letter and someone went a bit over the top on the delivery method.'

'I'm going to check my phone' – I get to my feet – 'see if Joe's got my message yet. Can you finish pricing the purses?'

'I would but it looks like Fenella and Co. are coming in.'

I glance over to the entrance, where I see a gaggle of Pippa's old school friends on the pavement pointing at the window display. 'Okay, Pip. Put the pricing on hold. You're up. Make sure you bankrupt the lot of them.'

Pippa smirks and stands up, passing the price gun back to me and taking a deep breath. 'Consider it done.'

I know it's hard for Pippa. Her family used to be one of the wealthiest around, and now she can no longer afford to socialise with all her old friends. But she never complains about it. Just shrugs her shoulders and says that's life. Stiff upper lip and all that. It's not an uncommon situation for the British nobility to find themselves in. I should imagine the cost of running such enormous estates runs into thousands of pounds per month these days. The Manor House has been in Pippa's family for centuries and so it's hard for them to even consider selling.

By contrast, I was brought up locally by middle-class parents who had a mortgage on a perfectly respectable three-bedroom semi-detached house. I went to the local comprehensive school and would no more expect to be invited to Prince Charles and Camilla's for tea than I would expect to fly to the moon. So, Pippa and I live on different social planets, but we've always got on well. And, considering she's part of the nobility, she doesn't seem to have a problem taking orders from me, her manager. I guess she's… grounded.

'Pippa, sweetie!' Fenella Sherston-Moore sweeps into Georgio's followed by three of her equally privileged friends. They greet one another in a shower of exclamations and air kisses.

I retreat into the back room to check my phone. There's a text from Joe:

Got your message. What's the note about? Meet at The Crown for lunch at one?

My heart rate quickens. So, the note wasn't from Joe, then. I already guessed it wasn't, but now that I know for sure, it's made me doubly anxious. I tap out a quick reply:

Really busy so might be a bit late. Order me a cheese sarnie xx

I walk back out onto the shop floor feeling strange, like everything has shifted a little to the left. Someone – not Joe – left me an unsettling letter in my home. My mind is all over the place. Should I be worried?

Pippa walks past me with armfuls of clothes. Fenella and her friends haven't bothered to draw the fitting-room curtains; instead, they're stripping off in full view of the other customers with an enviable lack of self-consciousness. They stand in their Agent Provocateur underwear, tossing their hair and talking about Saturday's polo match while Pippa hands them item after item, suggesting matching jewellery, belts and bags. George is going to be over the moon with today's sales figures. I give Pippa an encouraging smile.

Somehow, for the rest of the morning, I manage to pull myself together enough to deal with the invoices that have become due. But my mind isn't on my work. It's on the letter and who could be behind it.

After a busy morning, I manage to slip away to meet Joe for lunch, leaving Pippa in charge of the shop. I walk quickly down the High Street, weaving between clusters of tourists who are blocking the narrow pavement, hovering outside restaurants and bars, checking out the menus on the wall. Or who, like me, are simply nipping out for a lunch break. The sun lasers down on my head and I'm looking forward to sitting down with a nice cold drink.

Malmesbury, our pretty market town, is situated in Wiltshire on the edge of the Cotswolds – the largest Area of Outstanding Natural Beauty in England, with its sweeping meadows, rolling hills, quaint cottages and stately homes. The Prince of Wales' Highgrove Estate is just up the road in Tetbury, and there are more than a few movie stars, models and musicians living in the area. We also get a lot of customers who live most of the year in London but have their second homes here. They love bringing their friends down for the weekend, spending their money in the local delis, boutiques and clothes and gift shops like Georgio's.

Finally, halfway down the street, I arrive at The Crown, a Cotswold-stone-fronted seventeenth-century pub where Joe and I sometimes meet for lunch. I push open the wooden door to the lounge bar. Thankfully, it's cooler in here. Joe is already sitting in our favourite spot by the window, his blond waves catching the light, making him look like a saint from a religious painting. He waves me over and I'm happy to see that my lunch has already arrived. He stands and we kiss.

'Got you a sandwich and a Sprite,' he says gruffly.

'Thanks.' I sit opposite him and stretch out my legs under the table.

'What was that message you left about a letter?' he asks through a mouthful of steak and ale pie.

I start filling him in on the details, telling him about the letter addressed to me with today's date on it.

Joe shakes his head slowly and lays his knife and fork down. 'Wow, Lizzy. That's weird. Are you okay?'

I nod, but his concern makes me wobbly. 'Someone must have been inside our house last night,' I say.

'I don't know about that. How would they have got in without us hearing something? Did you check for signs of a break-in?'

'I didn't notice any broken windows. And both doors were locked.' I take a sip of my drink. 'Did you notice anything weird in the kitchen this morning, before you left? Was Frank in there scratching at the floor?'

'You know what I'm like first thing. I just get up, get dressed and leave the house. Don't even have a cup of tea till I get to work.'

'So you definitely didn't go in the kitchen?'

'Nope. I was straight down the stairs and out the door, like always.'

I sigh. 'That's what I was afraid of. So the letter could just as easily have been put there sometime last night.'

'You really think someone broke in and put it there?'

'I don't know. It's odd. And the envelope… it looks really old. Here, see for yourself.' I reach for my handbag, pull out the envelope and pass it across the table.

Joe takes it from me in his oil-stained fingers and frowns at my name written on the thick envelope. He pulls out the sheet of paper, his frown deepening. 'This is today's date, right?'

'Yeah, the twenty-sixth. So what do you think I should do?'

Joe turns the envelope over in his hands once more, staring at it. 'I'll change the locks when I get home, okay?'

'Yeah, I think that would be good.'

With a disconcerting lack of concern, he takes another mouthful of pie.

'Joe, someone's broken into our house. I thought you'd be more worried about it.'

'I am worried, Lizzy. I'm just getting my head round it, that's all. Don't stress, it'll be okay.' His expression softens. 'Like I said, I'll change the locks.' He hands me back the letter and the envelope.

'Maybe we should tell the police?' I suggest.

'I dunno, Lizzy. It's just… after all that business last year, I'd rather not get the police involved if we don't have to.'

With a suspended sentence for the Leon Whittaker debacle, Joe has to be as good as gold for almost a year or he could find himself serving actual prison time. And while this letter thing is obviously nothing to do with Joe, the thought of the police being involved is naturally making him jittery.

'Of course,' I say. 'Yeah, of course, we'll leave the police out of it.'

'Thanks, Lizzy.' Joe reaches across and puts his hand over mine.

'I did have another thought…'

Joe raises his eyebrows questioningly.

'What about…' I begin hesitantly. 'What about *Emma*?'

Joe scowls and takes a deep breath in through his nose.

I plough on. 'Think about it. My sister's the only person I've ever truly fallen out with—'

'You haven't spoken to her for years.' Joe takes a swig of his drink. 'Why would she do something like that *now*?'

'Dunno. I'm just throwing out ideas.'

'It's more likely to be George,' Joe says. I can tell he's changing the subject. I guess I can't blame him – Emma's not exactly his favourite topic of conversation.

'Pippa said the same thing. But come on, you can't seriously think George would do something like that?'

'He doesn't seem the type, but then again he's the only other person with a key. Maybe I should have a word with him.' Joe rubs his chin, his eyes narrowing.

'No. Joe. *No*. You won't, will you?' I'm scared he'll wade in with his fists again and regret it later. 'George is my boss. I can't have you accusing him of all sorts.'

'Just because he's your boss doesn't give him the right to harass you.'

'He's not harassing me! We don't even know if it's him. It's not him. Don't say anything. I don't want to lose my job. I love my job.'

'Calm down. I won't speak to him if you don't want me to. But once we've changed the locks we're not going to tell him what we've done, okay?'

'It's George's house. We've got to let him know. I don't think we're allowed to just change the locks and…'

'The whole point is *not* to tell George. Completely defies the object if we tell him what we're doing. Anyway, if I catch him or anyone else sneaking into our place, I'll beat the crap out of them.'

'No you won't. You'll call the police.'

'I'll beat the crap out of them, then I'll call the police.' He grins to let me know he's joking. But I know what he can be like. He acts first and pays the consequences later.

'Well then, it will be you going to jail, not them,' I say, glaring at him. 'You don't really think George wrote that note, do you?'

Joe shakes his head. 'Dunno, Lizzy. But like you said, it's weird.'

I nod, realising I haven't touched my sandwich. But I'm no longer hungry; the strangeness of the morning is finally catching up with me as I wonder what on earth is going on. Has someone actually been in our house? And if so, will they try it again?

CHAPTER THREE

After a relatively quiet afternoon at work, I begin cashing up. Pippa's friends' spending spree this morning means we've already reached our monthly target, and there's still almost a week to go until the end of the month. Normally I'd call George with the good news, but I'm reluctant to speak to him today. The more I think about it, the more I see that, logically, he's the only other person with access to our cottage. But it doesn't fit. Yes, he can be a bit touchy-feely, but not in a creepy way. He's never made a pass at me and he's always talking about how wonderful his wife Sophia is. I'm sure the letter has nothing to do with George, so why am I scared to call him?

'Hello, Lizzy.'

I look up from the till receipts to see Pippa's brother Seb hovering over me like a stooped giant, his checked shirt tucked half-in, half-out of his shorts.

'Hi, Seb. Pippa's just getting her coat. She'll be out in a mo.'

'Uh, okay. I'm, uh—'

'Coming, Sebbie!' Pippa calls from the stockroom.

He shifts awkwardly from foot to foot. 'Hope she's quick. Had to leave the Land Rover parked on double yellows out there.'

'Have you had a good day?' I ask.

'Yes, yes, thanks. You?'

For a moment I think about mentioning the letter, but I hardly know Seb. I only ever see him when he comes to pick Pippa up, and he's always quiet around me. The polar opposite of his sister. 'It's been busy,' I reply.

'That's good, right?'

'It is.' I smile.

Pippa finally emerges from the stockroom in a cloud of perfume.

'Is that the new jasmine tester?' I ask.

'Yes,' Pippa admits. 'I had a quick spray. Hope you don't mind. Divine, isn't it?' She takes her brother's arm. 'Sebbie, can you drop me at Whittaker's? I'm meeting Fenella for drinks.'

'Pip, Mum's expecting you. We've got the—'

'Pleeease?'

'Fine.' Seb stuffs his hands in his pockets and gazes down at his shoes before letting his sister lead him out of the shop.

'See you tomorrow, Pippa,' I call after her, sliding today's receipts and cash into an envelope for George. He'll stop by the shop to pick it up later.

'Bye, sweetie!' Pippa calls back.

The door closes with a rattle and I walk across the shop floor to lock it behind them. It's a beautiful evening and there are still quite a few people out and about. If Georgio's were my shop, I'd stay open to make the most of the foot traffic, but it's not mine and my wages aren't enough to warrant the free overtime. Still, the thought of going home is making me uneasy. I switch off the shop lights one by one and retrieve my bag from the stockroom. As I slide the strap over my shoulder, I think of the offending letter in the side pocket. Is it something I should be seriously worried about? Hopefully it's simply an odd, one-off incident that I'll have forgotten about in a few weeks' time.

I set the alarm and leave work via the side door, the smell of car engines and hot tarmac hitting my nostrils in a not altogether unpleasant way. Turning right out of the shop, I head up the High Street, my mind straying towards thoughts of what to have for dinner tonight. I should probably turn back towards the supermarket, but I'm suddenly tired and just want to get home. I'm sure I can cobble something together from whatever's in the fridge, and if I can't, I'll ask Joe to pick something up later.

I cross over the road and pass by the familiar grey limestone of the Market Cross, its elaborate arches and pillars casting complicated shadows across the paving slabs. Seated inside, on its circular bench, a man is on his mobile phone, swearing at someone about something they did last night. I hurry on by, up the curvy lane with its too-narrow pavement, past the rows of pretty stone houses towards the Abbey. Even on the shaded side of the street, it's warm. The air thick with a sticky heat that clings to my skin and pulses at my temples.

Leaving the busy High Street behind, the sound of my clicking heels grows louder, echoing in the newly minted stillness. I've walked this route hundreds of times, but this evening the silence is suddenly oppressive and a little threatening. Rounding the bend, I turn into the Abbey grounds, giving a little start as something brushes my bare arm. But it's just a stray leaf from a horse chestnut tree, its branches dipping low over the gate.

The Abbey graveyard is empty and quiet, too early for a service, too early even for birdsong. Just the steady click of my heels and the sound of my own breathing. This is silly. I've nothing to worry about. A scuff of gravel behind me makes me whip my head round, but there's no one there. No one that I can see, anyway. I pick up my pace and wonder about doubling back, going home the long way round rather than cutting through the Abbey gardens. But this way only takes five minutes; the road way takes twenty-five. I'll be fine.

I square my shoulders and take a deep breath. This is the route I always take and I'm not going to let that stupid letter put the fear of God into me. Nevertheless, as I walk, I reach into my handbag and take out the big bunch of shop keys, holding them so that they spill through the gaps in my fist like a weapon. If anyone *is* following me and tries anything on, I'll ram the keys into their face and make a run for it.

And now I hear them – definite footsteps behind me. But this is a public footpath, people walk this way all the time. Footsteps don't necessarily mean anything sinister. So why are my heartbeats reverberating through my body? Why has sweat begun to prickle at my pores? I lengthen my strides, too scared to turn around and look. Instead, I just keep walking, the thrum of blood in my ears drowning out the sound of footsteps – theirs and mine. Here, the path veers away from the graveyard and narrows with high hedgerows on either side, a couple of Abbey buildings looming ahead. Is someone coming up behind me? I break into a hobbling run, almost sobbing now.

Laughter. I hear laughter up ahead. Wiping away a frightened tear, I see a group of teenagers heading my way. Young lads, laughing, shouting, clutching four-packs of cheap beer. I exhale, thankful for their appearance. They pay me no attention as I walk by, and I risk a fleeting look over my shoulder, but apart from the teens, there is no one else there. The pathway behind me is empty. It must have been my imagination. This letter business must have unsettled me more than I thought.

As I speed-walk down the rest of the lane, my breathing is still shallow, my pulse is still racing. I cross the small stone bridge, which spans a narrow section of the River Avon, until I finally emerge out onto the public highway once more, the distant sound of sparse early-evening traffic filling me with relief. I'm such an idiot, letting myself get spooked like that. I walk through the out-of-town public car park and then, two minutes later, I finally turn into Richmond Gardens. It's a grander sounding road than it really is. In reality, it's a dead-end lane, home to a pretty row of Cotswold stone cottages. Ours sits in the middle of a terrace of three. And I've never been so relieved to reach home.

Joe's nine-year-old BMW is parked out front next to my Polo. The shop keys in my fist have dug into my palm leaving painful red marks. I drop them back into my handbag and take out my house keys instead, but there's no need because as I go to put the key in the lock, Joe opens the front door, a scowl on his face. He's already changed out of his work clothes and his hair is damp from the shower.

I smile, but his scowl remains and I'm confused by his hostile expression. 'Hi,' I say tentatively.

Instead of replying and leaning in for a kiss, he steps back to let me into the cramped hallway, a waft of shower gel and deodorant following me through to the kitchen, where Frank miaows and winds himself around my legs. I reach down to scratch behind his ears, trying to work out what's got Joe so moody.

'How was your afternoon?' I ask.

'Okay,' he grunts, coming into the kitchen and standing there like a spare part.

'Something the matter?' I set my bag and keys on the counter before picking Frank up and burying my nose in his fur, taking comfort in his purring warmth.

Joe doesn't reply.

'It's hot in here.' I walk over to the sink and turn on the tap and let it run. After a brief moment, I wash my hands and splash my face, the cool liquid a balm on my hot skin. I pour myself a glass of water and turn around.

'I've been thinking about that letter,' Joe says, leaning against the counter top.

'What about it?' I drain half the glass and start to feel more normal, cooler and less panicky.

'It's obviously like… a love letter or something.'

I stare at Joe, trying to work out just what it is he's getting at. 'A love letter? I wouldn't have said that. For starters, it's creepier than a love letter.' I set my glass on the draining board and unlock the back door, opening it wide in the hope of letting a breeze into the house. But the air is still. Warm as ever.

'It's just…'

'What?'

'It's just, if you weren't so flirty with everyone, this type of thing, well… it probably wouldn't happen.'

I set Frank down on the floor and turn back to my boyfriend, whose face is now flaming red in what I'd like to hope is shame for insinuating what I think he's insinuating.

'*This type of thing*?' I repeat. 'What type of thing is that, Joe?' Joe has always been quite an insecure and jealous boyfriend, and I often find myself having to reassure him that he has nothing to worry about in terms of my fidelity. His last girlfriend cheated on him and I still think he can't quite bring himself to trust me completely. But we've been together for years, and I've never once given him cause to doubt me. So this accusation is a low blow and is completely unfounded.

'Sorry.' He rubs the back of his head.

'No, what type of thing, Joe?' I can feel my blood pressure rising. I can't quite believe that my boyfriend is trying to blame some creepy stalker's note on my own innocent behaviour.

'I didn't want to bring it up,' he says. 'It's just, well, I was telling the lads at work about the letter, and Brycie mentioned that you're always really friendly with everyone. And the thing is, Lizzy, if you're too friendly with your customers, well, it might have given some lad with a crush the wrong idea.'

I realise my mouth is wide open so I snap it shut. My heart is beating out of my chest, not from fear any more, but from anger that is gradually morphing into a white-hot rage. 'Oh, well, if Brycie and the lads at the garage said that, then it must be true. I mean, how dare I actually be friendly towards people. Maybe I should walk around glaring at everyone. Would that be better?'

Joe's shoulders drop. 'You know what I mean, Lizzy.'

'Do I? Do I, though? Maybe you should show me the exact expression I need to wear on my face to ensure that I don't attract a stalker. Can you do that for me? Can you show me now?' I shake my head and resist the urge to lob my glass at his head.

'All right, Lizzy, I'm only trying to help!'

'Ah, but you see, you're not trying to help. You're picking a fight. You've been gossiping with the lads at work about me and they've decided that it's all my fault. That I'm too smiley or some such shite. Honestly, Joe, I can't believe you're taking advice from Terry knobhead Bryce. He's an idiot. And so are you for listening to him.' I barge past Joe, out into the hall and up the stairs, tears of anger pricking behind my eyes.

'Lizzy!' he calls after me. 'Lizzy, I'm sorry!'

I march into the bedroom and try to slam the door, but my dressing gown – hanging from a hook on the back of the door – swings into the gap and prevents the door from closing properly, so I'm denied even that small satisfaction.

How dare Joe accuse me of bringing this on myself? I thought I'd be able to come home to a bit of support, and instead I'm faced with ridiculous sexist paranoid accusations.

Seconds later the door flies open. 'I'm an idiot, Lizzy. I'm sorry.' Joe hangs his head and comes and sits by me on the bed.

'Yes, you are,' I say through tight lips.

'I shouldn't have listened to the lads. They don't know what they're talking about. I'm just worried about you, that's all.'

'Funny way of showing it.' I cross my arms over my chest.

'I couldn't get the words of that letter out of my head,' he says. 'The fact that someone else is obsessed with you, it's made me crazy.'

'And how do you think it makes *me* feel!' I cry. 'When I was walking home, I was convinced someone was following me. It was terrifying. And then I come home to some Godzilla macho boyfriend trying to blame me for someone else's weirdness.'

'I know, I know. I'm sorry. It's because I'm worried about you.' He sits up straighter and his eyes narrow. 'Wait, was there actually someone following you?'

I shake my head. 'Probably not. Just me being paranoid. Thought I heard footsteps behind me, but when I turned round there was no one there.'

'You didn't walk through the Abbey gardens, did you?'

'It's fine. I always—'

'It's not fine. Don't walk through there again. It's too dangerous. Too deserted.'

'Fine.'

'And I really am sorry…' He hangs his head. 'About before.'

'Okay,' I say, without really meaning it. I'm still mad at him.

'Let me make it up to you.' Joe leans in to kiss me. But I don't return the kiss with any enthusiasm, so he tries harder, letting his hand ride up under my dress. 'What can I do?' he murmurs. 'To make it up to you?' He thinks he can win me round with sex, but he's wrong.

I get to my feet and face him. 'If you want to make it up to me, you can go and get some shopping. We've got absolutely no food in the house.'

His face falls. 'I've just got in from work.'

'And where have *I* been all day? At the spa?'

'Fine.' His shoulders sag. 'Can you do me a list of stuff, then?'

I sigh. 'Sure.'

Ten minutes later, Joe huffs out of the house with a shopping list and I collapse onto the sofa with a glass of wine, wishing I could erase today. Wishing my boyfriend was a little more sensitive. Wishing that whoever wrote that note, hadn't.

CHAPTER FOUR

In a rare moment of quiet, I busy myself with rearranging and restocking the jewellery displays, pinning some new silver necklaces and bracelets to the rectangular black felt boards that hang on the walls. It's a satisfying, creative task that also helps me become familiar with the new stock. It's been another busy day at Georgio's. More deliveries and lots of wealthy tourists popping in to buy expensive souvenirs and summer outfits.

I'm grateful we've been busy as it's taken my mind off the note, and off Joe's ridiculous behaviour yesterday. After our row, he was super-apologetic. He went grocery shopping without too much of a fuss, so I decided to forgive him. Hopefully we can put the whole weird episode behind us. I can't wait to get home, put on some summery tunes, crack open a bottle of wine and chill in the garden with him this evening.

'Do you mind if I slip off early today?' I turn to see Pippa standing behind me with a hopeful expression on her face.

'Is this anything to do with the man you met last night?' I ask with a smile, pinning a silver necklace onto one of the fabric boards.

Pippa laughs. 'He just sent me a text. Asked if I wanted to go out this evening. But look at me, I'm a sweaty, hideous mess.'

This is a total exaggeration. Pippa has never looked sweaty or hideous in her life.

'I need to go home and beautify myself, so I was hoping you'd let me go early?'

I glance at my watch. It's only four twenty. Still over an hour until closing time. 'Can you bear to stay till five o'clock?' I ask. 'Just in case it gets busy again.'

'Yes, sure,' she replies. 'I'll text Seb, tell him to fetch me in half an hour.'

'Perfect,' I reply, thinking actually it isn't perfect. Five o'clock is in forty minutes, not half an hour, and we often have a mad rush of customers between five and five thirty – people who finish work at five and come to the shop on their way home. But, well, I can't begrudge Pippa. She doesn't go on many dates, and she seems so excited by this new man she met while she was out with Fenella.

'Thanks, Lizzy. You're a star. Appreciate it.'

'That's okay. If you could tidy up the clothes rails before you go, that would be great.'

'Absolutely!'

But rather than tidying up the rails, what Pippa actually does is to call her brother to pick her up, then proceed to spend the next ten minutes holding up various outfits against her body and asking me what I think. Seb appears in the shop at four forty.

'Afternoon, Lizzy,' he says, in a stiff, deep voice. He's lurking awkwardly beside me, a little too close, so I take a small step back.

'Hi, Seb.' I glance at my watch. 'You're a bit early. Pip's got another fifteen minutes.'

But Pippa rushes past me with her handbag and a bag of shopping. 'Sebbie! Thanks for this, Lizzy. You're an absolute darling.' She blows me a kiss and I take a breath, muttering something about taking the piss. But I don't say it loud enough for her to hear, and I'm not bossy enough to make her stay until five on the dot. I'm supposed to be her manager, but I guess I've always treated her more like a friend and equal than an employee. I'm good at managing the shop, but not so great at managing my one member of staff.

Sure enough, the minute she leaves Georgio's suddenly becomes the most popular place in Wiltshire. As well as the usual last-minute customers, we're graced with a coachload of Welsh sightseers and a couple of well-to-do ladies who need personal shopper-type assistance. Normally I love to help customers out with selecting outfits and accessories, but it's tricky when there's a queue of tourists almost out the door wanting to buy postcards and local fudge, and I'm flustered and irritated that I'm having to do all this on my own. 'Bloody Pippa,' I murmur. But I have no one to blame but myself. I should have told her she had to stay until five thirty.

Finally, at 5.35 p.m. the shop empties and I quickly bolt the door and turn the sign to 'Closed', heaving a sigh of relief that I managed to serve everyone without having a nervous breakdown. I always find in these situations it's best not to worry about how long the queue is, or how huffy the customers get; you just have to deal with one customer at a time and accept that you can't serve everyone at once. Easier said than done, though.

I make a start on the till receipts and see that it's been another exceptional day, although something is niggling me and I can't work out what it is. I scan the till roll again and then it hits me. A dress was sold from the window display this morning, but I can't see it listed here. It's not showing up on the roll and it's not been written down in the receipt book either. But the takings add up just fine. The only other explanation would be that the dress was stolen. But I remember the woman who tried it on, and I remember seeing her queue up to pay. Pippa served her while I was dealing with another customer. I must be mistaken. Only I don't think I am.

I put the receipts into an envelope and push away an unwelcome thought. Pippa wouldn't do anything like that, would she? I mean, I know she has money worries, but… No. I'm going to ignore this for now. It could just be that I'm tired and remembering things wrong. I'll take another look tomorrow.

Remembering that it's Mum's birthday on Sunday, I head over to the scarf display where there's a patterned silk scarf that I really can't afford, even with my staff discount. But I'm sure Mum will love it. I slide it off the spigot and run my thumb across the soft fabric. I know Mum won't show me any appreciation for the gift, but I take it into the stockroom anyway. I've already cashed up, so I'll buy it tomorrow. Every year I get her something beautiful for her birthday, and every year she acts like it would kill her to say thank you. Although if the scarf was from my sister, Mum would talk about what excellent taste she had, and how generous she was. It's always been this way – our screwed-up family dynamic – so I guess I'm used to it. But it still rankles. And I'm annoyed with myself for trying so hard to please her when I know it will end in my own disappointment.

The thought of our upcoming family lunch makes my insides clench. It's always a trial for Joe and me, and not only because of my mum's demanding nature. No; it's due to something far worse than that.

Five years ago, my elder sister Emma bumped into Joe in the pub while he was out with his mates. She was single at the time and she tried to kiss him. Joe didn't know whether to tell me or not, but in the end he came straight home and admitted what had happened. He said he didn't want us to have any secrets. He swore he didn't kiss Emma back. He told her that he would never cheat on me, especially not with my own sister. That night tore apart my relationship with my sibling, but cemented mine and Joe's.

I waited for Emma to ring me up and apologise, but she didn't. I gave her a week's grace, and after that time I went to visit her to confront her about it. I wanted her to give me an explanation that made sense. But then she had the cheek to suggest that it had been Joe who'd tried it on with *her*. I said if that was the case, then why did *he* come straight over and tell me what had happened while *she* stayed silent?

We had a massive row about it where she said that there was no point her trying to defend herself because she knew I would take Joe's side. She even had the nerve to call me disloyal. It was like talking to a stranger. I mean, our relationship has always been a bit rocky since we were teenagers – the usual arguments over clothes, boys, our parents' attention and all that sibling stuff – but nothing as bad as this. Nothing as bad as her trying to steal the love of my life. But then Emma is used to having everything her own way. I usually found it easier to give in to her. I've always been more laid-back, more easy-going. She's a high-maintenance type of girl. But I still loved her. She was my sister. I guess she still is. Although I'd rather she wasn't.

Emma is a total brainiac, a genius with a worthy career as a cancer research scientist. Plus she's slim and super-pretty, so goodness knows why she did it. She's always had plenty of attention without resorting to trying to steal my boyfriend. But Emma always had to be the best at everything. Maybe she was trying to prove to herself that she could have Joe if she wanted to. Or maybe she was just drunk and didn't know what she was doing. Either way, she should never have done it. And after it happened, she should bloody well have apologised. Even thinking about my sister these days sends my blood pressure skyrocketing. Seeing her on Sunday will be as painful as always. I wonder if she feels the same. If she feels any remorse for what she did.

I push my hair back out of my face and glance around, realising the shop is in a bit of a mess. I can't leave it like this for George to see when he comes in later to collect the day's takings. I'd better have a quick tidy-up. I make my way around the clothes rails, ensuring that all the garments are hanging straight and in the right order. Next I rearrange the gifts on the shelving units, getting rid of any gaps and bringing old stock to the front. My gaze lands on a discarded chocolate wrapper near the window. I march over to pick it up when I see a plain white envelope face down on the doormat. It wasn't there when I locked up a few minutes ago.

Thump, thump, thump, thump. My heartbeats are suddenly too loud. No need to panic; it could be anything. It will be junk mail, that's all. So why are my hands trembling? Why don't I want to pick the thing up? I could leave it there, pretend I haven't seen it. But then it would niggle at me all evening.

I glance out through the window. A middle-aged couple walk past; she's talking, he's nodding. A girl is looking in the window of the shoe shop opposite. A man darts diagonally across the road in this direction and then strides away up the street. No one is hanging around suspiciously or looking in at me. I snatch up the envelope and turn it over in my hand.

Thump, thump, thump, thump. Handwritten in that recognisable blue ink, my name is stark across the front of the pristine envelope. Someone has pushed this through the letterbox within the past ten minutes. I unbolt the shop door and pull it wide open, the jangle of the bell harsh, like a warning. I step out onto the pavement, a breeze cooling my warm cheeks. Still clutching the envelope, I whip my head back and forth, peering up and down the road in case I see… in case I see *who*? I don't know. A guilty man running away? Whoever it was will probably be long gone by now.

A grey-haired woman puffs up the street towards me, a harried smile on her face. 'Oh, great, you're still open. I thought I'd missed you.' I recognise her; it's the woman who works in the chemist.

'Sorry, we're closed,' I say.

Her face falls. 'Just need a birthday card. I'll be ever so quick.'

'I've already cashed up… Oh, go on then. I'll add it to tomorrow's totals.'

'Thank you, you're a life saver.' She pats me on the arm and follows me inside. I close the door behind us in case anyone else gets the same idea. True to her word, she quickly makes her selection and pays. 'Sorry about that,' she says. 'I know what it's like when you just want to go home and you get a straggler.'

'Don't worry about it,' I murmur, not really listening.

She finally leaves and I bolt the door behind her, realising I've had the envelope in my hand all this time. I stare at the front of it once more, at my name written on the thick white paper. Not aged this time, but white and new. In a daze, I open it, pull out a single sheet of paper. The paper looks similar to yesterday's letter – only this time, instead of an aged sheet, it's a brand new white rectangle of paper, unremarkable in its plainness. I unfold it and make myself read what's written:

Dearest Lizzy,
I love to watch you.

The words blur in front of my eyes, like I'm reading them from far away. The blood thrums in my ears and my fingers tingle. Okay, this is not good. This is definitely not good. Standing by the glass door, I feel exposed, vulnerable. Is the person who wrote this watching me now? I turn off the shop lights and take a step back, and then another until I'm standing in the dim interior. Perhaps whoever it is works in one of the shops opposite? Or maybe they live in a flat above one of the shops? Will this person make themselves known to me? What do they hope to get out of it? This is more than some admirer with a crush. These letters are not romantic. No. They're scary. They make me want to hide. To cry. This is stalker territory. They've been written by someone who gets off on doing this type of thing. And they've sent two of them now, which means they're not going to stop, are they? They'll write more, won't they?

Something suddenly dawns on me. Whether Joe likes it or not, I'm going to have to call the police. I'm going to have to call them right now.

CHAPTER FIVE

Our local police station isn't far away, so within minutes of making the call a marked police car pulls up outside the shop on double yellows. By this stage, I can't even bear to touch the letter and it's back in its envelope, lying on the counter. I unbolt the front door and let the two uniformed officers – a spotty male and a female with a short, no-nonsense haircut – into the shop. The female officer looks like she's my age, late twenties or thereabouts. The male officer looks a bit younger, or maybe he just has a baby face. But, however young they are, dressed in their black uniforms with their boots, stab vests and utility belts, they seem to fill the whole shop with their official-ness.

'Are you Elizabeth Beresford?' the female officer asks in a Wiltshire accent.

'Yes, I'm Lizzy,' I croak.

'You reported an anonymous letter?' she says.

I gesture to the back of the shop, to the counter where the envelope now sits, pulsing with menace. The two officers wait for me to lead the way. Will they think I've overreacted by calling them? After all, it's just a harmless piece of paper. But no, it's not. It's a threatening statement. A statement that's letting me know someone is watching me. And that's not normal behaviour, surely?

I lead them over to the counter and point to the envelope.

'Have you touched it?' she asks.

'Uh, yes. Sorry.' I feel foolish. Of course I shouldn't have touched it with my fingers, I should have used something to pick it up with.

The female officer slips on a pair of gloves, picks up the envelope, slides out the letter and reads it. She shows it to her colleague who gives a single nod.

'When did you receive this?' she asks.

'It was posted through the letterbox just after I locked up at five thirty-five.'

'Did you get a look at the person who posted it?'

'No.' I take a seat on the wooden stool behind the counter, suddenly feeling wobbly on my feet. 'I was cashing up, here, by the till. So I wasn't looking towards the front of the shop. After I finished, I had a quick tidy round the shelves and that's when I noticed it… the envelope lying on the doormat. It wasn't there before, when I locked the door.'

'Have there been any other letters or anything else unusual?' she asks.

I nod.

They stare at me encouragingly, waiting for me to continue.

I slide off the stool. 'There's another note. I'll fetch it.' I go into the stockroom to get my handbag and return to the counter where I slide the dusty envelope out of the side pocket and give it to the woman officer.

'This came through the door, too?' she asks.

'No.' I shake my head and sit back down. 'I found it yesterday. At home.'

She takes the first note out of the envelope and they both read it.

'You found it?' the male officer asks.

I take a breath and tell them how I discovered the note sticking out of the floorboards in the kitchen. Then I point out that the note has yesterday's date on it, even though it looked like it had been under the floor for years. 'Someone must have left it there. Which means they came into my house.'

The female officer lays both letters flat on the counter next to the envelopes with my name on. 'Do you live alone?' she asks.

'With my boyfriend.'

'Could he have—'

'No. It definitely wasn't Joe.'

She takes a phone out of her pocket and fiddles with it for a moment. 'How long have you lived together?'

'Just over five years.'

'And he's never done anything that might make you suspect him of—'

'Never. He wouldn't do anything like that.'

She starts taking photographs of the letters and envelopes. 'Do you have any idea of who it might be? An ex-boyfriend? Someone with a crush?'

I make a pretence of thinking, but in reality my mind has gone numb. I'm so shaken up that I can barely string a thought, let alone a sentence, together. 'Can you find out who it is?' I ask. 'Test the letters. For fingerprints, or something?'

'Unfortunately, as there's nothing specifically threatening in the letters, there's not a lot we can do,' she says, putting her phone away. 'But I've taken photos, so we'll keep those on file in our system, just in case.'

'But someone's admitted they're watching me! Someone has broken into my house!'

'Was there any sign of a forced entry?' she asks, gathering up the letters and envelopes and passing them back to me.

I take a breath. 'No. Not that I could see.'

'Was anything taken?'

'No, not that I know of. But someone must have come in to leave the letter.'

She peels off her gloves and puts them away in one of her many pockets. 'Does anyone else have a set of your house keys? Or have access to them?'

'Only my landlord, but he's been our landlord for years and he's also my boss. He wouldn't do anything like this, I'm sure of it.'

'I'd strongly advise you to change the locks,' she says.

'My boyfriend was going to change them last night, but he never got round to it.'

'Well, I'd make that a priority. And if anything else untoward happens, please let us know.'

'So, is that it? Can't you do anything? Try to catch the person responsible?'

'I know this has probably been unsettling for you, but we find that in these types of situations, whoever it is will usually get bored and stop. Once you've changed the locks, your house will be more secure. In the meantime, please try not to worry.'

Easy for her to say.

I want them to tell me they have it all in hand. That they'll catch the person doing it and make sure they never come near me again. But I guess that type of policing only happens in the movies. In reality, they're too understaffed to waste resources on a couple of weird letters. I toy with asking the officers to give me a lift home, but would that be cheeky? Being a taxi service isn't part of their job description. The thing is, though, I don't feel safe. Not at all. Someone out there has said they like to watch me work. So that means they could be watching me right now. They might know that the police are here, but they may not even care. It may not faze them in the slightest.

I can't bring myself to ask the officers for a lift, and they don't offer. They leave, and I lock up once more, watching them get back into their car and drive off. Now that they've gone, the shop is suddenly bathed in a menacing silence. My skin itches. My stomach swirls. How am I supposed to leave the safety of the shop and walk home on my own? I can't do it. Not even if I walk the long way round and avoid the isolation of the Abbey. I can't believe this is happening. Who could be doing this? Who is behind these awful letters?

I could have kept my distance.

I could have carried on with my pathetic life as though nothing had changed. But that wouldn't have been right. Because everything has changed.

I'm not stupid. I know that life isn't fair. I know that some people get lucky and others get the shitty end of the stick. But I'm tired of it. And I can put up with a bit more shit for a little longer if it means I get what I want in the end:

To even things out a little.

Call it karma.

CHAPTER SIX

With shaking fingers, I call Joe from the shop phone.

'I've had another letter!'

He pauses for a second. 'Another one?'

'Joe, can you come and get me from work? I don't think I can—'

''Course I can. Be there in ten minutes, okay? How are you doing?'

'Just please come and get me.'

I sit on the stool behind the counter, fairly confident that no one can see me back here. I hope George doesn't show up before I've left. I don't think I can face talking to anyone right now. And what if Pippa and Joe are right? What if it really is George behind the letters? I can't see it myself. He's never made a pass at me before, so why would he start now? We always kiss on the cheek. But it's nothing you wouldn't do with a friend. Nothing *dodgy*.

Finally, Joe pulls up outside in his navy-blue Beemer. I jump to my feet, my heart lifting. I try not to think about the implications of what's happening. That it may not be safe to go out on my own, at all. I set the alarm and lock up. As I step out onto the pavement, I get that instant feeling of being exposed. I've never felt like this in my life. I've always been a confident person. I love going out and about. But now…

I open the car door and slide into the passenger seat, feeling smaller somehow. Joe reaches over to give my hand a squeeze. Then leans across to kiss me. The car indicator is on while Joe waits for a gap in the Friday-night rush-hour traffic. It's not busy by most town's standards, but it's busy enough that we have to wait.

'What happened?' Joe asks, his face hot and red, the front of his hair streaked with oil. He notices my stare. 'Sorry, didn't have time for a shower. I'm all mucky from work.'

'It's okay, I don't care about that.'

'I know. I'm just saying. So, what about this note, then?'

I explain what happened, how I found the letter.

'I don't believe it. Sick bastard, whoever it is.' His fingers tighten around the steering wheel.

'And, Joe… I had to call the police.'

'You called the police?'

'I'm sorry, I had to. I know you said you'd rather I didn't, but—'

'No, of course you had to. Of course. I wasn't saying you shouldn't, I was just commenting.' A white Nissan flashes Joe, and he pulls into the light stream of traffic, waving his hand in thanks. As we leave the shop behind, I wonder if my stalker is watching me now. If they saw me get into Joe's car. If maybe they're in one of the cars behind us. Maybe he's the one who let us out just now. I crane my neck to see. But the people in the car behind are an elderly couple. I doubt either one of them is sending me intimidating letters.

'So what are the police going to do?' Joe asks.

'Not a lot.'

'What do you mean? Surely they have to do something. Isn't there a law against stalking? It's harassment, isn't it? Can't they get fingerprints off the letters?'

'I asked them that, but they just told me to get the locks changed at home. They said whoever it is will probably lose interest.'

'I doubt whoever did it would be stupid enough to leave their fingerprints all over the evidence anyway. Probably wore gloves,' Joe adds.

'So, can you change the locks tonight?' I ask.

''Course I will, Lizzy. I should have done it yesterday, but you wanted me to get the shopping and it was too late after that.'

It annoys me how Joe makes out that I wanted him to get the shopping, like he was doing something special to help me out. We both eat the food, so we should both take responsibility for the shopping. But I don't have the energy to argue, and, well, I guess he is going to change the locks, so things work out equal-ish in the end.

'What about Pippa's brother – what's-his-face? Sebastian?'

'*Seb*?' I picture Sebastian Hargreaves, tall and bumbling, painfully shy. I guess he is a little odd, but not creepy. Anyway, he's Pippa's brother. 'No. No way.'

'Think about it, Lizzy.' Joe's face becomes animated. 'And it makes sense, too. He could have swiped your keys from the shop and had a copy made. Then he could have let himself into the house. Much more likely that it's Seb rather than George.'

I think Joe is jumping to conclusions. He loves his TV police dramas and always thinks he has the bad guys figured out long before the police do. But he invariably gets it wrong, and then he spends ages after the show criticising the scriptwriters for not following his own logic. Which is fine when he's watching TV, funny even. But this is real life, and Joe playing amateur detective isn't helping matters.

'Seb's harmless. And kind,' I reply. 'Always running around for Pippa, looking after their house and his parents.'

'Has he got a girlfriend?'

'Don't think so, no.'

'There you go!' Joe cries triumphantly. We've left the High Street behind and Joe puts his foot down, taking the bends far too fast.

'Just because he hasn't got a girlfriend doesn't make him a stalker.'

'No,' Joe agrees, 'but it makes it more likely.'

'Well, I think you're wrong. Seb wouldn't do anything like that.'

'Lizzy, you don't realise what effect you have on men.'

I splutter out an incredulous laugh. 'Now you're talking crazy.'

'It's not crazy. You're gorgeous. You have this kind of Jessica Rabbit vibe going on. And don't get mad at me again, but you do flirt a lot – whether you mean to or not.'

'I do not!'

'It's not necessarily a bad thing, it's just who you are.'

'Well, if being friendly is now called flirting, then I guess I'm guilty.'

'Well, doesn't matter how friendly you are, still doesn't give scumbags like Seb the right to send creepy letters.' Joe flicks on the indicator to turn into our road.

'I really don't think it was Seb. He knows I've got a boyfriend. He's met you before.'

'It doesn't stop some blokes. They think of it as a challenge.'

'Well, in a way, I hope it *is* him,' I say.

'What!' Joe slams on the brakes, coming to a halt in the middle of the road in a screech of white noise. Luckily there's no one behind us. Up ahead, our neighbour Ruby, who's letting herself into her house, glances up to see what's going on. She raises a hand in a tentative wave, which I return.

'Not like that!' I clarify. 'I just mean that if it's only Seb, then it's not so scary as if it's a total stranger. He's obviously doing it to try and be romantic, and doesn't realise it's coming off as creepy.'

Joe restarts the engine and pulls into a space outside our house. 'You go in,' he says with a scowl. 'I'm going round to their manor house, or whatever it is, to have a word.'

'Uh, no you're not.'

'Lizzy, I'm your boyfriend. I'm supposed to look after you and stick up for you.'

'Thanks, Joe, but I'm quite capable of sticking up for myself.'

'You just called me to come and pick you up from work because you were too scared to walk home on your own!'

He's got a point. I sigh and feel my shoulders sag. 'Sorry, you're right. I'm just a bit tense, on edge. Look, can't we just have a nice relaxing evening? Some good food? An early night?'

Joe's expression mellows. 'Sounds good. But we still need to do something about Seb.' Joe has never been keen on Pippa or Seb. I think it's a bit of inverse snobbery. Because they're from a privileged background, Joe thinks they look down their nose at him. But Pippa isn't like that at all. She takes people as she finds them, and I'm sure Seb is the same.

'I'm not convinced it's him,' I say, 'but if it'll make you feel any better, I'll bring it up with Pippa tomorrow at work, okay?'

Joe nods. 'Fine. Make sure you do. I know you, you're too nice sometimes.'

As we get out of the car exhaustion hits me like air going out of a balloon. I feel like I've run a marathon or fought in a war. But I don't want Joe to see how weak this situation is making me. He'll only worry even more. Instead, I plaster on a bright smile and follow him into the house.

After a quick cup of tea in the kitchen, Joe says he's off to B&Q to buy some new locks.

'Want me to come with you?' I ask.

'No, that's okay. You relax. You've had a stressful time.' He sticks his empty mug in the sink, runs a hand through his hair and gives me a cheeky smile.

I smile back, feeling incredibly lucky to have such a caring boyfriend. I'm sure I would be ten times more terrified without Joe's support.

After he's gone, our little cottage feels still and claustrophobic. I wonder where Frank has got to. He's usually here to welcome me home from work. A quick sweep of the house confirms he's not home, so I open up the back door and give him a shout. After two or three calls he usually comes running, eager for a treat or some affection. But the garden is still. No sign of him. I go into the kitchen and pick up his ceramic food bowl from the mat on the floor. Banging a fork against its side usually does the trick. I stand at the door, clang the bowl a few times and wait, my eyes scanning the fences and bushes, squinting in the lemon-bright sunlight. Still no sign. I hope Frank is okay. I'm sure he'll come back when he's ready.

Without Joe or Frank to keep me company, my mind starts veering down dark corridors. The air is too close, too hot. The cottage no longer feels like a homely refuge. Instead, I imagine that someone is out there watching me, which is crazy because unless they're lurking in the bushes at the back of the garden, there's nowhere for them to hide. But I suddenly feel exposed and vulnerable again. I pull the door closed with a scrape and a thud. I don't like this feeling. I don't like it at all.

CHAPTER SEVEN

I close and lock the back door. Frank can use the cat flap once he's ready to come home. I wish he hadn't picked today to go off roaming – I could do with his company while Joe's out. Sure, he's only a cat, he can't do anything to protect me against a stalker, but just having him here would make me feel less alone, less unsettled. I'm kicking myself; I should have gone with Joe to B&Q. Why didn't I? I put Joe's mug in the dishwasher and peer through the back window, hoping to spot Frank, knowing I won't.

This is silly. I should be able to relax in my own home. What would I normally do? I'd have a shower, get changed and pour myself a glass of wine. Start cooking supper. But I'm antsy. I keep imagining that someone is watching me. If the person who sent those letters did it to unnerve me, then they've succeeded in their mission. My handbag sits on the kitchen table, the two letters in its pocket like twin unexploded bombs. How can two pieces of paper have so much potency?

Rather than drifting around the house, I decide to do something proactive. I get my keys out of my handbag and leave the house, pulling the front door closed behind me with a decisive thunk. But I'm not going far. I walk the few steps it takes me to reach my neighbour's house. Mrs P, my old chemistry teacher, is retired now. She owns the cottage next door and has always been the perfect neighbour – friendly without being too nosy. I ring the bell and wait.

No one comes, but her car is parked out the front so I'm hoping she's in. I ring it again, trying to see if I can make out any movement beyond the half-glazed stained-glass door. After another long moment, I hear footsteps.

'Hellooo! I'm coming, coming!' Mrs P's cheery voice immediately puts me at ease. The door rattles as she pulls it open. Her wrinkled face is flushed and she wipes her forehead with the back of her hand, or rather with the back of her gardening glove. She's holding a muddy garden fork in her other hand. 'Lizzy,' she beams. 'How lovely. Have you been standing here long? I was just out the back doing some gardening, wasn't sure if that was my bell I could hear. You coming in?'

'I don't want to disturb you if you're busy.'

'Come through. I was going to stop for a drink anyway. Thirsty work, gardening in this heat. You'd have thought it would have cooled down out there by now.'

'If you're sure.'

'Yes, I'm sure. Always nice to have a visitor.'

I follow her through to the kitchen. The layout of her cottage is the same as ours, only in reverse. And hers is much more tumbledown and homely, with framed prints covering almost every inch of wall space, bric-a-brac and knick-knacks adorning all the surfaces.

'Lemonade? Iced water?'

'Water would be great, thanks.'

Mrs P lifts a patterned jug out of an old cream-coloured buzzing fridge and pours the icy water into a couple of green dimpled glass tumblers.

She gestures to a wooden stool and I take a seat while she downs her glass of water and pours herself another.

'Mmm, that's better. I think you might have saved me from heatstroke.' She barks out a laugh. 'Is this a social call?'

'I just wanted to…' But I'm not sure how to begin. Mrs P lives on her own, and I don't want to alarm her.

Her faded blue eyes fill with concern. 'Best way is to just come out and say it.'

'Okay, well, I wondered, have you seen anyone hanging around outside our house recently?'

'Hanging around?' Mrs P perches on the other stool, a puzzled look on her face.

'Someone, I don't know who, has been leaving me these weird letters. They left one at the house and one at work.'

Puzzlement turns to worry. 'Oh dear, how upsetting. What do the letters say, if you don't mind me asking? Nothing too awful, I hope.'

'One of them says: *You're my only obsession.* The other says: *I love to watch you.*'

'Gosh.' A hand flies up to her mouth. 'Did you call the police?'

'Yes, I did, but they can't do anything. So I thought I'd ask my neighbours if they've seen anything. Which is why I'm here.'

Mrs P thinks for a moment and then shakes her head. 'I wish I could be more helpful, but I haven't noticed anyone unusual. I take it they were hand-delivered, these letters?'

I nod. 'And they both had my name on the envelopes, so they were definitely meant for me.'

'Oh, Lizzy. I am sorry. There are some awfully strange people in the world. I hope it hasn't upset you too much.'

I bite my lip, trying to keep from welling up.

'Probably some lad with a bit of a crush, going about it all the wrong way.'

'I hope that's all it is.' I take a sip of water.

'Well, I'll definitely keep an eye out. And if I see anything unusual, I'll be straight round to let you know.'

'Can I give you my phone number? In case anyone comes round to the house while Joe and I are at work?'

'Of course, dear. No problem.'

We exchange numbers and I reluctantly leave the cosiness of Mrs P's kitchen.

'Let me know if you find out who's behind it,' she says as we walk through the hallway.

'I will.'

'Oh, that's made me feel quite upset on your behalf,' she says. 'If you ever feel worried, you know you can pop over here any time.'

'Thank you,' I reply, feeling warmed by her offer. 'I really appreciate that.'

She pats my arm and stands in the doorway as I walk back out onto the pavement. I turn to give her a wave before heading over to my other neighbours.

Ian Clutterbuck and Ruby Davies live on the other side of our house. I'll pop round and ask them the same thing. Maybe they will have spotted something, although I doubt it. I press the doorbell but it doesn't appear to be working, so I knock on the frosted glass instead. It's Ian's dad's house. He used to rent it out to three students from the local agricultural college, but they were nightmare neighbours, always having parties and playing loud music. They ended up trashing the place. So he rented it out to his son, who's far more considerate. Ian's girlfriend, Ruby, moved in six months ago.

Ruby answers the door barefoot, wearing short shorts and a white crop top. 'Hiya!'

'Hey, Ruby.'

'Who is it?' Ian yells from the living room over the sounds of sports playing at full volume on the TV. Thankfully their lounge isn't adjacent to our side of the house.

'It's Lizzy, from next door!' Ruby yells back in her faint Bristol accent.

As the lounge door opens, the sound of stadium cheers becomes deafening. 'Hi, Lizzy,' Ian says in his Wiltshire drawl. 'Is the TV too loud? Want me to turn it down?' He's wearing a pair of football shorts without a T-shirt, and his skinny, hairless chest is the colour of Frank's salmon supper. I don't want to be shallow, but I have no idea how he managed to land a girlfriend as beautiful as Ruby, who is tall, slim and big-boobed, with auburn hair straight out of a Titian painting.

'I already told him to turn it down.' Ruby tuts. 'But he won't flippin' do it for *me*, will ya?'

Ian disappears back into the lounge and sudden silence descends. He pops his head back round the door. 'Sorry 'bout that.'

'No, no, you're fine,' I say. 'I'm not here about the telly. I just wanted a quick word.'

'Oh, right.' Ian grins and pokes his girlfriend in the ribs with his forefinger. 'See, Rubes, told you they wouldn't be able to hear it.'

She pushes his finger away. 'What's up, Lizzy?'

I give them a potted history of the letters I've been receiving, and ask them if they've seen anyone suspicious hanging around.

'That's well creepy,' Ruby says, looking at Ian for reassurance.

Ian puts his arm around her. 'That's mad. If anyone did that to our Rubes, I'd kill 'em. Any idea who it is?'

'I don't know. Joe thinks it's this guy, Seb, but I'm not sure. I'd be really grateful if you could let me know if you see anyone hanging around near the house.'

'Yeah, 'course we will, won't we, babe?' Ruby gazes down adoringly at Ian, who's a smidgen shorter than her.

'Too right we will,' he agrees. 'I'm learning mixed martial arts, so if I see anyone weird, I can sort them out for you.'

I nod, looking at his lanky frame and thinking that I could probably take Ian in a fight myself. But I'm being uncharitable. Sure, he's skinny, but that doesn't mean he isn't handy with his fists. 'Thanks, guys. I appreciate it.'

'You're welcome,' Ruby says.

'Yeah, totally welcome,' Ian says.

'Oh,' Ruby says, her eyes lighting up, 'while you're here, me and Ian have been meaning to ask if you and Joe want to come round for dinner one night, haven't we, babe?'

'Yeah. Yeah, we have.' Ian's not very good at hiding the fact that this is probably the first he's heard of it. But it's sweet how he's going along with her.

'What about next Tuesday?' Ruby asks. 'Just bring a bottle or some beers or something. We'll cook the food.'

'Thanks,' I say. 'That'll be really nice.'

'Yeah,' Ruby says. 'It'll be a laugh, won't it, Ian?'

'Yeah, Joe's cool,' Ian replies. 'I mean, so are you, Lizzy,' he adds hastily. 'Didn't mean you weren't…' His face and neck turn crimson.

'Thanks.' I give him a smile. 'So, see you both on Tuesday.'

'Yeah, Tuesday,' Ruby confirms. 'Seven o'clock okay?'

'Perfect.'

Before they've closed the door, Ian starts kissing Ruby, putting his hand up under her top. I turn away, embarrassed, but they don't seem in the least bit self-conscious. I leave them to it, feeling a little better than I did earlier. Knowing that both my neighbours are keeping an eye out for me is reassuring. Joe should be back from B&Q any minute. I think I'll go home and make a start on tonight's pasta. We can have it in the garden after Joe's finished doing the locks. We'll be eating late, but that's fine. It'll be worth it to know that whoever broke into our house won't be able to get in so easily if they try it again. But is changing the locks going to be enough? They know where I live, but they also know where I work.

What else do they know about me?

CHAPTER EIGHT

Saturdays at work usually feel different to the rest of the week. The atmosphere is buzzier, the customers happier. And it's always nice to know that I have the next two days off. Only today, the shop feels different. Yesterday's letter has shifted everything, so that instead of feeling fired up and ready to smash sales targets, I feel vulnerable and suspicious. It feels as though every customer who comes in could be the person responsible for leaving me the letters.

'Are you okay?' Pippa asks. 'You've been staring at that man by the perfumes for ages. Do you think he might be a shoplifter?'

'What?' I turn to my friend. 'Sorry. No, no, just a bit spaced out this morning.'

'Heavy night?'

'Something like that.' I've already told Pippa about the second letter, and she was sympathetic. But since their second date, she's so wrapped up in her new boyfriend Toby that she can't focus on anything else for more than a minute.

'Toby's taking me to Castle Combe tomorrow. For lunch. Did I tell you his parents own an estate there – several hundred acres?'

'Wow. So he's loaded, then?' I reply.

'You could say that. But you know that's not why I'm going out with him. He's funny and sweet, and very attentive. I've only known him a few days, but I really think he could be the one.'

'I'm happy for you, Pip. But…'

'What?'

'Just be careful, okay? Don't fall too hard, too quickly. Not until you know a bit more about him.'

'You sound like Sebbie, now. He's gone all "protective big brother" on me.'

'Of course. That's because he cares about you. We all do.'

'What do you think of the new dress?' She gives a twirl.

I've been so preoccupied that I hadn't noticed Pippa is wearing one of the new floral cotton dresses that came in earlier this week. 'Looks gorgeous, Pip.'

'Thanks. Toby's picking me up after work tonight, so I want to look good.'

I don't remember Pippa buying it. George has a rule that if staff want to buy something, they have to get another member of staff to ring it through the till. As she and I are the only ones who work here, I wonder how she managed to buy it. Maybe she hasn't paid for it yet.

'Do you need me to ring it through the till for you?' I ask.

'Oh.' Pippa flushes. 'Sorry, Lizzy. Hope you don't mind, but I rang it through myself earlier in the week.'

'George won't like that,' I say, trying to keep my voice light. 'He's a stickler.'

'Thing is, Liz, I used your admin code to ring it through. You were busy. I just did it to save time.'

'Pippa! You can't do that, George will go mad.'

'I know. Sorry.' She gives an awkward laugh.

I'm not at all comfortable with Pippa using my code to ring goods through the till. I didn't even realise she knew the code. I'll have to change it now. And I also have the niggling suspicion that she might not have paid for the dress at all. I don't remember seeing the sale when I was cashing up this week. But I can't accuse her without proof. I wish I could check back through the till receipts, but George will have them filed away by now, and I can't ask him without bringing up my suspicions about Pippa. Although on second thoughts, I can't imagine she would have brought the dress to my attention if she'd taken it without paying. I think I'm just feeling paranoid about everything at the moment. Quite honestly, my mind is all over the place.

Pippa nudges me as Leon Whittaker saunters into the shop. My first thought is: *what the hell is he doing here?* Followed by: *what if he's the stalker?* My heart pounds with a strange anxiety as he catches my eye and smiles. I give an automatic little wave that feels robotic and awkward. Thankfully, a woman comes over to ask the price of something and I'm prevented from making a further fool of myself.

Several minutes later, Leon comes up to the counter with a basket brimming with cards and gifts, his broad shoulders blotting out most of the view behind him. Pippa is at the other end of the shop assisting another customer, so I have no choice but to serve him myself. I decide to be polite but cool. 'Hi. Would you like any of these gift-wrapped?'

'Yes, please.' Leon tries to catch my eye, but I'm staring resolutely into the basket. 'Can you wrap everything apart from the chocolate heart?' he asks.

'Sure. 'Do you want to choose some paper?' I gesture to the wall where all the sheets are displayed on a wooden rack.

'You choose,' he says. 'I trust your judgement.'

'Okay. Are the gifts for special occasions? Or do you just want a generic design?'

'Generic will be fine.' His voice is filled with humour, like he's enjoying my obvious discomfort. I think he's got a bit of a nerve coming in here, after what happened between him and Joe. I know Joe punched him first, but Leon was winding him up on purpose.

I slide several sheets of gold paper out from the rack and begin wrapping the various gifts. 'Would you like one of our carrier bags? They're ten pence.'

'It's okay, I have one here.' He pulls a folded cotton bag out of his chinos pocket and passes it across the counter to me. I can't help raising an eyebrow. 'What?' he says with mock indignation. 'Didn't think I was the type to be environmentally friendly?'

'I don't have an opinion either way,' I reply curtly.

Now it's his turn to raise an eyebrow. But I won't be drawn into this conversation. Joe's words are still ringing in my ears about me being too flirty with the customers. Maybe he's right. Maybe I've been giving people the wrong idea. Maybe they're assuming there's more to my friendly banter than meets the eye. But I can't simply treat each customer with dispassion and detachment. Most of my job satisfaction comes from connecting with people. From having a bit of fun. And if that involves a little mild flirting, is that so bad? Before this week, I didn't think so. Now I'm aiming for polite professionalism, and failing miserably.

I finish wrapping the gifts, totting them up on the cash register before placing each item in his bag. Lastly, I add up the cards and then the chocolate foil-covered heart that he wanted left unwrapped. He puts the latter in his pocket and passes me his credit card.

'That's ninety-three pounds, fifty-seven pence,' I say.

Leon doesn't flinch at the cost, just nods, his blue eyes downcast, suddenly not looking quite as confident. I resist the urge to ask him if everything is okay, and then immediately relent. 'Everything okay?'

To my surprise, his cheeks turn pink. 'Uh, yeah. Thanks.'

I feed Leon's credit card into the machine and turn it towards him so he can enter his pin number.

'The reason I didn't want you to wrap the heart, well, it's because I bought it for you.' He draws the chocolate back out of his pocket and places it on the counter. 'You've stolen my heart, Lizzy. I can't stop thinking about you. Will you please come for a drink with me?'

I freeze at his words, unable to believe he has the cheek to actually ask me out. I don't even know how to reply. And saying *I've stolen his heart*? Sounds like something my stalker would have written in one of his letters. Time seems to slow down until all I can see is the shiny red heart-shaped chocolate before me. It looks as though it's pulsing; oozing blood onto the counter. But of course that's nonsense, it's just a piece of foil-wrapped chocolate.

'What's going on, Leon?' I hiss. 'Is it *you*?'

Leon's screws up his face. 'Is what me?'

'Did you leave me those letters?'

'Letters? I don't know what you're talking about, Lizzy.'

'Don't say my name. You don't know me. You know nothing about me!'

He raises his hands in surrender. 'Calm down. All I did was buy you a gift and ask you out. I thought it would be cute. I thought you'd like it. Jeez, forget it, okay?'

'Why would I like it?' I cry. 'You know I'm with Joe. We live together. And he knows about the letters, so if you're thinking of sending any more of them… *don't*.'

'Christ, calm down,' he mutters, his face contorting into a sneer. 'I don't know anything about any letters. I was just doing something nice. Thought you might feel like a change from your Neanderthal boyfriend. Wish I hadn't bothered now.' He shakes his head and turns to leave.

'What about your presents?' I snap, holding out his cotton bag, my hand shaking along with my voice. I don't know why I'm worried about his purchases; maybe some subconscious part of me still wants to remain professional, even while my composure is crumbling.

He snatches the bag from me and walks away.

I watch him leave, the anger radiating off him. Did I overreact? I don't think so. But I can't think straight. And I can't stand here any longer. I need to sit down. There's a queue forming, and by the hushed whispers I can tell most of them witnessed the scene. I avoid eye contact, and instead I stagger into the stockroom, pulling the door closed behind me, the strip light buzzing over my head like an angry wasp. Pippa will have to deal with that lot out there while I pull myself together, try to figure out what just happened.

Sitting on the black leather swivel chair by the stockroom desk, I lean back and take a few deep breaths to slow my pulse. I pick up a sheaf of invoices and use them to fan my burning face. I'm trying desperately not to cry. I don't know which is worse – for Leon Whittaker to be my stalker, or for him not to be the stalker and I've just behaved like a lunatic towards him. But either way, he should never have asked me out. Not after what happened at Christmas. He knows what Joe's like. And he knows that if Joe steps out of line he'll end up in prison. Maybe that's it! Maybe Leon asked me out simply to goad Joe; to get him to lash out so he'll be arrested again. I'm going to have to keep all this from my volatile boyfriend.

Before I can change my mind, I pull my mobile out of my bag and dial the local police station, quoting the incident number they gave me yesterday. I have to wait while they find the right person for me to speak to. The silence on the other end of the line is interminable, painful. I go over the different ways I can explain what just happened. But my brain is becoming muddled, I don't know what I'm doing, what I'm thinking. So instead of holding, I end the call before they can find someone to talk to me. I press the cool metal phone to my forehead and close my eyes, Leon Whittaker's arrogant expression imprinted on my retinas, the blank tone of the cut call ringing in my ears.

CHAPTER NINE

The hubbub out in the shop is becoming louder. Someone calls out, 'Hello!' Probably an angry customer – someone who saw me disappear into the back room, annoyed that I'm not giving them my full attention. I can just imagine them all complaining about how I must be skiving out the back. Normally I'd be mortified to let down one of my precious customers. They always come first with me. But not today. Today I can barely hold it together for myself, let alone anyone else.

My phone trills in my hand, making me jump. It's a withheld number. I answer it.

'Hello?' I say in a quavery voice.

'Is that… Elizabeth Beresford?'

'Speaking.'

'This is Sergeant Jenny Llewellyn. I came to see you yesterday at Georgio's.'

'Oh, yes. Hello.'

'Did you just call the station? I've been passed a memo with your incident number, but the line was dead when the call came through to me.'

'Uh, yes, I did. But the thing is, I don't know if I should have called. It might be nothing.'

'Well, now we're on the line together, why don't you tell me anyway?' She sounds friendlier than she did yesterday, almost comforting.

'Okay, well, I just had Leon Whittaker come into the shop, and he gave me a gift – a chocolate heart – and asked if I'd go out with him.'

She doesn't reply, so I continue.

'He had a bit of a situation with my boyfriend, Joe, last year…'

'Oh, yes. I remember,' Llewellyn says matter-of-factly.

'I thought it might be him – the person who left me the letters.'

'What makes you say that?'

'Well, his history with Joe, for one thing. And the timing of everything – asking me out when I've just started receiving these creepy letters…'

'Want us to go and have a word with Mr Whittaker for you? Get his version of events?'

'Maybe… No. No, it's fine.' I'm nervous of what his reaction might be if the police turn up on his doorstep. It might make things worse. 'Don't worry about it.'

'Are you sure?' she presses. 'It's no trouble for me to pay him a quick visit. And in light of what happened last year, with Joe…'

'I know, it's just, it might not have been him who left the letters. I might have jumped to conclusions. But him giving me that heart today, after everything, it just seems a bit…'

'Coincidental?'

'Exactly.'

'So maybe we should just pop down to Whittaker's this afternoon. Have a friendly chat…'

I think about it for a few seconds. If the police don't speak to him, I'll most likely be worrying about it all day. And if Leon is doing this to rile Joe, then I guess it's better if the police act on it and warn him off. 'Okay then. Yes, if you think that's best.'

'Don't worry, Elizabeth. We'll have a quiet word with him. Put your mind at rest.'

'Thank you. And please call me Lizzy.'

'No problem, Lizzy.'

'Can you let me know how it goes?' I ask. 'Your chat? If you find anything out?'

'We'll stop by Georgio's after, if we get time. See how you're doing. Will you be there later?'

'I'll be here until five today.'

'Great,' she says. 'I felt a bit bad leaving you alone yesterday. We should have offered you a lift home. I could see that note had shaken you up.'

'It's okay,' I reply. 'Joe came and got me.'

'Good. Well, you take care, and try not to worry.'

The stockroom door bursts open and Pippa's red face appears. 'Lizzy, can you come and help? It's mayhem out here!'

'Thanks, Sergeant.' I end the call feeling decidedly less shaky. I get to my feet and give Pippa a nod. 'Coming.'

Pippa's face shows relief as I follow her back out into the fray, fixing a rictus smile on my face, losing myself in the all-consuming task of customer service.

Things become a little quieter over lunchtime. Pippa and I take turns eating our lunch in the stockroom. Neither of us takes a proper lunch break on Saturdays as things can get crazily busy within minutes. After lunch, things calm down even more. It's such a beautiful day out there that most people are probably out enjoying the sunshine. I notice that the greetings card section looks as though a hurricane has blown through it, so I decide to restore some order. Hopefully sorting the cards will help to still my racing brain.

Pippa comes over. 'You were serving Leon Whittaker for ages. What were you two chatting about? Did he declare his undying love again?'

Normally I'd have laughed it off, but unfortunately she's not too far off the mark. 'He asked me out,' I say through gritted teeth.

'Nooo!' Pippa gasps, her eyes sparkling with the promise of some juicy gossip.

'I think he might be my stalker.'

'I thought we already ruled him out? He's too good-looking to be a stalker, darling. Honestly, he's not the type. He could get pretty much any woman he wanted. He doesn't have to resort to scrappy bits of paper sticking out of the floorboards.'

'I thought so too, but then today he gave me one those chocolate love hearts, you know, the ones over there.' I point to the glass shelving unit displaying an assortment of chocolate and candy gifts.

'So? That's romantic. Hearts equal romance. Breaking and entering equals psychotic tendencies. No?'

'Oh, God.' I put a hand to my forehead. 'Have I gone and accused him unfairly?'

'What did you say?'

'I accused him of writing the letters, and then I shouted at him and told him not to use my name. I can't remember exactly what I said, but I was… pissed off.'

'Well.' She tilts her head. 'I suppose it is a bit cheeky of him coming in here after what happened with Joe. All I can say is, he must like you an awful lot.'

'And then…' I begin.

'What?'

'I called the police.'

'Really?' Pippa's mouth drops open. I can see that this snippet will be worth millions in gossip currency.

'Yes, really. I mean, how well do we actually know him? We don't know what he might be capable of. A pretty face is no indication of character. Plus I thought he might be doing it to make Joe angry. To get him put behind bars.'

'That sounds more likely. But Leon Whittaker is not your stalker. I mean, come on. No way.'

'Well, he might be,' I say stubbornly, my lips pressing down into a hard line. 'That love heart was just as creepy as the letters. Anyway, the police are popping down to see him this afternoon.'

She opens her mouth to say something and then clamps it shut again.

'You think I've overreacted, don't you?'

'We-ell… I mean, he came in here and asked you out face-to-face. That isn't exactly the same as leaving creepy anonymous letters.'

'Okay, so if it isn't Whittaker, then who is it?'

'Could be any sad little loser, sweetie. You're better off trying to put it out of your head.'

'I would if I could, but I've already started looking at everyone differently. Thinking that every man who comes into the shop could be guilty.'

'Get Joe to take you away this weekend. Change of scenery. Do you the world of good.'

'Hmm.' Joe's not the type to go away on a whim. He needs time to get used to the idea of things. But I don't say this to Pippa. I know she doesn't have a very high opinion of Joe. Although she hasn't said as much, she thinks I could do better. But Joe and I have been together for six years. We know one another inside out. And there's still that spark of passion. Which is rare after so long.

'Nice little country hotel, that's what you need,' Pippa says, warming to the subject. 'Four-poster bed, cocktails, a spa. I might even suggest that to Toby.'

'Don't take this the wrong way,' I begin, knowing as I open my mouth that this line of questioning is not going to go down well with Pippa. But now that I've started voicing my fears, I can't seem to stop myself. 'But, you know Seb…'

'My brother Seb?'

'Yeah. You don't think it could be him sending the letters, do you? Not in a creepy way, but in a he's-got-a-bit-of-a-crush way?' I wince, waiting for her response.

'I'll pretend I didn't hear that.' Pippa flashes me the darkest scowl before her expression closes down.

I persevere. 'It's just, you seem so convinced that it's not Whittaker. And Seb always seems to be embarrassed and uncomfortable when he's around me.'

'For goodness sake, Lizzy! Seb's embarrassed around *all* women. I love him to bits, but he's just so painfully shy. Sure, maybe he does have a crush on you – half the bloody population of Malmesbury has a crush on the wonderful Lizzy Beresford – but Sebbie would never do anything remotely resembling what you're accusing him of. I'm hurt, quite frankly, that you would even suggest such a thing!'

Shit. I've messed everything up. What was I thinking? 'I'm sorry, Pippa. You're right. 'Course you are.'

She holds out a hand to silence me. 'Don't talk to me right now, Lizzy. I'm too upset with you.' She turns her back and walks to the other end of the shop.

My heart plummets. It's going to be a very long afternoon.

CHAPTER TEN

Luckily the shop is nicely busy this afternoon, meaning that Pippa and I can stay out of each other's way while the dust settles over our argument. Maybe I should apologise to her for suggesting that Sebastian could have been responsible for the letters, but Pippa won't even catch my eye, and anyway, there are too many people in the shop for us to have a proper conversation. I'll apologise at the end of the day – if she'll even listen.

I'm restocking the perfumes when I catch a glimpse of a black uniform heading my way. I set down the cardboard box I'm carrying, straighten up and wipe my dusty hands down the sides of my skirt. It's Sergeant Jenny Llewellyn, without her colleague this time. I wonder if she's already been to see Leon Whittaker, or if she's popped in here on her way to his wine bar.

'Hi,' I say.

'Hello,' she says with a brisk smile. 'How are you doing?'

'Still a bit shaky, to be honest.'

'Sorry to hear that. Hopefully I'll be able to put your mind at rest. I've just had a quick word with Mr Whittaker. Asked him about the heart, and the letters.'

My shoulders tense. 'And?'

'He denied any knowledge of the letters, but admitted coming into the shop to give you the heart and ask you out on a date. He said he's been trying to pluck up the courage to ask you for ages.'

'Well, I know he asked me out on a date. And if it was him sending the letters, he's not exactly going to admit it, especially not to a police officer.' I know my tone is a little sharp, but *really*... how is that supposed to put my mind at rest?

'True,' she replies, unruffled by my reply. 'I asked him if I thought his actions were wise, given his history with your boyfriend. But I did get the sense that he was telling the truth about the letters. He seemed too shaken up to be lying. I think the last thing he expected was a police visit.'

'So you believe him then?'

'It's hard to say. We've only got his word for it. But there's no evidence he has anything to do with the letters.'

'You could test them for fingerprints. See if his DNA is on them.' I realise we now have a bit of an audience. Our customers are getting more than they bargained for. I shouldn't really be having this conversation out on the shop floor, so I guide Sergeant Llewellyn into the back room and close the door behind us.

'First,' she says, 'I doubt anyone would be so stupid as to handle the letters and not wear gloves. And secondly, there's actually no law against sending a letter. If it happens again, and they contain threatening content, we'll test them for you and see what we come up with, okay?'

'I suppose it will have to be.' I shrug, annoyed they can't do more to help me while I'm feeling so vulnerable.

'You were absolutely right to contact us, Lizzy. Especially given Joe's situation with his suspended sentence. And we will certainly respond if anything like this happens again. Please be assured of that. Let's hope whoever's behind the letters has lost interest now.'

I know she's trying to be reassuring, and she probably sees way worse things than this every day, but I really had hoped she would try harder to find out who the culprit is. Instead, I feel a bit daft. Like I've caused a fuss over nothing. And yet I'm still terrified about what will come next. Somehow, I know this isn't the end of it.

I thank her for coming and for speaking to Whittaker, and follow her back out into the shop, wishing I'd never bothered calling the police today. Llewellyn leaves and I get back to restocking the perfumes, trying to concentrate on the exotic names of each fragrance, rather than on the chaos in my head.

Pippa eyes me from across the room. I bet she's absolutely dying to find out what's going on, but it's a testament to how mad she is at me that she doesn't ask me to fill her in.

Fine. I'll just get through the rest of the afternoon, go home and try to forget about it. Maybe Joe and I could go out for a drink tonight. Somewhere a bit further afield, like Bath or Cheltenham, where I can relax knowing my stalker isn't nearby. But I already know what Joe's response will be. He'll say, *what's wrong with a local pub? Let's go to The Crown.* But I don't want to go to The Crown. I'm sick of The Crown. I dump one of the perfume bottles down on the shelf a little too loudly and tell myself to calm down. At least Leon Whittaker now knows I won't take any crap. If it is him, he's been warned by the cops, so that should stop him from doing it again. And if it isn't him… well, best not to think about that right now.

It's a little before closing time, and the shop has finally emptied out. Pippa still isn't speaking to me and I'm trying to pluck up the courage to apologise to her. I don't feel strong enough to face another argument, so I hope that if I grovel enough, she'll forgive me. But before I can approach her, I'm dismayed and unsettled to see Leon-freaking-Whittaker walking through the door. What's he doing here? I hope he's not going to have a go at me for calling the police. I wish I could run into the back room and lock the door until he's gone, but he's already seen me and is heading my way.

'No!' I cry, holding up a hand to ward him off. 'You can't come in here.'

He stops in his tracks and shakes his head.

Pippa is dusting one of the glass cabinets. She glances from me to Leon and then back again.

'I only came in to apologise,' he says, sounding anything but apologetic.

'Okay,' I say. 'Thanks. Now I'd really like you to leave. Please.'

He takes another step towards me, so I take a step back. Like we're dancing… or fighting.

'I didn't know about the letters,' he says. 'If I'd known about them, I would never have come in here and asked you out. The last thing I'd ever want to do is upset you, Lizzy.'

I have a hundred responses in my brain but I can't seem to get any of them out.

'You didn't have to call the police!' he adds.

Does he want me to apologise? Say sorry? Well, I'm not going to. I can't even speak. Leon's presence here has set my teeth on edge. I can't believe how much he's unsettling me. My nerves are shot to pieces.

'Can you say something?' he says. 'I've come here to say sorry – the least you can do is accept my apology.'

'She asked you to leave,' Pippa says, coming over and standing by my side. She takes my hand and gives it a squeeze.

I'm frozen to the spot. I have no idea why I can't speak. All I know is I want that man to go away.

Leon throws his hands up in the air. 'Okay, fine. I give up!' He spins on his heel and marches out of the shop. Once he's gone, Pippa closes and locks the door behind him.

'You can't close up yet,' I say quietly. 'It's only ten to five.'

'Who cares,' Pippa replies. 'You've had a rough day, we're closing early. Sorry I was such a bitch to you earlier.'

'No.' I shake my head. 'It's me who should apologise. I accused your brother of something awful.'

'Sweetie, shall we just forget about it?' She gives me one of her eye-rolling smiles.

'Yes, please. I'd like that.'

'Now, I'll make us a cup of tea, and you can tell me what happened with the police earlier and what on earth's going on with Leon Whittaker.'

I knew there had to be a reason Pippa wanted to make things up with me – she wants all the juicy gossip. I take a breath and follow her into the stockroom.

'Actually,' Pippa says, grabbing her purse, 'forget the tea, we're going for a proper drink.'

'Uh, Pippa, that's sweet of you to offer, but Joe's expecting me home.'

Pippa flashes me a look of disdain. 'What is he, your keeper? Text him and tell him you'll be late.'

I realise that going out for a couple of drinks with a friend is exactly what I feel like doing right now. I also realise that I need to rebuild a few bridges after accusing Seb. 'Okay,' I say, with a rebellious smile. 'Let me get my phone.' I'm a little nervous about telling Joe that I'm not coming straight home from work. It's not like he'll forbid me from going or anything like that, it's just that I know he won't be happy about it. But I push down my worries. I'll deal with the fallout later.

CHAPTER ELEVEN

Pippa reapplies her make-up in the fitting room mirror while I text Joe to let him know I'm going for a quick drink. I shove my mobile back into my bag, not waiting to see his response.

We leave the shop arm in arm, Pippa and I, and I feel suddenly reckless, like the past few days have all been an awful nightmare and I'm finally back in the real world again.

'We're not going to Whittaker's, obviously,' I say to Pippa as we walk down the High Street, our shoes clacking on the pavement.

'I'm not that insensitive,' she drawls. 'Although it is a shame. It's by far the best bar in town.'

My mobile starts vibrating in my bag and I toy with the idea of ignoring it. I'm pretty sure it will be Joe.

'Your phone…' Pippa says.

We stop walking for a moment while I root around in my handbag and pull it out. *Damn*. Two missed calls. 'Hang on, Pip, it's Joe. Let me just call him back.'

He answers after the first ring. 'Lizzy, what's going on?' he cries.

'What do you mean? Nothing's going on. I'm just going for a quick after-work drink with Pippa.'

'Okay, but I was worried when I saw your text. You don't normally go out. Want me to come and meet you?'

'No, that's okay, I won't be long.'

'Where are you going?'

'Hang on.' I turn to Pippa and mouth. 'Where shall we go?'

'The Crown?'

I shake my head. Joe's crowd will all be in there, and the last thing I need is them telling Joe that they saw his girlfriend having fun without him. 'What about The Black Sheep?' I suggest.

She shrugs and nods.

I put my phone back to my ear. 'Hey, Joe. We're just popping to The Sheep. See you later, okay? I won't be long.'

'Okay.' He doesn't sound impressed.

'Love you!' I say before ending the call.

'I haven't been to The Sheep in a while,' Pippa muses.

'One of my old school friends works behind the bar there. I haven't seen her for ages.'

'Milly Truscott?' Pippa asks.

'No, Abigail Samms.'

'Oh, Abi, yes.'

'You know her?'

'I know everyone, sweetie.' Pippa winks.

Luckily, The Sheep isn't too far down the road, so we won't have to walk past Whittaker's and risk seeing Leon. I'm beginning to get cold feet about this casual drink with Pippa. I've already pissed Joe off with my last-minute arrangements, and what if Leon decides to come into The Sheep for some reason? After our last encounter, it would be beyond awkward. I slow my pace a little, so Pippa links arms with me once more, making me speed up again. 'Stop being such a worrier,' she says. 'We're going to have a lovely, girly evening, all right?'

'All right,' I reply.

Seconds later, we push open the double doors and stroll into the warm, buzzing bar, an enticing tang of garlic and alcohol hanging in the air. It's Saturday evening and the place is already busy with the after-work crowd. Pippa and I weave our way through suited guys smelling of aftershave and groups of perfume-scented women, faint traces of smoke clinging to hair and clothes.

'Lizzy Beresford? Oh my days, it is!'

I turn at the sound of a woman's voice. A familiar face grins back at me, blonde waves tumbling around her face.

'Callie, hi!' I say, returning her smile. 'Haven't seen you properly since…'

'Sam and Lucy's wedding.' She finishes my sentence. 'And that was two flipping years ago.' Callie used to be a good friend of mine back when we were at school, but we've lost touch in more recent years. Nowadays she works as a cashier at the local bank.

'Thought you'd emigrated,' she says, taking a sip of her white wine.

'Emigrated?'

'I'm being sarcastic. We never see you any more. You've become a hermit since you got coupled up.'

It's a bit of a shock to realise that I've let our friendship fizzle out so easily. 'Do you know Pippa?' I ask, changing the subject.

They nod and smile at one another.

'Yeah, we've met before,' Callie says.

'Let me and Pip get a drink and I'll come and find you,' I say.

'Cool, we're in the corner. Me, Soph and Lins.'

Pippa and I carry on to the bar, where I buy us a glass of prosecco each, waving away her insistent offer to go halves.

'Thanks,' she says, squeezing my arm. 'I'll get the next one.'

'I'm only staying for one,' I warn.

'We'll see,' Pippa says with a smirk.

'I don't believe it!' Lindsay says, getting to her feet as I approach the table in the corner.

'Lizzy Beresford, bloody hell!' Sophie cries.

'Is there a blue moon tonight?' Lindsay asks, pretending to peer out of an imaginary window.

'Very funny,' I reply.

'I had to drag her out,' Pippa says.

'Well done,' Callie replies.

'She's had a crappy old day, so I thought a few drinks were in order.'

I realise that Pippa is going to tell them about Leon Whittaker. If she were sitting next to me, I could give her a little kick to get her to keep her mouth shut. I try to catch her eye, but it's too late. I may as well face the fact that this story is going to be all round the town before morning.

'What's happened?' Soph asks, her chocolate-brown eyes wide with concern, glancing from me to Pippa.

'Nothing,' I say, taking a huge slurp of prosecco. 'Let's talk about something else.'

'It's not nothing, darling. It's serious,' Pippa says.

I sit back and resign myself to Pippa blabbing about what's been going on. But actually, the girls are really sympathetic. It's nice to be fussed over for a change. It's lovely to be sitting around a table with my school friends again, like old times. I'm not sure why or how I managed to lose touch with them.

'So, do you really think that Leon's behind the letters?' Callie asks me.

'Honestly, I don't know, Cals. Everything's been really weird lately. Maybe I'm just clutching at straws because he showed an interest in me?'

'You should come out with us more often,' she says. 'Just because some of us are coupled up, doesn't mean we shouldn't catch up now and again.'

I nod, feeling guilty. But honestly, the amount of hassle it causes with Joe whenever I go out without him, it's just not worth it. I know it's only because he loves me. So why do I feel a fluttery, nervous feeling in my stomach at the thought of going back home? He won't be happy, and we'll have an argument. As these thoughts begin to take hold, the shine is rapidly coming off my evening. I love him, but sometimes I wish he'd give me a bit of space – and stop treating me like a two-year-old.

'Well,' I say, getting to my feet, 'it was amazing catching up, but I'm gonna head off.'

'Nooo!' my friends say in unison.

'Have another drink,' Pippa says. 'It's my round.'

'I can't, Pip. My car's in the car park. I've got to drive home.'

'A soft drink, then.'

They continue to try to talk me out of going, but I know I won't enjoy myself, thinking of Joe at home, sulking. I kiss everyone goodbye and promise to come out again soon for a 'proper' night out. As I leave, I hear Pippa telling the girls about her 'divine' new man, Toby. I'm sad to be heading home early. But it'll be nice, I tell myself. Just Joe and I cuddled up on the sofa. Isn't that what everyone wants? Someone to share their life with?

I leave the bar and step out into the evening sunshine. The street is quiet, just the odd car driving past and a few people on foot heading for a local night out in town. I only had one drink, so I hope I'm okay to drive back.

'Lizzy!'

I freeze at the sound of a man's voice. At footsteps running towards me. I jerk my head up to see who it could be. And then he comes into focus.

'Joe!' I'm relieved it's only Joe, but on the other hand, what's he doing here?

He jogs down the street towards me. 'Thought I'd come and join you at The Sheep,' he says with a grin.

'I've just left,' I reply, trying not to snap. 'I'm on my way back to the house right now.'

His eyes light up at my words, and he throws an arm around my shoulders. 'Great. Come on then, Lizzy. Let's get you home.'

Pippa's disdainful words, *he's not your keeper*, buzz around my brain. I want to tell Joe to give me some space, but I bite my tongue instead.

'I was worried,' he continues. 'I don't like you out here on your own in the evening – not with all this stalker stuff going on.'

'I wasn't on my own. I was with Pippa.'

'You know what I mean,' he says. 'You're out in town without anyone to keep an eye on you.'

I should tell him to ease off on the protective boyfriend role, but there's no point provoking an argument. I've got enough trouble in my life at the moment without creating more hassle at home. But my good mood is ruined. What with Leon's visit to the shop and Joe's macho bullshit, I'm sick of men at the moment. The girls were right – I've allowed our old friendships to slide. I need to put that right, and Joe will just have to accept that he's not the only person in my life. I need to see my friends too.

I know this is probably crazy, but a tiny part of me is even beginning to think that it could have been Joe who sent the letters – as an excuse to keep checking up on me. No, that's ridiculous. I shake my head, taking Joe's hand, dismissing the thought as soon as I have it.

I've realised something.

I've realised that this is not just about them. It's also about me.

About letting them know I exist.

The real me.

Not the person who's been invisible for years.

I'm only starting to discover who I am. Peeling away the veneer of my fake life to reveal someone new. Or maybe someone who was there all along but never had the chance to breathe. To shine. To be real.

These messages are simply my calling card. My introduction.

But what comes after the introduction?

CHAPTER TWELVE

The hallway is dark, apart from the yellow glow of a streetlight through the half-glazed front door. I stare down at the doormat, not quite sure what it is that I'm looking at – some kind of red, oozing mess. And there's a dull, rhythmic thump emanating from it. A creeping horror slides over me as I realise it's a bleeding body part, an internal organ of some sort. I want to look away, but I can't. Instead, I find myself crouching down to get a closer look, choking back the urge to throw up. When I realise what it is, I give a scream. It's a heart. A live, beating heart pulsing within a growing pool of blood that's spreading outwards towards my bare feet.

Submerged beneath my scream, a ringing sound emerges. A phone. I stagger upright and back away from the grotesque thing. I head instead towards the insistent ringing. But now I find the hall suddenly has no doors and I can't work out where the ringing is coming from. The sound is all around me, clanging bells inside my head. The air is thick and dark. I can't see anything and I'm terrified that I'm going to accidentally step on the heart. Feel its slimy squelch beneath my feet.

I wake with a start. The nightmare fades and I'm snapped into the present as I realise my phone really is ringing. Our bedroom is dark. It's the middle of the night. The luminous numbers of my clock read 3.40 a.m. Still groggy with sleep, I reach out a hand and bash about on the nightstand for my mobile, managing to answer it before whoever it is rings off.

'Hello?' I gasp.

'Elizabeth Beresford?' A male voice. Serious. Official.

'Yeah. Yeah, that's me.' My mouth is dry, my tongue thick and fuzzy.

'We have you listed as the registered key holder for Georgio's in the High Street. Is that correct?'

'Yes. What's happened? Who is this?'

'Who is it?' Joe murmurs next to me. 'What's the time?'

I ignore Joe for the moment, concentrating instead on the voice at the end of the line.

'This is Police Constable Matt Ryan. I'm afraid there's been a break-in at the shop. Are you able to come down?' It sounds like he's shouting, trying to make himself heard over a deafening clanging sound.

'You want me to come to the station?'

'No. If you can come straight to the shop that would be great.'

'Okay. Give me… uh, ten minutes or so.' I rub my left eye with the back of my fist.

'Great. See you shortly.'

I end the call and sit up, realising that the clanging noise in the background of the phone call was probably the shop alarm.

'Who was that?' Joe asks again. 'Is everything okay?'

'Break-in at the shop.'

'A break-in? What are they calling *you* for? Surely they should've called George.'

'Nope.' I swing my legs out of bed and get to my feet, trying to shake the sleep from my brain. 'It's part of my job description to sort out this kind of thing. All George's managers are key holders for his shops. So he can get his uninterrupted beauty sleep, I suppose.' I let out a huge noisy yawn.

'He should pay you more.' Joe rolls over onto his side and stares at me. 'Want me to come with you?'

I'm tempted to say yes, but there's no point both of us having a broken night's sleep. 'No, don't worry.' I open the wardrobe and root around in the darkness, managing to locate a pair of jeans and a sweatshirt. 'Go back to sleep, Joe. The police are already at the shop. I'll park right outside. There won't be any traffic wardens at this time of the morning. And if there are, the police can explain what's happened. Anyway, if I get a ticket, George can bloody well pay.'

Ten minutes later, I'm outside in the warm, damp night, unlocking my car and sliding into the driver's seat. The remnants of my dream still cling to me and I give a tiny shudder, closing the car door and pushing down the lock, testing the handle to make sure no one can get to me. All of a sudden, I'm overcome with the paralysing terror that someone could be hiding in the back of the car. Maybe they engineered the break-in at the shop in order to get me out of the house. The rational part of my brain tells me I'm being utterly ridiculous, but the other part – the part where nightmares live – is telling me to get out now and run back inside the house.

I grip the steering wheel, too scared to move. Too scared to breathe. Somehow I gather up the nerve to turn my head, even as chills are sweeping down my spine. The back seat looks empty, but I can't relax just yet. I ease myself round and kneel backward on my seat, peering into the back and down onto the floor. There's no one there. Of course there's no one there. What was I even thinking?

The roads are empty at this time of the morning. Even though last night was a Saturday, downtown Malmesbury tends to become quiet soon after pub kicking-out time. It's not exactly a heaving metropolis of action. Consequently, it only takes me a couple of minutes to reach Georgio's. I see the squad car parked out front and I pull up behind it, take a breath and wonder what I'm going to find here. Wonder if the damage will be great, and whether the thieves will have taken much stock. Straight away I notice that the glass front door has a jagged hole in it about three quarters of the way up. As I turn off the car engine, the deafening clang of the shop alarm makes me wince. I pity anyone who lives on the High Street. They won't get any sleep until that racket stops.

I get out of the car and nod at the two uniformed officers. I recognise one of them – he's the young male policeman who came to the shop on Friday with Sergeant Llewellyn. He looks older tonight. Less fresh-faced.

'Hello again,' he shouts above the racket. 'Doesn't look like you're having a great week.'

'Tell me about it. Did anyone see what happened?'

'Afraid not. There was no one around when we got here. The alarm company called us out.'

'Would CCTV have caught anything?' I ask.

'No cameras pointing in this direction. They're all focused up around the Market Cross and down the bottom of the High Street near the pubs. But we'll take a look at the footage, see if we can spot anyone leaving the scene. Do you have any security cameras on the premises?'

I shake my head. 'No, it's something that's been talked about, but we've never got round to it.'

'Okay. Do you want to go and open up? Turn off the alarm?'

'I thought you said the shop had been broken into?'

'Sorry, my mistake. The door is still locked, so it doesn't look as though they actually got inside the shop. It was either a failed attempt at a break-in, or vandals. Maybe even an angry drunk kicking it in or lobbing something through the glass.'

That's one bit of good news at least. If it wasn't thieves, then all George will have to do is get the glass in the door replaced. I pull the shop keys out of my handbag and fumble with them in the lock of the wooden side door until, finally, I manage to get inside. The alarm is absolutely deafening in here and I quickly punch in the code, sighing with relief when the clanging finally stops, although I think I'm going to hear that ringing in my ears for days.

I switch on all the lights, blinking in the sudden brightness, and make my way along the corridor and through to the main part of the shop. The two officers follow me inside and we stare around the interior. There's a small amount of glass on the floor by the door. One of the display units has been damaged, a result of whatever missile was used to break the front door.

'There.' PC Ryan points to a chunky black object on the carpet behind the display unit. It looks broken, like it's half a piece of something. I spot the other half wedged in among a smashed display of china mugs. Ryan walks over to the object on the carpet. 'Looks like marble.'

I reach down to pick up the other piece, but PC Ryan's voice stops me.

'Don't touch it. I'll bag it up and see if we can get some prints off it. Nice smooth piece of rock like that should yield some good prints, if the perp wasn't wearing gloves.'

I stare at the piece of marble. It's black, lined with silvery white veins. PC Ryan comes over to me with the other piece in his gloved hand. 'Looks like some kind of ornament,' he says.

'Or an ashtray,' I say. 'Look, it's got a deep indent, and there's a little groove on the edge where you rest your cigarette. My dad's got a similar one, but it's green.'

'Could be,' he replies. 'Strange thing to throw through a window, or rather through a door. Not the sort of thing someone would just happen to be carrying around in their pocket.'

'So you think someone came here with that ashtray deliberately?' I ask.

'Maybe.'

'But if it wasn't attempted robbery, or spur-of-the-moment vandalism,' I say, 'then it could be something more personal. An angry customer, perhaps.' I don't dare voice my biggest fear – that it has something to do with me. That it's the stalker who has done this. Possibly even Leon Whittaker. Would he be so vindictive? I have no idea.

The other officer pipes up. 'Could have been an attempted robbery, but they got spooked when the alarm went off, or maybe someone disturbed them before they could break in.'

'So what happens now?' I ask.

'It doesn't look like anyone actually made it inside the shop,' PC Ryan says. 'Both doors were locked and that hole isn't big enough for someone to climb through, but you should check nothing's missing, just in case. Do you keep cash in the till?'

'No, and we always leave the drawer open overnight – so if anyone does break in they can see there's nothing there but small change. We keep the float in a little safe.'

'Better check it's still there.'

I make my way to the stockroom and unlock the safe with one of my keys, but it looks like all the cash is untouched. I do a quick count-up – four ten-pound notes, six fives and twenty one-pound coins. The small change is still in the register. 'It's all here,' I confirm.

'If it was thieves, they would have gone for the cash first,' PC Ryan says. 'Will you be claiming on insurance for the door, and the broken unit?'

'It's not actually my shop,' I say. 'I'm just the manageress.'

'Okay, well, if the owner wants to get in touch with us for an incident number for insurance, tell him or her to give us a call.'

I nod. 'Thanks. So, you'll check the CCTV?'

'Yes. We'll let you know if we find anything.'

'Okay, great. You don't think…' I trail off.

'Go on,' he prompts.

'Could it be something to do with the letters I've been getting?'

'We can't rule it out,' he replies.

'What letters are these?' the other officer asks.

Ryan fills him in.

The other officer listens to his colleague and then turns to me. 'I shouldn't worry too much. I doubt the two things are connected.

If it was targeted at you specifically then I don't think they'd have thrown that chunk of marble through the shop window.'

I realise he's probably right. They would have aimed it through my house window instead. I let out a sigh, which turns into a yawn.

'You should go home,' PC Ryan says. 'Leave this mess until tomorrow.'

'You might want to board up the door first,' the older officer adds. 'Make sure it's secure so no one else tries to get in.'

I thank the two officers, who eventually leave with the bagged-up pieces of broken ashtray. I'm tempted to ignore everything and go back home to bed, but we've got that family lunch later today so I won't have time to clear up the mess later. I check the time on my phone. Almost 5 a.m. It should only take me half an hour or so to sort this lot out, then I can be home by 6 a.m to hopefully grab three or four more hours' sleep.

Joe has left me a text to see how I'm getting on, so I tap out a quick reply before heading to the stockroom to hunt for some kind of board I can use to cover the hole in the door. But before I open the stockroom door, I notice something on the floor outside one of the fitting rooms. A small box of some kind. I lean down and pick it up. It's a box of magnetic letters. We sell them in the shop. I wonder what it's doing all the way over here. Funny I never noticed it when I was closing up yesterday, or a minute ago when I was checking the cash. I guess I was too preoccupied. The cardboard is ripped, the cellophane hanging off. The box has been opened.

I swallow. The curtains to this particular fitting room are closed, which is also strange, as they're only ever closed when someone is using them. All of a sudden, my heart is beating painfully. Sweat breaks out on my forehead, my back, my armpits. There wouldn't be anyone hiding back here, would there? Surely not. Every particle in my body is screaming at me to run. To call the police back. But what if the fitting room is empty and I call them here for absolutely no reason?

This is silly. Of course there won't be anyone in there. The doors were locked. No one broke in. I draw back the curtain, ready to bolt if I see anyone.

A dark figure staring back at me makes me scream and jump backward, bashing my arm against the sharp edge of the counter. But then I realise, it's only my own reflection in the fitting room mirror. I put my hands on my hips and exhale, letting out an expletive and allowing myself to relax. Thank goodness I didn't call the cops back to the shop. That would have been embarrassing.

And then my eyes stray to the fitting room floor.

Spelled out in colourful magnetic letters are the words:

Hello Lizzy. Me again.

CHAPTER THIRTEEN

My mouth is dry as parchment, my stomach turned to slush. *They were here*. Whoever it was, they came into the shop. I grip the edges of the fitting room walls. There's no getting away from it – I really do have a stalker.

My mind races. Did they come in before closing time? Or did they come in afterwards? And if it was afterwards, then they must have had a key, because the doors were still locked and the hole in the glass was only the size of a fist. I fight the urge to reach down and mess up the letters. To erase their taunting words. But I have to leave them as evidence. The police need to see this. What will PC Ryan make of the message? Will he do something? Pass it on to a detective, who will try to find out who's behind all this? Surely they're going to take me more seriously now. I hope so.

After I call the police, the squad car pulls up outside the shop within a matter of minutes, back again having only just left. I open the door to greet the officers, realising that the dark strip of sky is already lightening. Dawn is here.

PC Ryan and his colleague follow me into the shop and I take them straight to the fitting room to see the letters. They glance down at the colourful pieces of plastic, and then they look at one another.

'And you just noticed this after we'd gone?' Ryan says.

I nod. 'I was going out the back, to look for something to cover the broken glass, and I noticed there was this cardboard box on the floor by the fitting room.' I hold the box out for them to see. 'Sorry, I probably shouldn't have touched it, but I didn't know what it was at the time. Anyway, it's been ripped open, as you can see. Then I saw that the fitting room curtain was closed, which is unusual as we leave them open unless someone's getting changed.' I'm speaking really quickly. Too quickly, almost manically. But I can't seem to slow my words down. 'So, I opened the curtains – I was nervous, thinking there might be someone hiding behind them, that maybe they'd been hiding back here the whole time – but when I opened the curtains… well, there was no one here, but then I saw the message. It's creepy. Don't you think it's creepy?' I babble.

'It is a strange thing to find,' the older officer says. He glances at PC Ryan once more, and I get the feeling they don't think it's as serious as I do. 'Could it be the work of a colleague? A prank, maybe?'

'What?' I'm not impressed with this suggestion at all. 'Ripping open an item of stock? Leaving the empty box on the floor, and then writing a threatening message directed at me? Not a very nice prank.'

'No, okay,' Ryan says. 'We take your point.'

'And the other thing is…' I say. 'You know Sergeant Llewellyn went to have a word with Leon Whittaker yesterday afternoon?'

'She did mention it,' Ryan says.

'Well, straight after that, he came into the shop to apologise to me.'

He frowns. 'After Llewellyn asked him to keep his distance?'

'And then he got angry, because I asked him to leave.'

'Was he threatening?'

'He didn't say anything threatening, but his demeanour was threatening.'

'And you think it could have been him who left this message?'

'I honestly don't know… But it feels a bit too coincidental.'

'Was he left on his own in the shop at all? Would he have had the opportunity to write the message?'

I shake my head, knowing that it was unlikely he did this while I was there. 'I don't know.'

'Does everybody call you Lizzy?' Ryan asks. 'Or do some people know you as Elizabeth? Because whoever left the message knows you well enough to call you Lizzy.'

'Everyone calls me Lizzy,' I say. 'The only person who calls me Elizabeth is my mum when she's cross with me. Which is most of the time,' I mutter.

'Okay,' Ryan replies. 'I'll ask Sergeant Llewellyn to have another word with Mr Whittaker. Tell him it's best that he leaves you alone.'

'Thank you. Will you also ask him if he knows anything about this message?'

'I'll speak to Sergeant Llewellyn,' Ryan says.

The older officer clears his throat. 'How did you manage to miss this when you were checking the till earlier? You walked right past the fitting room. Wouldn't you have noticed the closed curtains and the box lying on the floor?'

I stop myself from glaring at him. I much prefer PC Ryan; at least he seems to believe me. 'You think I did this? You think I wrote a creepy little note in magnetic letters to myself? You think I want to be here at my workplace, talking to you at five thirty in the morning, instead of tucked up at home in bed, asleep?'

'Please don't upset yourself,' the officer says. 'We don't "think" anything, we're simply trying to work out the sequence of events.'

'Do you know what?' I say, scratching the side of my head so hard it hurts. 'Just forget it. I shouldn't have called you. I should have said to myself, oh well, some nutter is writing me creepy letters, but it'll be absolutely fine. What I'll do is wait until he confronts me face-to-face – maybe with a knife, or maybe with a—'

'Okay, Lizzy,' PC Ryan interrupts, his voice annoyingly calm, highlighting my own increasingly hysterical tone. 'I can see what you're saying. In light of all the other recent events with the letters and so forth, I think you're right.' He turns to his colleague. 'CSI?' he asks.

His colleague gives a brief, reluctant nod.

PC Ryan turns back to me. 'We'll get CSI to come down to the shop and photograph the letters in situ, take prints.'

I'm surprised by their change of heart. My anger deflates and my nerves flare up once more. They must be worried if they're getting CSI involved.

'It's a pity you touched the box,' the older officer says.

'Sorry,' I reply. 'I didn't realise what it was. How long will it take to get the results back?'

'A rushed submission with the labs takes around three to four days for analysis,' he says.

'So this will be a rushed submission?' I ask.

'I can't promise, but probably,' he replies. 'I should imagine we'll also be briefing the neighbourhood team who covers where you live and also the town centre team. That way, if anything else happens, you won't need to spend time getting them up to speed.'

'Thank you. Can I tidy up the front of the shop and board up the door before they arrive?' I stare at the broken glass and the smashed display case. The last thing I feel like doing is clearing it all up, but the quicker I get it done, the quicker I can go home.

'You'll need to leave all that until CSI have been,' Ryan says.

'When will they get here?'

'Hopefully within the next few hours.'

'Okay. So, do I need to stay?' I ask, my heart sinking at the thought of waiting around for hours.

'No, that's okay,' PC Ryan replies. 'We can wait for them. I'll call you when they're done.'

It feels strange leaving the officers in the shop without me there. But I suppose the place is in safe hands. I wonder if CSI will find anything incriminating. I wonder if Leon Whittaker really could be involved. After my earlier adrenalin rush, I'm suddenly exhausted. I need to get home and lay my head on a pillow. Although whether or not I'll actually be able to get to sleep is another matter altogether.

CHAPTER FOURTEEN

After showering, I go into the bedroom and open the wardrobe door. I love this little cottage, but its one downside is the lack of storage space. All my clothes are crammed into one half – okay, two thirds – of a double wardrobe. Joe's clothes are squashed into the remaining third. He doesn't seem to mind, thank goodness. I pull out a suitable dress, ease the material over my head and smooth it down, watching it flare out over my hips. The burnt-orange colour brings out the reddish lights in my chestnut hair. Even so, I gaze critically at myself in the mirror. It needs a belt, so I root through the crush of clothes in the wardrobe and settle on a cream leather one that will go with my tan and cream Mary Janes.

I'm surprised that I actually look half decent. I suppose that's the miracle of good clothes and make-up. Inside, I feel frayed and unravelled, as though I've aged ten years. I barely managed one extra hour's sleep this morning after last night's episode, which all seems like an outlandish dream.

I haven't heard back from the police yet, so I assume they're still waiting for the crime scene officers to show up. I called George earlier this morning to break the bad news. Told him I'd sort out a glazier tomorrow on my day off. He thanked me and said he'd give me a bonus on top of this month's wages. So I guess at least that's something.

As for the hand-delivered letters and the magnetic letters message, I can hardly bear to think about them. I'm pinning all my hopes on the police finding the culprit, but I know this isn't a realistic hope.

Even with the authorities taking things seriously, there's no guarantee they'll find any fingerprints. If someone is going to the trouble of freaking me out, they'll probably have worn gloves to create their creepy letters and messages. To top it all off, I've got a potentially stressful family lunch to look forward to today, so my nerves would be frayed even without the break-in and the lack of sleep.

I take a breath and wonder if I could get away with a quick gin and tonic to settle my nerves. But the risk is I'd have a second, followed by a third, which would render me halfway to drunk, and then I'd end up saying something I shouldn't to my perfect sister and my critical mother. At least Dad will be there – a mellow port in stormy seas.

Another thing that's got me worried is Frank's disappearance. It's been almost two days now. And, yes, he's gone roaming for longer than that before, but I can't help worrying that something might have happened to him. If he's not back by this evening, I'm going to go out searching for him and put posters up. I twist my hair up into a French roll, pin it in place and then make my way downstairs, where Joe is waiting for me in the kitchen, dressed in chinos and a short-sleeved shirt.

I told Joe about the magnetic letters and about CSI, but I haven't mentioned that Leon Whittaker asked me out yesterday. If I tell Joe about him, he won't stop to think – he'll go round to Whittaker's wine bar and start throwing punches at Leon. And that will be that; he'll be sent to jail without passing Go.

Anyway, aside from all that business, Joe looks as miserable as I feel this morning.

'It'll be over in a few hours,' I say.

'Do we have to go?' His eyes are wide, pleading. 'Can you go without me?'

I give him my death glare and he holds his hands up. 'Joke!' he cries. 'You know I'd never let you suffer through it on your own.'

'I'm sorry, Joe. I know how awkward this is for you.'

But it's Mum's birthday today, and every year we always go out for lunch and pretend to be this wonderful, loving family. I wonder if Mum would still think my sister was such a golden girl if she knew the truth about what she did. That she tried to steal my boyfriend. I wonder if Emma will ever own up to it? Maybe it's easier for her just to pretend it never happened. Pretend I don't exist. But I can't deny that it still hurts.

'Come on then,' I say, putting my phone in my handbag. 'Let's get this over with.'

'Are you sure you're up to it?' Joe asks. 'After last night… that was pretty stressful for you. I'm sure they'd understand. I mean, you've had no sleep, a break-in at the shop, you're being harassed. Do I need to go on?'

'Nice try, Mr Lawrence, but you know as well as I do that nothing barring death keeps anyone from attending Mum's birthday lunch. I'd never hear the end of it. It's three hours of pain, and then we can come home and relax for the rest of the day.' I turn at a sound from the back door, my breath catching in my throat. But I relax when I see who it is.

'Frank!' I'm flooded with such joy at the sight of his marmalade face and white socks.

'Hey, Frankie boy.' Joe leans down and picks him up, scratches behind his ears while Frank purrs like a washing machine on its spin cycle.

'Where have you been, you naughty creature… is that blood?'

'Where?' Joe frowns and looks down at our errant cat.

'There! On his left, no, on his right paw. Looks like dried blood.' I gingerly reach across and pick up his foot, but Frank isn't happy about this. His ears flatten and he gives a low yowl like a dog. He's never done that before. Never. His paw must be hurting. 'Put him down a sec.'

Joe does as I ask and Frank walks straight over to his food bowl. But I notice he doesn't bear any weight on his bad foot.

'He must have cut it on something,' Joe says. 'Poor guy. Nothing wrong with his appetite, though.' Frank is tucking into his breakfast like he hasn't eaten for days, which I suppose he hasn't. I've been putting fresh food out twice a day since his disappearance.

'We should probably take him to the vet,' Joe says.

'I know. But if we go to the vet's, we won't make Mum's lunch. She'll use this against me for months. You know what she's like. I can hear her now: "Well, you know Lizzy, she thinks more of her cat than her own mother".'

Joe's shoulders droop, knowing this last opportunity to get out of the meal has been shut down. I'd rather take Frank straight to the vet, but apart from his paw he seems okay.

'I'll make an appointment to take him later,' I say. 'He seems all right for now, don't you think?'

Joe shrugs.

'What?'

'It's just, normally you treat Frank like a little prince, like he's your baby. I'm surprised you aren't rushing him round to the vet's in an ambulance.'

'Ha, ha, very funny. I'm not that bad.' In truth, I'm so tired I can hardly think straight. Everything feels a little surreal. All I know is, I can't give Mum an excuse to have a go at me. I couldn't cope with that on top of everything else that's going on. 'I'll lock the cat flap. Don't want Frank disappearing again.'

'Good idea. I'll put out a litter tray.'

After Frank has eaten his fill, he jumps into a basket of laundry, curls up with the tip of his tail over his nose, closes his eyes and goes to sleep. A glance at the kitchen clock tells me we're going to be late.

'Come on then,' Joe says. 'Frank looks happy enough, let's go and get this over with.'

I nod and follow my boyfriend out of the house.

*

We arrive at the Italian restaurant, in nearby Tetbury, twenty minutes late. My family are already seated around a rectangular table, but they get to their feet when we walk in. Joe and I wish my mum a happy birthday and I give her the beautifully gift-wrapped silk scarf I picked out from the shop, and a bouquet of roses.

'Lovely, Lizzy. Thank you,' Mum says, giving me a dry kiss on the cheek. 'Pretty roses. Although I hope they don't wilt while we're sitting here.'

'They'll be fine, Mum.'

Subtly made up, my mum looks as immaculate as ever, her brown hair tied back in a sleek chignon, her fitted floral dress perfect for her trim figure. 'You look tired,' she says, casting a critical gaze over me, then placing my gift in her handbag without opening it.

'I'm okay. Just been busy at work.'

'If you want to know about being busy, you should speak to your sister,' Mum says. 'Emma's been to a conference in America this month. A proper little jet-setter.'

'Nice,' I say, without looking at my sister.

'Hello, Joe.' Mum gives him a curt nod and lets him kiss her cheek.

'Happy birthday, Pam.' Joe catches my eye and grins.

Despite my dread at the lunch ahead, I stifle a giggle. If you can't laugh…

'Lizzy, love.' Dad comes over and envelops me in a huge bear hug. I'm overwhelmed with the aroma of his aftershave and cigarette smoke, that familiar scent of security and comfort. Unlike my mum, Dad has let himself go a bit. His once sandy hair is now grey; his belly hangs over the waistband of his suit trousers. And he would live in scruffy old shorts and T-shirts if he had his way. Mum nags him about what he eats and what he wears, but he pays her absolutely no attention. Despite this, Mum still adores him. I wonder, sometimes, if she's jealous of my relationship with him.

I've always been a daddy's girl, and he sticks up for me whenever Mum gets on my case about my weight, or my job, or any other lifestyle choice she doesn't agree with.

'Hi, Dad. How you doing? How's the microbrewery?'

'Good, love. I'm giving that Ray Tanner a run for his money. The man wouldn't know a good ale if it bit him on the arse.' Apparently Dad's best friend, Ray, has also turned his shed into a brewery and there's a bit of not-so-friendly rivalry going on.

'Hello, Joe.' Emma's fiancé Mike Prince holds out his hand for Joe to shake. Mike's far older than my twenty-nine-year-old sister. In his mid-forties, with greying hair, he's an orthopaedic surgeon who never says much at these family gatherings. Consequently, I don't really know him and he doesn't seem interested in getting to know me either. Emma and Mike live in Bristol in a fancy waterside apartment. Not that I've ever been there, but Mum likes to keep me informed about their ever-increasing upward mobility.

Mike nods at me and I give him a lukewarm smile. It's a testament to how bad things are between me and Emma that we don't even acknowledge one another. No eye contact. Not even a hello or a nod. But Mum and Dad don't remark on it. I guess if you ignore something, you can pretend it isn't happening.

I wish I could sit next to Dad, but there's no space. Instead, I find myself with Joe to my left and Mum to my right.

In actual fact, lunch isn't as bad as I was expecting. My *penne al salmone* is delicious and I spend most of the time chatting to Joe, which we never really get to do at home. United in our reluctance to be here, we end up having quite a laugh.

'You two are like a couple of children giggling in the corner,' Mum says. 'I can't hear a word you're saying. Like sparrows twittering away.' I think she's aiming for a light-hearted tone, but it comes across as critical. 'So, how are things at the garage, Joe?' Mum says 'garage' like it's a dirty word.

'Fine, thanks, Pam.'

'Good.' She transfers her gaze to me. 'Are you having dessert, Elizabeth?'

'Well, I was thinking about the raspberry cheesecake. How about you?'

'Have a coffee instead,' she says. 'I'll have one with you.' She pauses before adding: 'You know, I weigh the same today as I did the day I got married – eight stone.' This is Mum's subtle-as-a-brick way of telling me I'm overweight, but I've learnt the best way to deal with that is to ignore it.

'Mm, coffee. Good idea, Mum.'

She smiles and gives me a satisfied nod.

I turn to the waiter: 'I'll have a double espresso and the panna cotta, please.'

'Good for you, love,' Dad says, giving me a wink. 'I think I'll have the panna cotta too.'

I don't turn my head to check on Mum's reaction. I know what it will be – disappointment.

Of course, Emma has the same svelte figure as Mum. Mum loves saying how the two of them look more like sisters than mother and daughter. As for me, I'm big-boned like Dad, but I think my size suits me. I'm happy with it. And Joe has always liked me the way I am. I do have Mum's chestnut hair, though. Whereas Emma has Dad's auburn hair colouring and fair skin.

I glance diagonally across the table at my sister. She's fiddling with her napkin, and I notice she's hardly touched her food. She and Mike have barely spoken two words to one another since we got here. I wonder if they're going through a rough patch – not ideal if they're planning to get married next year. But I guess everyone has disagreements from time to time. These are the things we would have discussed if things had been different. If she hadn't betrayed me.

Mike says something under his breath to her and she snaps at him. I can't make out exactly what she says, but it sounded like the last word she spoke was 'letter'… 'Got the something, something *letter*.'

My skin goes cold. Why is she talking about a letter? Could my initial thoughts about Emma being behind the letters have been correct?

Joe has started talking to me about another car he's thinking of buying, but I'm only half-listening. Instead, my attention is trained on my sister and her hushed argument with Mike. She catches my eye and scowls. I'm taken aback by the venom in her stare, but maybe it wasn't directed at me, maybe it was for Mike. She doesn't seem very happy with him. She angles her body away from him and starts talking to Dad, leaving Mike brooding into his almost empty half-pint glass.

Did Emma actually say the word 'letter'? Or am I making connections where there are none? Would she really do something like that? Emma may not be my favourite person in the world, but I don't think she's capable of something so… awful. Is she?

But then again, I'm sure she said the word 'letter'.

CHAPTER FIFTEEN

George sweeps into the shop like a short, stocky, balding rock star, his designer suit and sunglasses probably worth more than two months of my rent. Pippa and I both subconsciously stand to attention.

'Morning, ladies,' he says in his Kentish twang. George moved to the local area from Sittingbourne in Kent twenty years ago with his wife Sophia and their young family. He opened up a shop in Gloucestershire, followed by two more, then this one and finally another in Wiltshire. They're all called Georgio's, and he's installed managers in each of them. Our branch has the honour of being the most profitable. I like to think it's down to my superb management skills, but if I'm being honest, Pippa's wealthy friends have probably got a lot to do with it.

'I see you've sold the Cavendish handbag!' George booms across at me to where I'm pricing up enamel pens at the counter. 'Nice work!' The Cavendish handbag is a trial item of stock – George is trying to add in some pricier pieces to test whether our customers' wallets are deep enough for such rare designer delights. This particular handbag is priced in the low hundreds, and I wasn't sure if it would sell. Pippa must have sold it yesterday, which was my day off.

'Pippa?' I enquire. 'Did you sell it?'

'What?' She's half-heartedly dusting a jewellery cabinet, her face like a wet weekend. She's convinced Toby is already going off her, and she doesn't know how to keep his interest.

‘Did you sell the Cavendish bag from the window yesterday?’

She shakes her head. ‘No.’

‘I hope it hasn’t been nicked,’ George says, his face darkening.

‘I suppose it could have been stolen during the break-in,’ Pippa says.

Pippa and I spend the next few minutes scouring the shop and the back room, but the elusive bag is nowhere to be seen. The shop is absolutely immaculate after the break-in. I came in on Sunday afternoon after CSI had done their thing, and after Mum’s birthday lunch, and I painstakingly swept up every piece of glass and logged every item of damaged stock. I was there until early evening. Finally, at around seven-ish, Joe turned up with fish and chips, which I banned him from bringing into the shop as the smell would have got into all the clothes. So we sat beneath the Market Cross, like a couple of teenagers, and stuffed our faces.

I catch up with George, who’s flicking through the invoices on my desk in the stockroom.

‘We’ve looked everywhere for the bag. It’s not here,’ I admit.

‘Do you remember seeing it in the window on Sunday after the break-in?’ he asks.

I cast my mind back. ‘I’m pretty sure it was still there. I had a scout around the whole shop at the time, checking for missing stock. I would have noticed if it wasn’t there. But, then again, I could be mistaken… can you claim for it on insurance?’

‘Nah. Bloody insurance isn’t worth a damn, Lizzy. My excess is a grand, so there’s no point in claiming.’

I haven’t told George that the break-in might have been carried out by the person who is stalking me. I’m not sure whether he’d be sympathetic, or annoyed. Now that I’m faced with my boss, I’m 99 per cent sure it isn’t him who’s behind the letters. It’s just not his style. George is brash and loud and in-your-face. Leaving creepy letters doesn’t fit his personality. Unless he’s schizophrenic.

'Well…' George leans back in the chair and locks his hands behind his head. 'That's a right pain in the derrière, isn't it? I'll have to order another one. Next time, stick the bag in one of the locked display cases, Lizzy.'

I nod, feeling chastised.

Another possibility is needling away at me. I know it's unfair, and I don't have any hard evidence, but I'm starting to believe that Pippa might be stealing goods from the shop. I also think she's taking money from the till. I don't know how I'm going to broach the subject. I can't accuse Pippa outright, and I don't want to mention it to George in case I'm wrong. I'll have to do a little more digging…

'Are you coming, Joe?' I yell up the stairs. 'It's almost seven!'

Earlier this morning, I remembered we were supposed to go for dinner with Ian and Ruby next door. I texted Joe to let him know, and received a grumpy message back. He's not a great socialiser, unless it's with me or his mates from work. But it was too late to cancel – Ruby and Ian would have already bought food for tonight, and as they're our neighbours, we can't get away with pretending to be sick. Besides, I like them. They're harmless. And I want to keep friendly with all our neighbours in case my stalker shows up and I need moral (or physical) support.

'Joe!'

'Coming!' He stomps down the stairs and I laugh at his expression.

'What's so funny?'

'You are, Mr Grumpy. You will be nice to them, won't you?'

'Mmm,' he says in a non-committal way.

I pop back into the kitchen to check on Frank before we leave. He's absolutely fine now, thank goodness. We took him to the vet's on Sunday evening and they gave him the once-over, confirming that, yes, he had cut his paw but it was healing nicely and didn't need any treatment. They suggested keeping him inside until he could bear weight on it. Consequently, Frank has been alternately miaowing at the back door and sulking.

'It's for your own good, Frankie,' I say, stroking his head. He flicks his ears and turns his head away. 'Fine, be like that,' I say. 'But just remember who gives you your supper.' I take the wine out of the fridge and grab the bouquet of pink tulips from the kitchen counter. 'Ready?' I ask Joe.

He gestures to his 'going out' clothes that he's wearing, and we leave the house and walk the few steps to our neighbours' front door.

Joe rings the bell and we hear clattering footsteps and cries from the other side of the glass. 'Get the door, babe!' Ruby yells.

'I'm upstairs!'

'Fuck's sake, I'm trying to put this stuff in the oven!'

Joe and I glance at one another, our eyes wide, trying not to laugh. A few seconds later, there's the clip-clop of more measured footsteps on the hall floor, and the front door finally opens.

Ruby stands before us in a skintight, black micro-dress that barely covers her bits, and three-inch-high gold strappy sandals. Her face is beautifully made up, although her eyebrows are a bit heavily drawn in. She looks like she belongs in an exclusive nightclub. I feel way underdressed by comparison in my pink flared skirt and white voile blouse.

'Lizzy! Joe! Come in.' Ruby beams at us and then turns towards the stairs. 'Ian! Get your arse downstairs! They're here!'

'You look amazing, Ruby,' I say.

'Thanks. So do you.'

I pass her the wine and the flowers.

'Aw, these are lovely – really classy. Thanks.'

We follow her into the lounge, where an assortment of cereal bowls have been filled to the brim with crisps and peanuts. 'Sit down. Help yourselves.' She gestures to the snacks.

Joe and I dutifully sit on the leather sofa and scoop up a few crisps.

'Can I get you a drink?' she says. 'We've got beer and vodka, or I've got some WKDs in the fridge if you want?'

'I'll have a beer, thanks,' Joe says.

'I'll have some of the wine I bought, if that's okay,' I say.

'No problem. Back in a sec.' Ruby leaves the room.

When she's gone, Joe eyes up the sea of bowls perched on every available surface. 'Do you think they like crisps?' he asks.

'Don't be mean,' I hiss. 'It looks like they've gone to a lot of trouble.'

'Yeah, they've obviously been on some kind of dangerous crisp expedition.'

I shake my head and try not to laugh. We sit there for another five minutes wondering where Ruby can have got to. 'Maybe I should go and see if she needs any help,' I muse.

Joe shrugs. 'If you like.'

I get to my feet and head out into the hall, peering into the kitchen, but it doesn't look as though anyone's in there. Then I hear voices coming from upstairs.

'You'll have to go and get one,' Ruby snaps.

'Where from?' Ian replies.

'I dunno. Supermarket, I suppose. Or the offy.'

'Why didn't she bring her own?'

'Everything all right?' I call up the stairs.

Ruby peers down, her face red. 'Sorry, we're coming down.'

'Is there a problem?' I ask as Ruby heads down the staircase followed by Ian.

'Hi.' I give him a little wave.

'All right.' He nods at me. 'Just gotta go out for a minute.' He gives Ruby an indecipherable look.

'Is something wrong?' I ask again.

'You're drinking wine, right?' Ian asks me.

'Er, yes, is that okay?'

'Ian, shut up,' Ruby says, elbowing him in the arm.

Ian ignores her. 'We haven't got a corkscrew. So I've just got to go out and get one.'

'A corkscrew?'

'For your wine.'

'It's okay,' I say. 'It's a screw top. Most wine bottles are screw top now.'

'Really?' Ruby says, her shoulders relaxing. 'It's just, we don't drink wine, and you see them on the telly opening wine bottles with corkscrews, so I just thought…' She dissolves into laughter.

'You dozy cow.' Ian gives her arm a friendly push. 'Give me that.' He takes the bottle off her. 'You go back in the lounge, I'll sort the drinks.'

Ruby and I return to the lounge, where she tells Joe what happened. The ice has been well and truly broken, and I see Ruby visibly relax.

'I know I'm twenty-three, but this is our first dinner party,' she admits. 'Feel proper grown up. I bet you have them all the time, don't you? I've been getting in a state all day. Worried I'm gonna make a mess of everything.'

It's touching how nervous she's been about having us over. 'Don't worry,' I say, trying to put her at ease. 'We're used to having our tea on our laps in front of the TV, so anything's a step up from that.'

'Okay.' She gives us a warm smile, and I can see that even Joe is charmed by her openness.

'Here we go.' Ian kicks open the lounge door and comes in with a tray of drinks. Two cans of lager, a bottle of vodka, a bottle of Coke, an empty glass and a glass of wine. Joe clears a space in the sea of crisps and Ian sets the tray down.

'Cheers!' We all clink cans and glasses.

After about ten minutes of chatting on the sofa, we squeeze around the four-seater dining table set up in the corner of the lounge. Dinner is pizza, garlic bread and salad. We all dig in, helping ourselves to the hot slices, which have been served up on two bread boards. The evening is relaxed and fun. Ruby is sweet and Ian is a bit of a lad, but he's okay.

'You work in that shop down town, don't you?' Ruby asks me.

'Georgio's. Yeah, I manage it.'

'Cool,' Ruby says through a mouthful of garlic bread.

'They had a break-in on Saturday night,' Joe adds.

'That's terrible,' Ruby says, her eyes filling with concern.

'Did they take much?' Ian says, getting to his feet. 'Want another beer?' he asks Joe.

'Please,' Joe replies.

Ian starts towards the door, but stops to listen to my reply.

'They only cracked the glass,' I say. 'No one actually got inside the shop. We don't think they did, anyway.'

'Tell them about the magnetic letters,' Joe prompts.

I give him a look. It's not something I wanted to talk about this evening. Tonight was going to be a break from all that. 'It's nothing,' I say.

'It's not nothing,' Joe persists.

'Fine.' I sigh.

'You don't have to tell us…' Ruby says.

'No, it's okay,' I reply. 'I don't mind.'

'Wait till I get back from the kitchen,' Ian says. He returns a few seconds later with two cans of cold beer and passes one to Joe before sitting back down next to Ruby.

'So,' I continue, 'you already know about the letters I've been getting.'

Ian and Ruby nod, their eyes wide, waiting for me to go on.

'Well, the glass in the shop door was cracked, but the doors were locked when I got there, and nothing was stolen. But in the fitting room on the floor, someone had used magnetic letters to write me a message.'

'What message?' Ian asks.

I swallow. 'It said: "Hello Lizzy. Me again".'

'Shit,' Ruby says. 'That's dark.'

I take a breath. 'Anyway, I'm not going to let it bother me. It's just some saddo trying to make their life more interesting.'

'So you've got no idea who's done it?' Ian asks.

I shake my head. 'None whatsoever.'

'Yes, we have,' Joe growls. 'It's that toff Sebastian Hargreaves.'

'Erm, we don't know that,' I say. Again, thoughts of my sister climb unbidden into my mind.

'No, but it's pretty obvious,' Joe says.

'No, it's not. Anyway, I asked Pippa and she said no way is it Seb.'

'Well, she would say that, wouldn't she? He's her brother.'

I try my best to keep my cool and not come back with an angry retort.

'Once the cops get the results back from the lab, they'll know one way or the other.'

'Results?' Ian asks.

'CSI,' Joe explains. 'Fingerprinting and stuff.'

'Cool,' Ian replies.

I try to catch Joe's eye to glare at him, but he's not looking my way. Giving up, I turn to Ruby. 'So, do you work at all?' I figure that changing the subject is the safest way of not having a full-blown argument in front of the neighbours.

'Yeah,' she replies with a curl of her lip. 'It's not anywhere near as glamorous as your job, though.'

'Believe me, my job isn't glamorous,' I say, trying to play it down. 'It mainly consists of unpacking boxes and sticking prices on stuff.'

'Well, give me cardboard boxes over rich people's toilets any day.' She wrinkles her pretty nose.

'Our Rubes is a cleaner,' Ian explains.

'Not just any cleaner.' She grins. 'I work for a posh holiday letting company – Cotswold Country Retreats.'

'Ooh, I've heard of them,' I say, impressed. 'Their holiday homes are supposed to be amazing. Pippa, who I work with… she's always going on about them.'

'Yeah, well, the guests might be loaded, but most of them are filthy slobs. The state of some of the places!' Ruby goes on to tell us about some of the messes she's had to clear up. And I'm almost put off my pizza by the grossness of some people.

As Joe polishes off the last pizza slice, the conversation dries up and there's a brief awkward silence. Ruby gets to her feet. 'Does anyone want afters? I've got Ben and Jerry's Rocky Road ice cream.'

Everyone nods.

'I'll give you a hand,' Joe says, gathering up the empty plates and following Ruby into the kitchen.

'So, those letters,' Ian says, leaning forward. 'Do you really not know who's behind them?' His eyes gleam, and for a moment I get a horrible feeling that he's going to admit to having sent them. But that's ridiculous. He's with Ruby, and seems besotted by her – Ruby is way out of his league in the looks department. Why would Ian be interested in someone like me when he's got her?

'No idea,' I say, clenching my fists beneath the table. There's something disturbing about Ian and the way he's looking at me, but I can't put my finger on exactly what it is. I'll be relieved when Ruby and Joe come back into the room. On second thoughts, I'm not waiting. I push my chair back and stand up. 'I'll go and see if they need any help.'

Ian leans back in his chair and belches. 'Okay. See you when you get back.'

I leave the room feeling shaken. I'm not even sure why. Maybe it's simply from being left in a room with a man I barely know. But as I head towards the kitchen, I tell myself that it's madness to suspect every single person I come into contact with. That's exactly what this psycho wants – they're trying to unsettle me, to ruin my quality of life. But I can't let them succeed. I won't play the victim. Not any more.

CHAPTER SIXTEEN

After an uneventful day in the shop, I gather up my bag and keys and lock up the stockroom. Pippa left a few minutes ago, and I'm looking forward to getting home and putting my feet up. I'm nursing a mild hangover after last night at Ian and Ruby's. We didn't stay late, but I did manage to polish off a bottle of wine, and my head isn't thanking me today.

At least I won't have to walk all the way home alone tonight. I've taken to driving to work and parking in the NCP car park around the corner. The car park fees are extortionate, but I'd rather pay the money than have a terrifying walk home thinking someone is following me.

I head towards the staff exit and catch my breath as I hear a door bang shut. It sounds like the side door, but the only other person with another set of keys is George, and he doesn't normally come to the shop at this time.

I should do something – unlock the front door so I can make an escape, or barricade myself in the stockroom. Instead, I am frozen in place, standing next to the counter, unable to make a decision.

'Hello!' My voice is quavery. 'Anyone there?'

Footsteps down the side passageway, and then the door to the shop creaks open.

'Evening, Lizzy.'

My hand flies to my chest and I exhale in relief. 'George! You frightened the life out of me.'

'Not that hideous, am I?' He pats his face and grins.

''Course not.' I attempt to smile back, but my heart is still beating frantically, I haven't quite recovered from the shock. 'It's just, after that attempted break-in I'm a bit edgy, that's all.'

'Sorry, I should have let you know I was coming. Remiss of me.'

I shake my head. 'No, no, it's *your* shop. It's just me being paranoid.'

'Can we chat for a minute?' George asks, his expression turning serious.

'Of course. What's on your mind?' I set my bag and keys on the counter top.

'It's delicate,' he says, 'but I'm just going to come out and say it.'

'Okay.' He's got me worried now.

'There's stock going missing.' George puts his hands in his pockets, jingling some loose change, or keys. 'So either we've got a serious case of customer shoplifting, or…' He opens his hands wide, leaving me to imagine the end of his sentence.

'Or what?'

George raises an eyebrow.

'You think it's *me*?' My hand flies to my chest. I can't believe George is accusing me of stealing.

'I didn't say that.'

'So, what are you saying?'

'I'd like you to tell me what *you* think's going on, before I get the police involved. Do you know why stock is going missing, Lizzy? You must have noticed, so I'm wondering why you didn't speak up.'

My face goes hot, and I have to admit I'm shocked by George's bluntness. I feel guilty, even though I've never stolen a thing in my life. 'How do you know stock's going missing?'

'For starters, there was that handbag yesterday. But it's been going on longer than that. A few months back, there was a hundred-quid candle in the window.' He points to the front of the shop. 'I noticed it had gone, but there was no sign of it on the till roll. Fine, I thought to myself, it's been nicked. I was going to tell you about it, Lizzy. Tell you to keep a better eye on the customers, but then I bumped into an old friend and she was wearing one of our outfits. Said she bought it the day before – it was a day when you and Pippa were both working. So I checked the receipts, and again, there was no sign of the transaction. I rang my friend up and asked her how she'd paid. She told me, *cash*, but she couldn't remember who'd served her. So, it looks like someone's being naughty and not been ringing all the cash sales through the till. I don't think it's you, Lizzy.' He pauses. 'Or is it?'

'No! I would never in a million years steal from you, George. Or from anyone else, for that matter.'

'That's what I thought. So it looks like Miss Hargreaves is our culprit.'

I should have told George my suspicions about Pippa when I first found out. Now it will look like I'm blaming her to cover my arse. But it's too late now. And I'm not about to take the blame for Pippa stealing. 'What are you going to do?' I ask.

'We'll set a little trap, get the evidence and then call our boys in blue.'

'Why didn't you just set the trap without telling me?' I ask. 'Because if it *is* me, you've just tipped me off.'

George throws his head back and laughs, loud guffaws that rumble through the stuffy air. 'Ah, I do like you, Lizzy. I knew it wasn't you. 'Course it wasn't. That Pippa Hargreaves hasn't got two pennies to rub together and she's trying to keep up with all her millionaire friends. But she's chosen the wrong person to steal from. I'm throwing the book at her. Setting an example to the rest of my staff, in case they think they can rip me off too.'

I know what Pippa's been doing is wrong, but I can't help feeling sorry for her. 'George, would you… could you let me speak to her? Ask her to return the stock and the cash? I know she's done an awful thing, but if she's arrested it will be terrible for her whole family.'

'She should have thought of that before she started helping herself.'

'I know.' I nod. 'I know.'

'And what if I let you speak to her and she denies it?' George cries. 'Then we'll have tipped her off and we won't be able to prove anything. I'll have lost my stock and my cash, and I won't be able to fire her because I won't have concrete proof.'

'Yes, but it won't be good for business,' I counter.

'How do you figure that?'

'Say you call the police and she gets arrested. Well, the Hargreaves are a well-known family, it will be all around the county in record time. The papers will get wind of it—'

'All publicity is good publicity,' George interrupts.

'Not necessarily. What about all Pippa's wealthy friends? You won't see them for dust. No way will they come back here after that.'

'Hmm.' George scratches his cheek. 'You could have a point there, Lizzy.'

'Not saying they'll all take Pippa's side, but they won't want to be associated with any scandal.' I'm not sure why I'm sticking up for Pippa – I certainly don't condone what she's been doing – maybe it's because she stuck up for me when Leon was in here the other day. Maybe it's simply because she's my friend and we've known one another since we were kids. It's no excuse, but I know she wouldn't steal unless things were really bad.

'All right, you've convinced me,' George says. 'For now, anyway. Tell her to return the stolen items and all the cash she's taken. Once she's done that, she can hand in her resignation. But there's no way I'll be writing any kind of reference for her, got that?'

I nod. 'Thanks, George. I really think it's the best way.'

'We'll see,' he replies, not looking at all convinced.

HOD

Transit items (s)

Current time: 08/08/2022,
15:44
Item ID: C902961716
Title: Silent Sister : A
Gripping Psycholo
User ID 1002093379
Transit to: Holywood
Library
Transit to group: Full
access to all libraries,
FLOATING, Lisburn Group

Libraries NI

I may have stopped George from getting the police involved, but now I'm going to have to bring the subject up with Pippa. How the hell am I going to do that? I've as good as promised George that I'll get her to return everything she's taken. But whether or not she'll even admit to the thefts is anyone's guess. I really don't think this is going to end well. And I don't know how Pippa and I will remain friends after something like this. I think I've just made a big error in judgement. But it's either *this* way, or George getting the police involved. And I can't do that to my friend. I just can't. I only hope she understands…

CHAPTER SEVENTEEN

As I walk in through my front door, all my thoughts are of Pippa and how I'm going to bring up the subject of her stealing from the shop. Why did I tell George I'd speak to her? I should have just kept out of it and let him call the police. Instead, I've given myself a massive headache. Pippa won't thank me for saving her from arrest. She'll blame me. She'll think it was me who told George in the first place. I'm going to have to approach the whole thing carefully and take some time to think about how to bring it up. Thankfully, George is off on holiday for a week, so I've got a few days to work out how to broach it.

'Hi!' I call out to Joe.

'I'm upstairs!'

I slip off my work shoes, dump my bag on the floor and climb the stairs, resolving to ask Joe what he thinks about the Pippa situation. Although I can guess what he'll say – don't get involved. Mainly because he doesn't like her.

I go into the bedroom where Joe is towelling his body dry. As I walk in, he looks up, a worried expression on his face. My hello smile dies. 'What is it?' I ask.

'You better sit down.' He wraps the towel around his lower half, sits on the edge of the bed and pats the space next to him.

'Why do I have to sit down? What's happened?'

'Just sit, Lizzy.'

I do as he asks. Thoughts of Pippa evaporate as I try to guess what's got Joe so worried.

'Don't panic,' he says, 'but it looks like you might have got another letter.'

I make a noise in the back of my throat, put my fingers to my forehead and try to let his words sink in.

'Are you okay?' he asks. 'Stupid question.'

I exhale and then square my shoulders, trying to prepare myself for whatever weirdness I'm about to face. 'Where is it?'

'On the dressing table.' He turns his head towards the cream and gold dressing table by the window.

I follow his gaze to see a pink envelope on the table. 'Did you touch it?' I ask.

'Yeah, sorry. It was on the front doormat with a load of flyers when I came in from work. Didn't realise what it was until I picked it up to take a look.'

'Shit,' I say, my nerve endings tingling. 'I kind of knew there'd be another one, but I was hoping there wouldn't be, if you know what I mean.' I should go over and take a look at it, but I can't seem to move.

Joe wraps an arm around me, brings me into his side and kisses the top of my head. His skin is warm and damp. 'I'll kill the bastard when we find out who it is.'

'Did you open it?' I ask.

'No.'

'So how do you know it's from… *them*?'

'It's got your name on it. Looks like the same old-fashioned writing as the other envelopes.'

'Oh. Right.'

'Want me to open it for you?' he asks

I pull back from his embrace. 'No, I'll do it. Or…'

'What?'

'Maybe we should wait and let the police… deal with it.'

'Maybe.' Joe shrugs. 'I don't know. You'd think the cops would have told you what to do if you received another one.'

I make myself stand up and walk over to the dressing table, hardly feeling the floor beneath my feet. Sure enough, my name is written on the front of the envelope, those looping letters now increasingly familiar, producing a tight feeling of dread deep in my guts. The only difference with this envelope is that it's pink, not white. I wonder what the contents of the letter will say. I wish I didn't have to find out. But the not knowing is killing me. Against my better judgement, I snatch up the envelope and untuck the flap. Like the others, it hasn't been sealed down.

'Do you think you should be doing that?' Joe comes over to my side.

I don't reply. I slide out the thin sheet of paper and unfold it.

The paper is pink and white with a cartoon image of a black and white cat in the bottom right-hand corner. Handwritten in the centre of the page, are the words:

Don't worry, Lizzy. Frank will be fine.

Beneath the words is a smear of something red. Bile rises to the back of my throat when I realise it looks like blood.

The letter and envelope fall from my hands and float to the floor.

'FRANK!!' I yell.

'What?' Joe says, getting to his feet. 'What is it?'

'Where's Frank?' I can barely breathe.

'I... I don't know.'

'FRANK!' I cry once more. 'Did you see him when you came in?'

'Er, I don't know, I can't remember. No, I don't think so.'

I push past Joe, tearing out of the bedroom and down the stairs.

'Lizzy, wait!'

As I reach the bottom of the stairs, I have terrible visions of my little Frank being held somewhere by a crazy nutter who won't think twice about harming him. They'd better not have done anything. Not my little Frankie. An image of Leon Whittaker flashes into my mind. Then an image of Seb. Then George. Then Ian from next door. It could be any bloody one of them doing this to me. *Why?* But then, anyone who does something like this has got something seriously wrong with them.

I make my way into the kitchen. The wash basket stands empty by the machine. Frank isn't here. I peer out through the kitchen window but can't see him outside either. I barely register Joe's footsteps on the stairs. He comes through to the kitchen, now dressed in shorts and a T-shirt, damp in patches where he hasn't dried off properly. In his hand he has the letter.

'Did you read it?' I ask.

He nods. 'Is Frank down here?'

I shake my head. 'We locked the cat flap, so how can he have got out?'

Joe takes hold of my shoulders. 'It's okay, Lizzy, we'll find him. Whoever wrote that letter said that Frank is okay. So even if… even if they have somehow got hold of him, doesn't mean they've hurt him.'

I'm finding it hard to breathe. The thought that anybody would threaten me or my pet is absolutely crazy. How can this be happening? I can't comprehend it. What sick bastard would threaten my beautiful cat? But as I sit here, I realise something – it wasn't necessarily a threat. It was a statement: *Don't worry, Lizzy. Frank will be fine.*

Does that mean…

'Joe, last week when Frank went missing for a couple of days… he came back with a cut on his paw. You don't think…'

'Shit.'

'I know.'

'That red mark at the bottom of the letter…' Joe begins.

'It could be Frank's blood.' The horror of it hits me in the solar plexus. I stare at Joe, my shock mirrored in his eyes. 'We need to find out who's doing this.'

CHAPTER EIGHTEEN

'Have you tried the lounge?' Joe asks.

'What?'

'The lounge,' he repeats.

I shake my head.

'Frank could be in there, couldn't he?'

As one, we rush back down the hall into the sitting room. I'm not expecting to see Frank, though. After reading the letter, I'm expecting the very worst. So when I follow Joe through the lounge door, I sob with utter relief when I see my beautiful cat curled up asleep on the corner of the sofa. 'Frank!'

I cross the room and sit next to him, stroking his head before picking him up and putting him on my lap. Typical of him not to come when I called him earlier. He's always gone his own merry way. His default position is 'ignore', but I still love him to bits. Even now, he doesn't look too impressed with being disturbed, but he makes the best of it, deigning to curl up on my lap with a half-grunt, half-sigh. We've had him since he was a kitten. Found him mewling, half-starved at the end of our street about three years ago. Aretha Franklin's 'Respect' was playing loudly through someone's speakers as the little guy followed us home. It gave us the idea for his name. No one came to claim him. So that's how Frank became part of our family.

Joe exhales. 'Whoever wrote this… this shit, is twisted.' He waves the letter at me.

'Can you get my phone from my bag?' I ask.

'Sure. Where—'

'In the hall on the floor.'

Joe spins on his heel and leaves the room while I kiss the top of Frank's head. Seconds later, Joe returns and hands me my phone. With a pounding heart, I call the police station and explain to them that I've received another letter. They tell me someone will be here as soon as possible.

'We can't let Frank outside again,' I say. 'Not until they've caught whoever's doing this. Do you really think it could be his blood on that letter? Or is it maybe someone who just wants us to think that?'

'I don't know.' Joe shakes his head and comes to sit by my side. 'Either way, whoever's doing this has got a screw loose.'

We wait in the lounge, both of us making a fuss of Frank, who is happily oblivious to the drama going on around him. His paw is almost healed now and he's been walking normally again, thank goodness. But that still doesn't stop me feeling sick at the thought of someone doing something so terrible.

After a while, I couldn't say how long, I hear a car pull up outside. A car door slams, and then another one. Joe stands and peers out of the window. 'It's them,' he says.

I lift Frank off my lap and put him back in his cosy corner on the sofa, where he makes himself comfortable.

When the doorbell rings, both Joe and I go into the hall. He pulls open the door and I see two familiar faces on the doorstep. 'Hi,' I say, unable to manage a smile. 'Come in.'

They step inside.

'This is my boyfriend, Joe Lawrence.'

'Hi Lizzy.' She turns to Joe. 'Hello, I'm Sergeant Jenny Llewellyn and this is my colleague, Constable Matt Ryan.'

'Hi,' Joe replies.

They follow us into the lounge and I gesture to the two armchairs and they each take a seat. I sit back down on the sofa next to Frank.

'Would you like a drink?' Joe asks. 'Tea?'

'Water would be great,' Llewellyn says.

'Not for me, thanks,' Ryan adds.

Joe goes to the kitchen to get Llewellyn her drink.

'Would you like to tell us what happened?' she asks me.

'I got another letter.' I point to the letter and envelope, which are now lying on the coffee table.

'Did you touch it without gloves?'

I flush. 'We both did. Me and Joe. Sorry. Stupid, I know.'

'Easily done,' she says. 'But if you receive anything further, or see anything odd, try to remember not to touch it or disturb it in any way. The less it's been tampered with, the more chance we'll have of finding the perpetrator.'

I nod.

Llewellyn takes a small plastic bag out of one of her pockets and lays it on the arm of the chair. Next she takes out a pair of black nitrile gloves and puts them on before reaching down and picking up the envelope. Ryan gets up and goes to stand by the side of her chair. They look at the name on the front of the envelope and then she opens the plastic bag and slides the envelope inside.

'Evidence bag,' she explains.

Joe comes back into the room with Llewellyn's glass of water.

'Thanks, Joe,' she says. 'Would you mind putting it on the table for now? I'll have it in a minute.'

He does as she asks and then comes back to sit by my side, taking my hand in his. I wish I'd asked him to bring me a glass of water, too. My mouth is dry, my skin hot and clammy.

'When did you find the letter?' Llewellyn asks me.

'Joe found it, not me.'

The two officers turn their attention to my boyfriend. I know Joe is jittery around the police after spending so much time in the local station last year because of his ABH charge. Thankfully, different officers were dealing with his case back then, but I bet these two know all about his history. It's a small town, and everybody gets to know everybody's business.

'I found the letter when I got home from work today,' he begins.

'What time was this?' Llewellyn asks.

'Uh, about quarter past five. I came in and saw all the usual crap, er, flyers and junk mail on the doormat. I picked it all up and flicked through to see if there was any post and I saw the pink envelope with Lizzy's name on the front.'

'Did you open it?'

'No.'

'If you did,' Llewellyn says, 'you should say so, because we'll be testing it for prints.'

Joe scowls. 'I just said I didn't.'

'Okay, that's great. Was the envelope on top of the flyers, or at the bottom? Reason I ask is to give us some idea of the time of day it was posted through your door.'

'I'm sorry, I don't remember.' Joe turns to me with an apologetic expression. 'I wasn't really concentrating. I just picked the whole lot up and sifted through. Not sure if I might have turned the pile over and started from the bottom.'

'Okay. And how long were you out of the house for today?'

'I left around seven thirty this morning, came home at five fifteen.'

'And you, Lizzy?' she asks.

'I left about an hour after Joe, at eight thirty.'

'And are these times usual for both of you?'

Joe and I nod. 'Yes,' he says.

The sergeant now has the letter between her thumb and forefinger. Her brow creases as she reads it. 'Do you know what they're talking about in this letter?' she asks, looking over at me and Joe. 'Who's Frank?'

'He's my cat,' I reply, glancing down at his sleeping shape.

'That him?' she nods in Frank's direction. 'He's a beauty.'

'We think that might be his blood… on the letter,' Joe explains.

'Why would you think that?' Llewellyn asks. 'It could be smudged ink, or any kind of stain.'

I notice that Ryan is scribbling in a notebook. I wonder what he's writing.

'Because,' Joe replies, 'Frank was missing for a couple of days last weekend. And when he came home, he had a cut on his paw.'

'I see,' she says, her frown deepening. 'Do you remember exactly when he went missing? And when he returned?' she asks, dropping the letter into the evidence bag.

I cast my mind back. 'I noticed he wasn't home on Friday when I got back from work. But I wasn't too worried, as it's not unusual for him to go off for a few days. He didn't reappear until Sunday morning. That's when we noticed the blood on his paw. We just assumed it was an accident – that he'd trodden on a sharp stone, or broken glass.'

'Who else knows you have a cat called Frank?' she asks.

'Lots of people,' I reply. 'It's not exactly a secret.'

'Can you write me out a list?'

I shrug. 'Sure.'

'Although…' Joe begins. 'There was that time just after Christmas when we thought he was missing and we put up signs in the local area with his name and photo. He was gone for a few days, but turned up of his own accord. So anyone local could have seen the notices and found out his name.'

'Do you have the other letters, the previous two you received?'

'Yes.' I get to my feet. 'Do you want me to…?'

'Yes, could you get them, please? We'll send them off with this one.'

I retrieve my handbag from the hall and bring it into the lounge. The letters are where I left them in the side pocket. I've been carrying them around with me for days because I couldn't think of where to keep them in the house. I didn't really want them in the house. I'd like to have burnt them, or ripped them into pieces, but thought I'd better hang on to them, *just in case.*

And here is the *just in case*. I pass them both to Llewellyn, who puts each of them into separate evidence bags.

'Have either of you been fingerprinted?' she asks.

I shake my head. 'Not me.'

'You've got mine on file,' Joe mumbles.

'Okay, Lizzy, Matt will do yours now, if that's okay.'

'Oh, yes, that's fine.'

'And Lizzy,' Llewellyn says, 'I don't want to worry you unduly, but it's best if you don't go out alone for the next few days at least.'

My stomach lurches at her words.

'Why?' Joe asks.

'It's just a precaution, until we know what we're dealing with.'

'You think she's really in danger?' Joe asks.

'The important thing is not to jump to conclusions. Frank's cut could simply be a coincidence. We'll send the letters off to be analysed. Discover whether that smudge on the paper is feline blood, or something more innocuous.'

But I don't believe it's a coincidence, any more than she does. Whoever sent that letter is responsible for hurting my cat. And if they're fine with harming an innocent creature, then who knows what else they're capable of?

How far do I go?

Is their fear enough to balance out the lies?

The thrill of seeing that pale face and trembling lip. Hearing the telltale tremor in their words. The tension, the glances to their left and right. Always wondering when they talk to someone: is it you? Could it be you?

But it's got to the point where I need more. What good is a letter on its own? Anyone who knew the truth would understand my point of view. My desire to hurt them is only right. Only human.

Inevitable, really.

CHAPTER NINETEEN

'Well, it's official,' Pippa announces outside the shop as I'm opening up, unlocking the side door. Her usual buoyant manner is subdued, her face pale. Even her normally glossy hair is lank and dull.

'What's official?' I ask, as she follows me through the side passage while I deactivate the alarm.

'Bloody Toby. He dumped me last night. By text!'

I turn to face her, my expression suitably sympathetic. But all I can think is that I can't possibly quiz her about the thefts after her new boyfriend has just dumped her. George would have no such qualms about bringing it up, I'm sure. But I'm not George.

'Oh, Pippa. I'm so sorry.'

'I know I'm bonkers for thinking it,' she says, 'but I really thought he was *the one*. We got on so well. We were perfect for one another.'

'Maybe he'll change his mind,' I say, flicking on the shop lights one by one.

'Doubt it,' she says glumly. 'I'm destined to die a spinster.'

'Don't be daft. And anyway, that word should be banned from the dictionary – *spinster*.' I tut. 'You might find a man to share your life with, you might not. But either way, you'll be fine, Pippa.'

'Easy for you to say. You've got Joe.'

'You don't even like Joe!' I say with a smile.

'What? Of course I do... Well, I hardly know him. But that's not the point. The point is that *you* like him, and that's what it's all about, isn't it? Finding someone you like, or love even, whatever love is. I thought I'd found my Joe. But all I'd found was another liar.'

We head into the main part of the shop and I try to comfort Pippa while we go about our early-morning routine of unlocking the front door, setting out the A-board, putting the float back in the till and generally preparing for the day ahead. But we're both subdued. Pippa because of Toby, and me because of yesterday's letter. I barely slept last night and I could tell Joe was really shaken up, too. And I hated the idea of leaving Frank alone in the house. Even though we've locked the cat flap and changed the locks, I'm sure someone could find a way into our house if they wanted to. I can't bring myself to tell Pippa about the new letter. I want to try to put it out of my head if I possibly can.

I text Joe to tell him I've arrived at work safely. He wanted to drop me in this morning. Part of me wanted to say yes. Part of me was terrified to drive in alone. But I told him that I didn't want to make him late for work. That I'm not putting my life on hold because of some weirdo who wants to freak me out. So he reluctantly agreed, as long as I let him know I got in to work okay. I feel like a child again.

After texting Joe, I notice I've got a voicemail so I have a quick listen. It's George calling from the airport, reminding me to speak to Pippa about the thefts. I can't face calling him back, so I send a text instead:

Don't worry, George, I'll speak to her. Enjoy your holiday. Catch up when you get back.

I'm hoping this is enough to keep him off my back. He responds instantly:

Text me when you've done it.

I text him a thumbs-up emoji, hoping he'll be too wrapped up in relaxing to bother me again. However, I know George. He's a workaholic, and never truly switches off.

'Everything okay?' Pippa comes into the stockroom and I move my phone out of her eyeline.

'Fine,' I lie, thinking how she doesn't know the half of it. Why on earth did she have to go and start stealing? Now I'm going to have to fire her, lose a friend and hope that the repercussions aren't too awful.

The morning goes by so slowly that I keep thinking my watch has stopped. Pippa is miserable, and I feel like I have a bag of sharp stones in my stomach. Just before one o'clock I'm helping a customer decide on a necklace to go with a dress when I see the familiar figures of Sergeant Llewellyn and Constable Ryan walk past the shop window. I want to drop what I'm doing, run outside and ask them if they've made any progress on my case, but I can't abandon my customer.

'Do you think the silver or the rose gold?' she asks, holding both necklaces against her throat and staring critically at her reflection in the fitting room mirror.

'Definitely silver,' I say, with one eye on the front of the shop. My heart simultaneously lifts and drops as both officers walk into the shop. 'The rose gold is too close to your skin tone and gets lost, look.'

'Oh, you're absolutely right,' she says. 'Yes, I'll take this one.'

Llewellyn catches my eye and I raise my index finger to say I'll be with her in a minute. Pippa has gone to the bank to get some pound coins, so I can't pass my customer on to her to deal with. It takes what feels like centuries for her to get changed and make her final decisions, but eventually I'm able to ring through her purchases and my customer leaves happy but staring with undisguised curiosity at the officers on her way out.

'Hello, Lizzy,' Llewellyn says as the two of them make their way down the shop towards me.

'Hi.' I nod at her and at Ryan, whose acne looks angrier than usual today. I bet the heat makes it worse, poor guy.

'We've got a bit of news,' Llewellyn says.

I dig my thumbnails into the pads of my forefingers.

'Nothing to move things on, I'm afraid,' she adds.

'What's the news?'

'We've had the first lot of test results back from the lab.'

'And?'

'No prints on the ashtray or magnetic letters, I'm afraid. They were perfectly clean. Which means whoever threw the ashtray and arranged those letters was probably wearing gloves.'

I take a moment to digest the information. If they were wearing gloves then they're serious about what they are doing.

'We've sent the letters off to the lab, so we should get the results back beginning of next week.'

'Along with the blood test?' I ask. 'To see if that smudge is… Frank's blood?'

'Yes, that's right.'

'Thanks,' I reply, feeling suddenly queasy.

'Sorry we haven't got more news for you but these things can take time,' Llewellyn says. 'How are you feeling today? Are you holding up okay?'

'Ah, you know,' I say, shrugging my shoulders. 'I'll be happier once we find out who it is.'

'I know.' Llewellyn sighs. 'We're doing everything we can on that front. Do get in touch if you hear or see anything else suspicious.'

'I will.'

Llewellyn and Ryan leave and I have to sit down on the stool for a moment. My head is swimming, and with the police gone, I suddenly don't feel safe in the shop on my own. Anyone could come in, close the door behind them, and… and *what*? What do they even want from me?

I've never been a nervous kind of person. I've always stuck up for myself, and others. Despite my mother trying to chip away at my ego over the years, I've managed to retain my confidence. I'm proud of it. It's who I am. But I'm gradually realising that, given the right circumstances, anyone can have their self-esteem eroded. That you can be strong one day and faint-hearted the next. That no one is immune to fear.

Pippa comes back from the bank and I ask her to watch the shop while I go into the back to catch up on some paperwork. I also want to avoid making small talk with her, but that's not the only reason I'm going into the stockroom. No. I've had a brainwave – an idea of how to find out who's behind the letters. It may be a little over the top, but this kind of thing doesn't happen every day. And I refuse to sit around waiting for another threatening letter or intimidating situation. Instead, I'm going to do something proactive.

CHAPTER TWENTY

After a fraught drive down the M32 during morning rush hour, followed by almost forty minutes trying to get parked, I make my way on foot up Whiteladies Road, the heat already uncomfortable even though it's not even 9.30 a.m. It's Monday, my day off. Pippa works Mondays with Clarissa, one of George's part-time members of staff who's also a friend of his and a key holder. I have the sudden thought that maybe it's Clarissa who's been stealing from Georgio's, but then I remember George saying that his friend's dress was bought on a day when Pippa and I were in the shop, so it couldn't have been Clarissa who pocketed the cash.

Joe wanted to come to Bristol with me today, but he's working so I said I'd be fine on my own. The weekend has been quiet with no more scary incidents or letters, but I still feel the threat in the air, looming like an axe about to fall. I can't imagine that the person responsible for the letters has finally lost interest, given up. This morning is a way for me to try to take back control.

Finally, I reach the café where my appointment with the private investigator is to take place. It's a traditional greasy spoon-type establishment, a tatty relic squatting between an organic artisan bakery specialising in soda bread and an upmarket vegan restaurant. I'm almost twenty minutes late for our meeting, so I hope he received my apologetic text and hasn't given up on me.

The front door to the café has been wedged open with a scrap of folded cardboard, presumably to let in the non-existent breeze. I step inside the steaming café, drawing attention from the crowded tables where groups of workmen sit drinking tea and shovelling down late breakfasts. Ignoring their stares, I glance down the length of the plate-glass window. Sitting in the corner, at a table by himself, a medium-built olive-skinned dark-haired man in his thirties leans over a laptop. Spread out before him, various papers, mugs and plates litter the table. I'm assuming this is the PI, as he explained on the phone that this particular corner of the café doubles as his makeshift office.

I wipe a light sheen of sweat from my forehead with the back of my hand and walk over to the man. Hopefully he will prove to be the answer to all my problems.

'Paul Nasri?' I ask.

He looks up, smiles and closes his laptop. 'Lizzy?'

'Yes.'

'Call me Nas. Good to meet you.' His accent is thick Bristolian. Reminds me of Ruby. He gets to his feet and we shake hands. 'Can I get you something to drink? Have you had any breakfast yet? They do a great full English here.'

'Just a lemonade or Sprite would be lovely.'

He shouts over to the guy behind the counter to bring us a Sprite and more tea. I sit opposite Nas on a somewhat sticky chair and wait while he tidies all his papers away, stacking them in an untidy pile on his laptop.

'Sorry I'm a bit late,' I say. 'Traffic was scary.'

'Have you come far?'

'Malmesbury.'

He gives me a blank look.

'It's in Wiltshire,' I explain.

'Wiltshire? Okay. So, how did you hear about me?' he asks.

'Google,' I reply. 'It said you're ex-police, with lots of experience in all types of situations. Your name came up at the top of the page.'

'My sister works in search engine optimisation,' he says. 'Comes in handy for bringing in the business.'

Our drinks arrive, plonked on the table by a stocky man in an apron. I tear off the ring pull, pour the Sprite into my glass and take several huge gulps. The sugar instantly perks me up.

'So, why do you need a private investigator then?' Nas asks.

'I need you to find someone for me.'

'Missing person? That's not always easy, but I've got a good track record.'

'Not a missing person as such.' I start to worry that maybe stalkers aren't his area of expertise. I should have explained what I wanted when we spoke on the phone. But he insisted on an initial face-to-face meeting. Said it weeded out the time-wasters. If someone wasn't serious, they wouldn't bother to schedule a meeting. Otherwise they'd spend hours picking his brains for free on the phone.

'Okay,' he says. 'Why don't you explain what the problem is, and I'll see if I can help.'

I take a breath and launch into the events of the past ten days. Nas doesn't interrupt, but lets me tell the story in one huge, splurging monologue.

He takes a moment to digest what I've said and then inhales deeply. 'At least it sounds like the police are taking you seriously now. So why come to me? Why not leave it with them to deal with?'

'Because it's all so slow. They're no further along. I mean, they're helpful, and sympathetic and everything, but until this… *stalker* shows themselves, the police can't do anything. And this person isn't stupid. They haven't left any prints, or let themselves be caught on CCTV. I'm scared. I need someone on my side twenty-four/seven.'

'I do sleep, you know.' He gives me a lopsided grin.

'I don't mean twenty-four/seven. Sorry, I'm not explaining myself very well. I just mean, I'd feel more secure if someone was actively trying to find whoever's doing this.'

'Look,' Nas says, leaning back in his chair, 'I'll be honest with you. The police are probably better placed to do this kind of work than I am. Plus, they're local to you. I'm all the way over here in Bristol, and it sounds like the person doing this probably lives in the same town as you.'

'Really?' My heart sinks. Ever since I had the idea last week to hire a private investigator, I've been placing my hopes on this being the answer. After I called Nasri and he agreed to meet me, I rang the bank and had a loan agreed in principle. I was that convinced he would be able to help me.

'I could lie to you,' he says. 'I could take your cash – which, by the way, would probably have racked up into the thousands – but the chances of me finding this person on the evidence you've got… well, they're slim to none.'

I rest my chin on clasped hands as new waves of disappointment hit me. What a total waste of time. I get to my feet. 'Okay, well, thanks for being so honest.' I root around in my purse until I find a couple of pound coins. 'For the Sprite,' I say, placing them on the table.

He raises an eyebrow. 'Thanks. Look, I can see I've disappointed you. Why don't you sit back down a minute?'

I hesitate, then do as he asks.

'There is something simple you can do which might help.'

I sit up straighter.

'Do you live in a house or a flat?' he asks.

'A house. A little cottage.'

'Good.' Nas flicks through his pile of papers and tears a strip off the bottom of one of the sheets. He pulls a pen out of his pocket and starts writing. 'Here.' He slides the scrap of paper across the table towards me.

'What's this?' I ask, looking at the words, which don't seem to make much sense.

'It's the make and model of a great little spy cam you can use to try and catch your stalker. You said they've delivered letters to your house twice now?'

I nod, suddenly understanding what he's getting at.

'Chances are they'll do it again. Stick the camera in a plant pot underneath a leafy plant, or something. If I was local I'd set it up for you. Make sure the lens is pointing upwards to catch their face. Experiment with angles. Okay?'

I don't know why I didn't think of this in the first place. Hope replaces disappointment. 'That's a great idea! Thanks so much. Where's the best place to get one of these cameras?'

'Online's cheapest.'

'What if I wanted to get one today?'

He reaches out to take the scrap of paper and scribbles something else on the back. 'That's the name and address of a place I use not far from here. Ask for Reuben and tell him Nas sent you. They'll give you a good discount.'

'Thank you so much.'

He shrugs. 'Didn't really do a lot.'

'You did. Do I owe you anything, a consultancy fee or something?'

'Nah, you're all right.'

'Okay. Well, thanks. Is the camera place walkable from here?'

'Yeah. Take you about ten minutes. Turn left out of the café, keep walking and it's your fourth turning on the right, off the other side of the main road.'

'Thank you, Nas.' I down the rest of my Sprite and leave the café, feeling like I have a real purpose now. Why on earth didn't I think of putting a camera up before? It's so obvious now that Nas has mentioned it. But I guess everything is obvious with hindsight.

I find the electronics shop, tucked away down a side street. Nas's friend Reuben spends about half an hour showing me how to use the camera and how and where to position it. He knocks fifty quid off the asking price and I put it on my credit card, part of me relieved that at least I won't have to take out a loan for Nas's PI services.

Leaving the shop, I clutch my carrier bag tightly, thrilled with my new purchase. I'm dying to get back to my car, drive home and set the thing up. I can't wait to catch whoever it is in the act of posting another letter through my door. My mind flashes forward to me presenting my video evidence to the police and them arresting whoever it is.

The air outside is thick and heavy. I'm betting that slice of blue sky above will be eaten up by thunderclouds soon enough. I make my way back to the main road that's suddenly heaving with shoppers, workers, people eating and drinking in pavement cafés. Cars and bikes whizz down the wide street as I stand on the kerb, trying to get my bearings. A group of foreign students crowd past me, moving at a snail's pace, their backpacks bashing into passers-by.

As I wait for a gap in the traffic, I hear the slap, slap of running footsteps growing louder, but they're on the periphery of my hearing. I'm not paying too much attention until the noise approaches, a heavy thud on the pavement behind me. And then I feel a sudden, shocking push at my back and I'm flying into the road. Into the oncoming traffic.

It's like a slowed-down movie where the sound is turned down and then suddenly turned up loud. A scream rips through the air. It could be my own, but I'm not sure. And in the distance a flash of auburn hair flying away down the street. It looks like… it looks like Emma. Like my sister Emma. But I mustn't be thinking straight. I'm still flying, and then falling, falling to the accompaniment of car horns, screeching tyres and screams. More screams.

And then silence.

CHAPTER TWENTY-ONE

The noise starts up as quickly as it stopped. Voices, car horns, doors opening and slamming. I'm lying on my front in the middle of the road, the odour of burning rubber and hot tarmac in my nostrils. The taste of blood in my mouth. *Am I okay?* I don't know. I really don't know.

'She just stepped out into the road.'

'Is she hurt?'

'Has anyone called an ambulance?'

I open my eyes to brightness, my left cheek pressed into the gravelly road. A man's face hovers above me.

'You all right, love?'

I swallow and try to speak, but my throat is dry. 'I… I don't know. She pushed me.' I lift my head off the ground and it feels like I've left a layer of skin on the tarmac.

'Not sure you should be moving. You took quite a tumble there. Lucky my car's got good brakes. What the hell was you doing, stepping into the road like that?'

I push myself up with scraped palms, shakily sit back on my haunches. Everything feels bruised, but nothing is unbearably painful.

'Lucky you wasn't killed,' the man says, shaking his head, his eyes wide. He's middle-aged, grey-haired, wearing denim shorts and a FatFace T-shirt.

He keeps saying I'm lucky, but it doesn't feel that way to me. I glance around at the halted traffic, at the people crowded on the pavement, staring. A sea of mobile phones point my way. Great. I'm probably going to go viral. Just what I need.

The man takes my hand and helps me to my feet. He puts an arm around me and guides me back onto the pavement. The crowd parts like the Red Sea, letting me through. A café waiter gestures to a chair and I sit. A glass of water is placed in front of me, but I'm too dazed to touch it.

'What happened?' the man asks. 'It looks like you threw yourself into the traffic back there. You wasn't trying to kill yourself, was you?'

'What? No!' I try to think back, but I can't be sure what actually occurred, it all happened so quickly. 'I was waiting to cross. And then… someone ran past me and pushed me into the road.'

'You got knocked over?'

'I… I think they did it on purpose. It felt like I was shoved.'

'On purpose?' The man stares at me like he's trying to work out whether I'm telling the truth or not. 'You sure?'

'Yes. I felt someone push me.'

He looks around and calls out to the people milling around. 'Anyone see what happened? Anyone see this lady get pushed into the road?'

A few people shake their heads, some slide their gazes away and walk off. Others don't take their eyes off their phones. Too busy tweeting about what happened. But no one actually steps forward as a witness.

'Are these yours?'

I glance up.

A teenage girl stands next to me, holding out a carrier bag and my handbag. 'I think you might have dropped your bags.'

The handbag is mine. I look at the white plastic carrier bag, trying to register it. I think I must be in shock because I can't seem to find the words to reply to her. The girl looks to the man for assistance. He takes the bags and thanks her. 'You see what happened?' he asks. The girl shakes her head, mumbles an apology and leaves.

'These yours?' the man asks.

I nod. I remember; it's the security camera I bought earlier. That seems like hours ago. I feel bad for not saying thank you to the girl for rescuing my belongings.

'Okay, look,' the man says, 'I better move my car out of the way. Everyone's going mental over there. Traffic's probably backed up all the way to Gloucester.'

I realise that there are car horns blaring quite a way down the road. People yelling, 'Move the fucking car, dickhead!' They don't realise that I could've died. That this man's quick reactions probably saved my life.

'Of course,' I say. 'You go. I'll be fine.'

'I'll come back,' he says. 'Just gonna move my car over to the side of the road. The Old Bill will probably want to speak to me, anyway.'

'Okay,' I reply. 'Thank you.' As he moves away, I think about what he's just said – that the police will arrive, and probably an ambulance. In fact, I can hear the sirens now, drawing closer. What will I say to them? That someone pushed me? But how can I even be sure that's what happened? Could it have been an accident? Someone nudging me as they ran past? I don't know. It didn't feel that way. It felt deliberate. And… I thought I saw Emma running away, dodging and weaving through the crowd. But that's crazy. My sister may not like me any more, but does she hate me enough to push me into oncoming traffic? The thought makes me nauseous. I swallow down bile.

I can't stay here with all these people watching; even though they're pretending not to, I can see them still milling around, sneaking sideways glances through their phones – a socially acceptable way to excuse a lack of decency.

I need to get home. It's so hot out here I can hardly breathe. I put a hand to the side of my face, my fingertips running over the grit that's embedded in my skin, in my hair. My knees and arms are scratched up, too, the heels of my palms red raw. But the pain feels distant from myself. I stand shakily, steadying myself on the table. The waiter asks if I'm okay, if I need anything, but I give him some non-committal answer, thanking him for the water, which I haven't touched.

'You should stay where you are. An ambulance is on its way,' he says.

'I'm fine,' I say, picking up my bags. I don't think about where I am or which direction I need to go in, I just start walking. Needing to get away from the curious stares. To escape from the drama of the situation. I need to be somewhere cool and quiet.

I shamble down the street as though in a dream, weaving through the crowd, attracting curious stares. I glance down to see that my green dress is covered in black marks, torn in places. Goodness only knows what state my face is in. The skin on my cheek and forehead is beginning to burn. I probably should have waited for the paramedics to clean me up. I'll do it later. I feel irresponsible that they were called out for nothing. Should I go back? I stop walking for a moment. My mind skitters all over the place. I really do think I must be in shock.

'There she is!' A cry from behind. The sound of footsteps coming closer. I cover my head and sink down onto the pavement. Is it them? Are they going to push me into the road again?

'Hey, it's okay. Are you okay?'

I peek out from my cowering position on the ground. It's the man who almost ran me over. I find that I can't speak, can't move.

'Sorry if I scared you,' he says. 'I was worried when I saw you'd gone. The ambulance is on its way. Come on.' He takes my hand and helps me to my feet. I keep my head down, staring at the dusty pavement, too nervous to look up and see if people are staring. I feel like a freak.

We walk back the way I've just come and stop outside the café where I was sitting moments ago. I see that an ambulance is pulling up outside. A man and a woman wearing green uniforms get out and start speaking to me, but their words just sound like a buzzing in my ears. They turn their attention to the guy I'm with. I hear the words 'shock' and 'she can walk okay' before they lead me into the interior of the vehicle.

I sit down on a fold-out chair while they get to work cleaning me up, checking me over for anything serious. Turns out I bit the tip of my tongue, which is why I can still taste blood. The rest is just scrapes and bruises.

'How are you feeling, love?' the female paramedic asks. 'You can talk to me here, if you like. Or we can take you somewhere where you'll get some proper support.'

'Support?'

'The man who brought you here, he said you might have stepped out in front of his car.'

The implication jolts me out of my stupor. 'I didn't try to harm myself, if that's what you think! I'm not… I'm not suicidal or anything.' I wince as she cleans the dirt and grit out of my hairline.

'Sorry, love, I know this stuff stings. The gentleman was quite concerned about you.'

'Well, it's nice of him to be worried, but I didn't do it on purpose. I think someone tried to push me.'

'Push you?' She frowns. 'Are you sure? Whatever happened out there, we can sort it out, okay? Look, here's the police now. They'll be wanting a chat. Best thing is to tell them the truth. No point keeping any problems to yourself. We're all here to help you, love. Do you feel up to talking to them yet? Or shall I tell them to hold fire?'

'I'm okay. I'll talk to them.' Part of me is touched at her concern, but the other part is annoyed that she actually believes I tried to kill myself. Do they really believe that? Is she going to try to section me? I spy a couple of uniformed officers through a gap in the ambulance doors. Exhaustion hits me at the thought of having to explain what happened. I wish my local officers were here instead. Knowing my recent history, Llewellyn and Ryan would be more likely to take me seriously. Now I'm going to have to tell these guys everything that's been going on. I close my eyes and try to gather my strength.

One of the officers climbs up into the back of the ambulance. He's dark-haired with a few flecks of grey at his temples; his face is kind. 'You okay?' he asks, his eyes flicking to the paramedics.

'A bit shaky, that's all,' I reply.

'You up to telling me what happened?'

I nod.

He whips out a notebook and pen.

'I'd been shopping,' I begin, 'and I was heading back to my car, waiting for a break in the traffic so I could cross the road. And then…' I break off, remembering the feel of those hands on my back.

The officer waits patiently while I get myself together.

'… and then someone shoved me into the road.'

'Shoved you?' he asks.

I nod.

'Shoved you how?'

'I felt hands on my back pushing me hard.'

'You think it was deliberate?'

'Yes.'

'Could you have been mistaken?'

I pause, and think. As the seconds go by, my memory shifts and becomes less set. Like a solid cloud dispersing into wisps. 'I felt them push me,' I say.

The officer looks up at the female paramedic once more.

'We'd like to take her in,' she says. 'Just in case.'

The officer nods.

'Take me in!' I cry. 'Where?'

No one replies.

'You still think I tried to hurt myself?' I get to my feet, shaky, hot, a little dizzy.

'Please, love, just sit down,' the paramedic says. 'Let me finish cleaning you up.'

'Listen,' I say to the officer. 'You don't know what's been going on. This isn't an isolated thing. I'm being harassed. Threatened.'

The officer holds out his hand to try to calm me down. 'Can you tell me what's been happening?'

'Speak to Sergeant Llewellyn, in Malmesbury. They've got a log of everything. Someone's stalking me. I'm not mad. I'm not suicidal. You can check. Here…' I reach down and root about in my purse until I find Llewellyn's card. 'She gave me her contact details. The case number's on the back. Quote it. You'll see.'

The officer nods and takes the card. 'Wait here, okay?' he says, before stepping out of the ambulance.

The female paramedic continues cleaning my injuries while we wait for the officer to return.

'You had any alcohol today, love?' she asks.

'No,' I reply, stiffening.

'Any other substances I should know about?'

'No! I'm not on anything, and I'm not suicidal. You'll see in a minute, when that police officer's checked it out.'

'I wouldn't be doing my job properly if I didn't ask,' she says kindly. 'I need to make sure you're okay.'

I sigh. 'Thank you. I know. But I also know what just happened to me out there.'

Despite the oppressive heat, I start to shiver as the truth of it hits me. I'm worrying about what this paramedic thinks of me, when I should be worrying about something far scarier.

Someone followed me here today.

Someone pushed me into oncoming traffic.

Someone just tried to kill me.

CHAPTER TWENTY-TWO

Finally, after a couple of false starts, we find the residential road where I parked. The officer pulls up behind my car. He asks again if there's anyone who can come and drive me home. I suppose I could have called Joe, but he's working, and I'd have had to wait over an hour for him to get here. All I want now is to be home. 'I'll be fine,' I say, feeling anything but.

Back at the ambulance, the police officer managed to get through to Malmesbury Police Station, who were able to verify my story. So the paramedic reluctantly let me leave her care. I could tell she still wasn't entirely convinced by my story. Before I left, she gave my hand a squeeze and passed me a leaflet with a load of helpline numbers on it.

I realise the officer is talking to me and I attempt to concentrate on what he's saying. 'We'll pass the full details of today's incident, and your statement, on to your local station,' he says. 'So if they need any more information from you about today, I'm sure they'll contact you.'

'That's great. Thanks so much.' At least I won't have to repeat the whole thing to Sergeant Llewellyn. As I leave the air-conditioned interior of the police car and step out onto the pavement, a wave of dizziness hits me. But I fight my way through it. Last thing I need is for the police to stop me from driving home. Can they even do that? Not sure if they would, but I don't want to chance it. I give a little wave at them through the window and try to walk as steadily as I can towards my red Polo. I'm amazed that I was able to show such a calm exterior when my insides are like jelly.

I open the car door and slip inside, put my bags on the passenger seat. Thankfully I parked under a tree, so the interior isn't too hot. I don't have the luxury of air con, so I'll have to drive home with the windows open. But first, I'll sit for a while, calm down before I have to navigate the one-way system and the motorway. The police car drives off and I exhale.

I pull down the sun visor to check my face in the mirror. There's a plaster stuck down at an angle above my right eye, and the area around it is puffy, scraped and red, shiny with antiseptic cream. I can't bear to look any more, so I shove the visor back up.

Rather than calming down, I'm becoming more anxious. All I can think about are the hands at my back, the way they felt when they shoved me. Two firm hands pushing me into danger. I can still feel them, like they're branded onto my skin. I think I'm going into shock. I have to resist it. I wind down the window, turn the key and start the engine. I can do this. I just need to keep it together for another hour or so. Until I get home.

I jerk awake on the sofa as the front door slams.

'Lizzy?'

Joe. He must be back from work. I didn't mean to fall asleep. My mouth tastes disgusting. I sit up and stretch, wincing at the pain flashing through my bruised body. 'In here,' I croak.

His face appears round the door. His smile drops and he rushes over.

'Bloody hell, Lizzy, what happened to you?'

'It looks worse than it is.' After my nightmarish drive home from Bristol, I had meant to come in, have a shower, get changed and have something to eat. But instead, I collapsed onto the sofa, closed my eyes and fell asleep. I realise I must now look like hell.

'Your face!' Joe's eyes travel down my body, taking in the bruises and scratches. 'Your dress! What happened? Have you been attacked?' He rushes to my side.

'I'm okay. I'll be fine. I fell asleep. Bit groggy.'

'But what happened to you? I thought you were going to see that private investigator guy. It wasn't him who did this, was it?' He jumps to his feet again.

'No! Calm down, Joe.' I take his hand – black with oil from the garage – and pull him back down next to me. I tell him about my trip to Bristol, about being pushed into the oncoming traffic. How the car stopped just centimetres away.

'Pushed?' he says, his eyes wide.

'I'm pretty sure I was, yeah.'

'No way. Who was it? Did you see them?'

'It was so busy. There were all these students on the pavement. I heard these running footsteps, then felt these hands at my back.' I give a shudder.

'Could it have been an accident? Someone bumping into you or something?'

'It could have been. But I'm pretty sure it was deliberate. I definitely felt two hands push me.'

'Have you told the police?'

'It was all a bit full on. Someone called an ambulance and the police, so I've been checked over. I'm fine.'

'What did they say when you told them you'd been pushed?'

'They said they'd go door to door round the local shops and cafés, see if anyone saw what happened. But it was so busy, I doubt anyone saw. Surely they would've come forward at the time.'

'CCTV?'

'None on that part of the road.'

'Shit. I knew I should have gone to Bristol with you. I'm such an idiot. What a crap boyfriend…'

'Don't be silly. 'Course you're not. It's not like you knew someone was going to push me in front of a car.'

'But what with all this other stuff going on, I should've realised you might be in danger. You could've been killed!'

I blow out a breath. 'I'm fine.' I may be fine physically, but inside everything is going haywire. My heart is racing, my mind spinning. 'There's something else…'

'What is it?'

'I think I might have seen Emma running away.'

'What do you mean, *Emma*? As in, your sister Emma?'

'Yeah. I'm wondering… I'm wondering if it was her. If Emma pushed me.'

'No.' Joe shakes his head. 'I can't believe she'd do anything like that.'

'Well, it looked like her.'

'You saw her face?'

'Not exactly. Just the back of her, running away. But I know her. I'd recognise her anywhere. Like, if you glimpsed me in a crowd, you'd know it was me.'

'Did you tell the police?'

'About Emma? No.'

'Jesus, Lizzy. Why didn't you call me after it happened? I would've come to get you.'

'To be honest, I wasn't thinking straight. I was a bit all over the place.'

'Did you tell them? The police, that you think it might have been your sister?'

'No. I'm not a hundred per cent sure it *was* her, and if I accuse her of something like this, it'll break Mum and Dad.'

'You don't think it's her doing all the other stuff, do you? The letters and everything?'

'I honestly don't know. It's not her writing on the letters, but I suppose whoever's doing it would disguise their own writing anyway.'

'But why would Emma do it? What would be her reason? I mean, you hardly see one another, you lead separate lives.'

I shrug. 'Maybe she still likes you.'

'What! No.' Joe screws up his face. 'That was years ago. Water under the bridge. Anyway, she's marrying what's-his-face, Mr Personality.'

'I dunno. I can't think any more.' I drop my head back onto the sofa and close my eyes for a moment.'

'You okay?' he asks. 'Should I call the doctor?'

My head is spinning. 'Can you get me a glass of water, Joe? I feel a bit weird.'

''Course. 'Course I can. Hang on.' Seconds later, he returns with my water. 'Here you go. Do you want anything else?'

I gulp down the cool liquid. 'That's a bit better. Thanks. I'm bloody starving, actually. Haven't had anything since breakfast. Probably why I feel so spaced out.'

'Toast?' he offers.

'With jam?' I add.

'No problem.'

'Let me just have a quick shower and get changed.' I gingerly rise to my feet. 'On second thoughts, I might just have to wash with a flannel. Too many cuts and scrapes to have a shower.'

'Poor baby.' Joe gives me a gentle hug and I wince as his stubble scrapes my cheek. 'How did it go with the private investigator?' he asks.

'That's another story. The guy can't do anything.'

'Why not?' Joe frowns.

'He told me the police are the best people to help. But he did give me some good advice.' I step out into the hall and retrieve my recent purchase.

Joe follows me. 'What's that you've got?'

'A spy camera.' I perk up as I tell him about Nas's suggestion. 'He said to hide it in a plant pot out the front. That way we can catch whoever's posting the letters.'

'Brilliant.'

'I hope it's all right,' I say, peering into the bag. 'I dropped it when I was knocked over.'

'You go and get washed and changed,' Joe says, taking the bag from me. 'I'll make you some tea and toast. And then we can set this up.'

I nod, feeling a little better now that we might have a real chance of catching whoever's doing this.

I only hope it's not my sister.

CHAPTER TWENTY-THREE

Joe didn't want me to go to work today. He thought I should take the day off. But it's not so easy to call in sick when you're the manager, especially while George is away. I can't expect Pippa to manage on her own, and besides, if she is stealing, this would give her the perfect opportunity to help herself to more stock. Besides, George is still waiting for me to speak to her. I sit at my dressing table painstakingly applying make-up to my swollen, scratched-up face. There's not much I can do to disguise the damage. And despite my best efforts, I'll probably still end up frightening the customers away.

Frank winds himself round my ankles as I dab foundation on the worst of the scratches. He starts miaowing in an attempt to get me to hurry up and give him his breakfast.

'Come on then, Frank. Let's get you something to eat.' I give up on my face, deciding that I'll spend most of the day hiding away in the stockroom. Pippa can always call me into the shop if it gets really busy. I make my way down the stairs, trying to avoid the trip hazard that is my cat. I've already decided I'm not going to speak to Pippa about the thefts today. Before I have that talk with her, I'll need to line someone up to take her place. I might call Maggie in the Cirencester branch, see if she can recommend anyone. I'll use my accident as an excuse for George, in case he asks why I still haven't spoken to her.

The sound of Frank's purring fills the kitchen as I begin spooning his breakfast into a bowl. Switching on the kettle, my thoughts turn to the police. I'd have thought Llewellyn might have called last night to see how I was. But maybe the Bristol coppers haven't sent over the information yet. If I haven't heard anything from her by lunchtime, I'll give her a call to see what she makes of yesterday's 'accident'.

Joe enjoyed setting up the camera for me yesterday. We decided he would do it surreptitiously, after dark. Even though Reuben from the camera shop had shown me how to set it up myself, I was too shaken and exhausted to even try. Joe hid the camera beneath some foliage in one of the terracotta flowerpots in the back garden. Once he was happy that it was suitably camouflaged, he brought the pot around to the front porch and spent ages testing out the angles. Eventually, he was satisfied that he'd set it up in the best position to capture anyone stepping onto our pathway.

After a quick breakfast of coffee and toast, I leave the house, get in my car and set off for work. It's even hotter today, if that's possible, probably because yesterday's promised thunderstorm never materialised. A dull throb has started up in my temples; I should have taken some painkillers before leaving the house. Never mind, I'll pick some up on the way to work.

My glance lands on a yellow air freshener dangling from my rear-view mirror. It's in the shape of a VW Beetle and it smells of bananas, of all things. I hate bananas. Who would even want their car to smell like that? Joe must have put it up yesterday, but it's going straight in the bin because the smell is vile. Typical Joe; he must have put it up as a joke. I smile to myself. I'll text him to say his sense of humour is getting worse.

As I turn out of our road, the air freshener swings around and I notice there's writing on the back in thick black marker pen. Suddenly I get a tight feeling in my chest. A car horn blares, making me swerve and gasp. In a split second, I've veered onto the other side of the road. I turn the wheel sharply to get back onto my side as a male driver in a silver Nissan zooms past, hurling all kinds of abuse out of his window. Can't say I blame him. I nearly caused a head-on collision. I pull over onto the grass verge, my heart hammering.

With shaking fingers, I take a tissue out of my handbag and use it to spin the air freshener around so I don't get my prints on it. I'm dreading seeing what's written on the back, praying it's something innocuous, but knowing it won't be.

Shame that car missed you yesterday

The words seem to grow bigger on the card. It's written in the same rounded, swirly hand as the letters. I hear the tone of the words in my head – bitter, hateful. The words of someone who wants to hurt me. Kill me, even. I let go of the card, mindful that the police won't want my prints on it.

This proves that I was pushed. This is definitely no secret admirer. This is someone deranged. Someone who has been watching me. Following me. Stalking me. They've been inside my house. And it hits me that they've also been inside my car! How did they get inside here? I turn to look at all the windows, but they're all rolled up. I get out, unsteady on my feet and begin to check all the doors. At the side of the road, the dry grass tickles my ankles as I walk around the vehicle, careful not to slip down into the ditch.

Both my back doors are locked. I try the passenger door handle next, and to my dismay it opens. It's unlocked! Did I leave it that way? I wouldn't have been so careless, surely? I never sit on that side, anyway. My car is old, it doesn't have central locking or an alarm. Does this person have a copy of my car key? Or did I accidentally leave the passenger door unlocked? How would I even know?

I slam the door closed and remain standing on the grass verge, staring into space, my brain going into overdrive. Whoever wrote the message on the air freshener must have got into my car sometime last night or early this morning. Which means they were in my road, outside the cottage. For a brief second I have the hopeful thought that my new spy cam will have captured whoever it is. But then I remember that I didn't park right outside my house yesterday as there were no spaces; I parked a few doors down – out of the range of the camera. Even so, I'll be able to check to see whether anyone walked past the house to get to the car. The footage might be clear enough to reveal who is doing this. But what will I do if I spot my sister on the video? I know she hates me now. But to try to kill me…

Emma and I used to be so close. Sure, we were different – she's always been studious, serious, beautiful. Everything has always come naturally to her. She never had to work hard at school, but consistently got 'A's in her exams. Boys were always intimidated but fascinated by her at the same time. Whereas I was more of a regular girl – I had to work hard to get any decent exam results. I always struggled with my weight. Don't get me wrong, I was pretty enough and had my fair share of the boys' attention. Plus I was probably more popular than Emma, with more friends.

So, is that the reason? Was she somehow jealous of me for my popularity? She never showed any signs. She never said or did anything overtly nasty until the incident with Joe. Maybe she kept it all bottled up? Kept it quiet for years, and now it's all coming out in the shape of these awful letters. And worse.

Or is my imagination making connections where they don't exist? As I was falling into the path of the traffic yesterday, I thought I saw Emma running away. But did I? Or was it my mind playing tricks on me in a terrifying situation? Maybe, in some twisted way, it was Emma I wanted to see. But it's more likely it was simply someone with the same hair colour disappearing into the crowd. Someone who might actually be nothing to do with me. They could have been a random person in a crowd who I latched on to.

I do feel guilty for suspecting my sister. For thinking her capable of something so evil. And yet she's betrayed me before…

I walk round to the road again and get back into the car, anxious, but also eager to head home and check the camera footage. I'll check the spy cam, then give Sergeant Llewellyn a call. Waiting until the road is clear of traffic, I execute a clumsy five-point turn, almost reversing into the ditch. But eventually I'm facing the right way and I head back home. A couple of minutes later, I park in a newly free space outside my house, nervously wondering if the person trying to hurt me might be watching me now. What if it isn't Emma who's been harassing me, but it is in fact Ian from next door? I got very odd vibes off him when we were round there for dinner. Hopefully I'll discover who it is soon enough. But part of me is terrified to find out.

I sit in the car for a few moments, hands gripping the steering wheel, paranoia gripping my mind. I can't let them know about the spy cam, so my plan is to walk up the front path, pretend to drop my keys, and then while I'm picking them up, I'll block the plant pot with my body and detach the camera. The road is quiet. No one around at this time on a Tuesday morning. Well, no one that I can *see*. They're all either at work, or inside wishing for air con.

With a hammering heart I exit the car, lock it and walk up the baking path. I let my keys slip out of my hand and then crouch down to retrieve them, legs like jelly. I keep thinking someone is going to run up and attack me from behind. Much as I want to keep throwing glances over my shoulder, I don't.

I slide my hand beneath the foliage in the flowerpot, trying to stealthily detach the camera from its hiding place. But my fingers find only soil and leaves. *Where is the bloody thing?* I drop the pretence of picking up my keys, and instead begin frantically searching the plant pot, digging my fingers beneath the dry earth and pulling back the stems of whatever half-dead plant this is. There's nothing here. I shift the pot to the other side of the porch, scanning the ground in case the spy cam has become detached somehow, and fallen onto the flagstones.

But it's gone. The camera has disappeared.

Someone must have taken it.

CHAPTER TWENTY-FOUR

I fumble my way back inside the house, hot blood racing through my veins. Someone must have seen Joe setting up the camera last night. Are they out there now? Watching me? Laughing? I stand in the narrow hallway, take my phone out of my bag and call Joe. He answers straight away.

'Hey.' He sounds out of breath.

'Joe, did you take the camera out of the plant pot?'

'Take the camera out? No. Why?'

'It's not there. It's gone.' With my fingertips, I press at the scratches by my hairline. They're beginning to itch as they tighten and scab over.

'What do you mean *gone*?' Joe cries. 'I set it up last night. It's there, hidden under the leaves.'

'Not any more. Did you check on it this morning?'

'No, I was half asleep. You know what I'm like first thing – Zombie, Dawn of the Dead.'

'That means it could have been stolen any time. Either last night or early this morning.'

Joe growls down the phone. 'I thought I was being careful, but someone must have seen me setting it up. Do you think it was kids?'

'No. It has to be the person sending the letters.'

There's silence at the end of the line.

'Joe? You there?' I sit on one of the lower steps of the staircase, stare at the grubby paintwork on the wall.

'You're probably right,' he says. 'But I didn't want to mention them. Didn't want to freak you out. Do you really think they were watching?'

'I don't know. Seems likely.' I pause. 'They left me another message.'

'WHAT? Why didn't you say anything?'

'I'm telling you now.'

'Are you okay, Lizzy? What did the message say?'

I open my mouth to tell him, but the thought of saying the words aloud makes my stomach churn. Tears well up behind my eyes.

'Lizzy? You all right?'

'Not really. What am I going to do, Joe?'

'Did they threaten you?'

'The…' I take a breath. 'The message admitted that they pushed me into the traffic yesterday.'

'*Shit!* That's…' Joe exhales. 'That's not good, Lizzy. That's not good at all.'

'I know.' My voice wobbles, but I manage to keep it together.

'I'm coming home.'

'No, Joe. It's fine. *Don't.*' I can't deal with Joe's macho overprotectiveness at the moment. I love that he cares about me so much, but when he's too concerned it makes me emotional.

'Go and sit down with Frank,' he says. 'I'm calling the police.'

'I can call them, it's okay.'

'Just let me call them for you. I'll tell them they need to get there ASAP.'

'Okay, Joe, thank you.'

'And I'm coming home, too.'

'No, honestly. I'll be fine. There's no need for you to come home.' I want to be strong when the police get here so that I can speak to them rationally about what's happening. I don't want to be a blubbering mess. And I don't want Joe throwing his weight around either, demanding results from Llewellyn and

Ryan. That's only going to piss them off. 'Look, I'll ring you after they've been.'

'I want to be with you, Lizzy. I can hear how upset you are.'

'Honestly, please don't worry. I'm okay,' I lie. 'I'll call you after I've spoken to them.'

'I'm not happy about you being there on your own. I mean, someone tried to…' His voice trails off, but I know what he was going to say – that someone tried to kill me.

Finally, I persuade Joe to stay at work. But we agree that he will ring the police for me. They know who I am and what's been happening, so at least he won't have to go into the whole backstory of the past few days.

I get up and gaze around the hallway, not really seeing anything. As I wait for the police to arrive, it feels like I'm hiding, cowering in this place that is starting to feel unfamiliar. My cosy cottage isn't a safe space any more. My stalker has admitted they've tried to hurt me once, so surely it's only a matter of time before they do it again.

My teeth are chattering and my right leg has begun to twitch involuntarily like it has a life of its own. I don't know what to do. Should I go into the lounge? Into the kitchen? Upstairs? I end up doing none of those things, instead sinking down onto the hall floor and leaning back against the wall. Frank struts out of the lounge and sits by my side like a guard dog while I stroke his head absent-mindedly.

When the doorbell rings, I have to shake myself out of my stupor. I heave myself off the floor and pick Frank up so he doesn't run out through the front door when I open it. I'm pretty sure it must be the police at the door, but I'm not taking any chances. I pop into the lounge and peer through the window to double-check, relaxing my shoulders when I spy the familiar figures of Llewellyn and Ryan standing on the doorstep. I see more of them than of Joe these days.

'Hello, Lizzy,' Llewellyn says as I open the door. 'So sorry to hear about what happened to you yesterday.'

Ryan is staring at my swollen cheek. He gives an embarrassed smile when I catch his eye.

'Come in,' I say.

'Such a cute cat,' Llewellyn says, scratching behind one of Frank's ears. Once she's closed the front door behind her, I set Frank down on the floor and he trots off into the kitchen, obviously not in a sociable mood this morning.

The officers follow me through to the lounge, where I gesture to them to sit down on the sofa. I perch on the arm of one of the chairs, not sure where to start with my story. But Llewellyn speaks first.

'We got all the info from Bristol. I wanted to come round and see you yesterday, but we were kept busy last night with various other things, unfortunately.'

'That's okay,' I reply. 'I'm not badly hurt, just a bit shaken up. Actually, a lot shaken up.' My voice cracks.

''Course you are,' she says. 'Must have been scary.'

'And you think you were pushed?' Ryan asks.

'Actually, I *know* I was.'

'The information we received said you weren't sure,' Ryan says, looking down at his notebook. 'The report says it may have been deliberate or someone may have accidentally knocked into you.'

'That's what I thought before today.'

'You mean the latest letter?' Ryan asks.

I nod. 'Not a letter, though. More like a message.' I stand up. 'Come outside and I'll show you.'

I take the officers out to my car and point through the window to the air freshener still hanging from the rear-view mirror. 'Someone broke into my car and they put that there.'

'What does the message say?' she asks, peering through the glass.

'I'll show you.' I go to open the door but Llewellyn puts a hand out to stop me.

'If you could just tell me what it says. I don't want to go messing up a potential crime scene.'

I swallow, and just about manage to force out the words. 'It says: *Shame that car missed you yesterday.*'

'Nice,' Ryan says. 'Sounds like we're dealing with a right charmer.'

'Okay,' Llewellyn says, pulling a mobile phone out of one of her pockets, 'I'm going to get CSI down here to do a thorough check of the vehicle.' Her phone call connects and she walks a little way up the street to have her conversation. A minute later, she's back. 'Shall we go inside to wait for them to arrive?'

I nod. 'Okay. Actually, there's something else I need to tell you anyway.'

Back in the lounge, I explain how I went into Bristol to buy a security camera. I leave out the part about meeting Nas, as it feels kind of rude to tell them I was trying to hire a PI when the police are already working on my case. My mobile phone buzzes out in the hall, but I ignore it. It's probably Joe texting to see how I am.

'My boyfriend set up the camera last night,' I say.

'Have you looked at the footage this morning?' Ryan asks.

'That's just it,' I reply. 'After finding the message in my car earlier, I came straight home to get the camera in case it recorded anything. But it was gone. Someone's taken it.'

'Where did you place the camera?' Llewellyn asks.

I lead the officers back outside and show them the plant pot. 'Joe hid it under the leaves.'

'Okay,' Llewellyn says. 'We'll ask CSI to take a look at this area while they're here.'

Back inside, my phone is vibrating angrily on the hall table.

'Do you want to get that?' Llewellyn asks.

'Maybe I'd better, in case it's important.' As soon as I reach to pick it up, it stops buzzing. I gesture to the officers to go back into the lounge while I quickly check my messages.

Shit. I have six missed calls from Pippa, along with a bunch of texts. I check the time and realise I'm almost an hour late for work. Pippa has no keys, so she's been waiting outside the shop for me. Her latest voicemail says she hopes I'm okay, and that she's gone into Clare's Coffee Shop to wait.

I tap out a quick text to say I should be there within the next half hour. But I realise that's probably optimistic. I feel terrible for leaving the shop closed, but I reason that I'll explain everything to George when he gets back. Hopefully he'll understand. If he wants, he can dock any loss of earnings from my salary.

Can today get any worse?

CHAPTER TWENTY-FIVE

I keep hold of my phone and return to the lounge where Llewellyn and Ryan are talking in hushed tones. They fall silent when I walk in and give me encouraging smiles.

'So, do you need me to stay while you wait for the crime scene people to get here?' I ask. 'Because I'm really late opening up the shop this morning, and one of my staff has been waiting outside for me. That was her on the phone.'

'No,' Llewellyn says. 'That's okay. If you leave us your car keys, we can wait for them in our vehicle. But there is another reason we wanted to talk to you today.'

I take up my position on the arm of the chair once more – too tense to take a proper seat – and wait for her to continue.

'The results of the stain analysis have come back from the lab,' she says, her face expressionless. I wonder if it's part of police training to perfect a poker face.

'You mean the stain on the letter?' I ask.

'That's right.' She pushes a wisp of fringe off her forehead. 'Unfortunately, the lab tests determined that the stain is in fact blood.'

My skin goes cold. 'What kind of blood?'

'The technicians used what's called a precipitin reaction, to detect the presence of a specific antigen,' Llewellyn says.

I have no idea what she's talking about, and my face must show my confusion because she quickly goes on to explain. 'They used a test to determine whether the bloodstain is human, or from another source.'

'And?' I wish she'd hurry up and get to the point.

'The results are positive for feline blood.'

A wave of nausea rises up from my gut, but I manage to keep it down. I take a deep breath in through my nose to try to damp down the horror of what Llewellyn is telling me.

'Are you okay?' Llewellyn asks.

'Not really,' I reply. 'Frank's paw,' I continue. 'They must have cut it, mustn't they? Whoever is doing this, whoever is hounding me, it was them who cut my cat's paw, wasn't it?'

Neither of the officers replies.

'Wasn't it?' I say.

'We shouldn't jump to conclusions,' Llewellyn says. 'But it does look that way. Yes.'

I stand up and start pacing the room. 'I don't believe this. Did you get any prints off any of the letters?'

'I'm afraid not. But we're working on other avenues.'

'Like what?' I ask.

'Like where the paper and envelopes were bought. That kind of thing.'

'What about Leon Whittaker? Have you spoken to him again?'

'Not yet. But in light of all these new incidents we'll be finding out his whereabouts for yesterday and today. Checking if he has any alibis.'

'My neighbour…' I begin, and then tail off.

'What about your neighbour?' Llewellyn asks.

PC Matt Ryan is writing in his notebook again.

'Ian Clutterbuck,' I say. 'He…' But I have no evidence that my neighbour has done anything. I can't accuse him simply because he gave me this weird look one time. 'I'm pretty sure he's harmless, but then again, I'm not sure what to think any more. Maybe you should speak to *all* my neighbours. Find out if they've seen anything strange, or anyone hanging around.'

'We'll do that,' Llewellyn says. 'Any reason why you singled out this Ian Clutterbuck person?'

'No. Only that… he lives next door. If he's got anything to do with it, he'd be able to see my comings and goings. It would be easy for him to follow me.'

'And that's all? No other reason you mention his name? Has he behaved inappropriately towards you? Said anything strange?'

'No, he hasn't. In fact, Joe and I went round there for dinner with him and his girlfriend last week.'

She nods slowly. 'And what about your other neighbours?'

'I only know Mrs P, on the other side of us. She's my old school teacher. Really nice. Said she'd keep an eye out for me.'

'And your neighbours opposite?'

'I don't really know any of them.'

'Okay,' Llewellyn says, getting to her feet. 'Matt and I will start going door to door. We might have to come back to finish up later, as most people will probably be at work. Talking of work, feel free to head off to the shop, if you're up to it. But no one would blame you if you took the day off.'

'Thanks. But I'd rather go in than sit around at home worrying.'

'I know what you mean,' Llewellyn says. 'Actually, why don't I drop you in while Matt makes a start on the door-to-doors?'

Matt raises an eyebrow and then nods at his superior.

'Really?' I say, feeling relieved. 'Would that be okay? I don't feel safe walking on my own at the moment.'

'Of course,' Llewellyn says. 'And please make sure you get a lift home after work, too. I don't want you out on your own at all. Not until we've caught this person. I thought I told you that last time we met?'

'You did,' I say.

'Well, please, Lizzy, take my advice this time.'

'I will.' I nod, wishing I'd taken it the first time. 'Can you give me ten minutes to get myself together?'

'We'll make a start on the neighbours,' she says. 'Meet me outside when you're ready.'

The two of them leave and I sink into the sofa, pulling my legs up under me and closing my eyes. I can barely take it all in. Two weeks ago I was living a peaceful, normal life. Now I'm living in the middle of a nightmare. I don't know what to think. How to be. I feel absolutely exhausted and overwhelmed. I mentioned Leon and Ian to the police, so why didn't I tell them my suspicions about Emma? She lives in Bristol, so she could have been in that crowd yesterday, but what about all the hand-delivered letters? She works full-time, so how would she have managed that?

I should call her at work. See if she's in today. If she's not there, then it makes it more likely that she was here hanging up that air freshener and stealing my spy cam. But she could have done all that last night and still made it back in time for work in Bristol. The truth is, I don't want to believe it's her.

My phone buzzes in my lap. It must be Pippa. I'd better go. It's almost half ten. My customers will be going mad wondering why we're not open. I check my messages and see that I've received another text. It's from an unknown number. Part of me hopes it's a spammy marketing text, but the other part knows it won't be. My heart twangs as I open the text:

> *Surely you didn't think you'd catch me out with your oh-so-obvious camera, did you?*

I read it again, my stomach swirling.

They have my number! Who is it? *Who is it?*

My shock and terror suddenly morph into something harder. Before I can stop myself, I find myself tapping out a reply:

> *Who is this?*

There's no reply, so I write another text:

What do you want?

Still no reply. I furiously tap out another one.

Just leave me alone!

The phone buzzes in my hand, making me jump. A reply comes back with just a single emoticon – a crying-with-laughter face.

I clench my fists and throw my phone onto the sofa. It bounces onto the floor and lands face up, the laughing icon staring straight back at me, like my stalker is watching me through my phone screen. I kick the handset over with my toe so it ends up face down on the floor. But that laughing face remains stamped on my brain. How am I going to make this nightmare stop?

So now I'm getting closer to what I really want.

This is not about their fear any more. It's about getting revenge.

Proper revenge on the one who's to blame.

Nothing will make up for the wrongs I've suffered. But I can taste the sweetness of everything that's coming and it will be worth it.

I'll make sure of that.

CHAPTER TWENTY-SIX

'Darling, what on earth happened to you?' The horror on Pippa's face tells me just how awful I must look.

'Let's get inside,' I reply.

Pippa waits in the corridor while I disable the alarm and switch on the lights, and then we bustle through to the shop. I couldn't face coming into work yesterday. I was too shaken up by everything that happened. I messaged George to tell him I was unable to go in. To give him credit, he was sympathetic and arranged for one of his other shop managers to open up for Pippa. Luckily, he didn't prod me about the thefts. But I'm aware that Pippa is very much on borrowed time.

George gets back from his holiday in two days, so I'm going to have to speak to Pippa soon. I'm lucky George hasn't messaged me about it again. Hopefully his wife Sophia has banned him from any more work-related activities while they're supposed to be on holiday. But he's a proper workaholic, so I'm not banking on it. He could call at any moment.

I check my watch – still ten minutes until opening time, so I've got a few minutes in which to fill Pippa in, although the thought of talking about the attack makes me queasy.

I sit on the stool while Pippa rests her elbows on the counter.

'You said you were in an accident,' she prompts. 'So what happened?'

'I went to Bristol on Monday,' I begin.

'Ooh, Sebbie was there on Monday. He went to visit the auction house. We're going to sell some artwork. Poor Mummy's distraught.'

'Seb was in Bristol on Monday?' I'm getting an uncomfortable feeling in my chest. 'When was he there? What time?'

'Oh, he left home at the crack of dawn. He was there all morning.'

My stomach lurches. Could that be a coincidence? I decide not to voice my fears about Seb. My questions didn't go down very well with Pippa last time. But I make a mental note to tell Llewellyn that Seb was in Bristol at the same time as me. Maybe Joe's initial hunch was actually correct.

'So?' Pippa persists. 'What happened to cause all this?' She gestures to my face.

I decide to give her a simplified version of the truth. If Seb is something to do with the letters, I don't want Pippa blabbing to him about how shaken up I really am. So I tell her that I was knocked over by a pedestrian.

'You mean, on purpose?' Her mouth hangs open.

'I'm not sure. It happened so fast. It was busy, it could have been an accident,' I lie.

'But it might not have been! Sweetie! That's absolutely horrific! Who would do such a thing? And *why*? You must have seriously pissed someone off, Lizzy.' Pippa is so blunt, I'd laugh if the situation wasn't deadly serious. 'Any idea who it could have been?'

At the moment I'm thinking it might be your brother. 'It could have been anyone,' I say instead. 'The street was crowded.'

'Have you fallen out with anyone recently?' she asks. 'Someone who might have a bit of a screw loose?'

Thoughts of my sister flash into my head. 'No.' I shake my head slowly. 'I can't think of anyone I've fallen out with, not recently.'

'Except the lovely Leon,' Pippa drawls.

'Hmm. Yes, well, the police were going to have words with him again. But they haven't got back to me yet.'

'Who do the police think is responsible?' she asks. 'I take it you did call them?'

I shrug. 'They know as much as I do.'

'Poor you. Should you even be in work? I mean, no offence, but you look like an extra from a horror movie.'

'Thanks a lot!' I put a hand self-consciously to my cheek.

'Darling. You know I think you're drop-dead gorgeous. Just, maybe not today.'

'Yes, well, I thought I'd hide in the stockroom. You can come and fetch me if it gets too busy. Sorry I left you hanging around outside the shop for so long.'

'Excuse me, I don't "do" hanging around.' She laughs. 'Actually, I waited in Clare's with a cappuccino, and had a jolly nice morning being chatted up by one of the waiters.'

'Well, I'm glad my crisis perked up your love life.' I roll my eyes. 'Things feeling better after Toby?' I ask.

'Ah, you know. Can't let the bastards grind you down.' She drops her flippant tone for a moment. 'Seriously though, Lizzy. If you need anything, any time, I'm here for you, all right?'

'Thank you.' I lower my eyes, feeling wretched about her imminent redundancy. I hate being so two-faced.

'Gracious, it's past nine o'clock,' Pippa says, glancing down at her watch. 'Hadn't we better—'

'Yes, I'll sort out the till, you get the door. And then I'm going into the back to catch up on my paperwork.'

Being back at Georgio's is strange. What with everything that's gone on, it seems like weeks since I was last here, not a few days. I'm hoping that being at work will take my mind off the fact that someone out there is trying to kill me. But it's not working. Hurriedly, I slot the float into the till and retreat to the back room, relieved to be away from the openness of the shop floor.

I slide into the leather swivel chair that sits in front of the desk and close my eyes for a moment, wondering if I'm going to have the strength to get through a whole day. I could so easily fall asleep right now. Maybe sleep is a coping mechanism – a way to block out all the crap I'm going through. My mind slips back to yesterday. To the air freshener, the spy cam theft and then the text messages. I was sure Llewellyn would be able to trace the texts. But she said that they'd most likely have been sent from a pay-as-you-go phone with an unregistered SIM, which would be untraceable. So, no joy there. Whoever is doing this is smart. They know how not to get caught. But I'm hoping it's only a matter of time before they slip up.

I open my eyes, make myself a strong coffee and get to work ordering new stock. The morning goes by reasonably quickly and, before I know it, Pippa's asking if she can take her lunch break. My breath shortens at the thought of going out onto the shop floor, but I tell myself not to be silly. I can do this. I can't let whoever is threatening me ruin my life.

I slick on some lipstick, dab some more concealer on my bruises and leave the stockroom, feeling like I'm about to go on stage.

'I won't be long,' Pippa says. 'Twenty minutes or so, okay?'

'Don't worry, you can take your full hour,' I say.

'No, it's fine. See you in twenty.' She blows me a kiss and leaves.

I can cope with twenty minutes, can't I?

The shop isn't too busy. Just a few customers browsing the clothes rails. Normally I would try to catch their eye and give a smile to acknowledge that I'm here to help if they need me. But today I purposely don't look their way, hoping they don't want any assistance. Instead, I busy myself rearranging one of the china displays.

Someone taps me on the shoulder, making me jump. I drop the cream jug I'm holding, but manage to fumble and catch it.

'Lizzy.'

I turn to see my neighbour, Ruby, her hair pulled up into a ponytail, large silver hoops in her ears. Her mouth drops open when she sees my face, but she clamps it shut again.

'Sorry, didn't mean to make you jump,' she says. 'What happened to your face? Sorry, that was rude. Tell me to mind my own business.'

I bring a hand self-consciously to my cheek and set the jug back down on the shelf. Obviously I didn't do as good a job with my make-up as I thought. 'Hi, Ruby. No, that's okay. I know, I look a real sight, don't I? I fell over on the pavement earlier this week.' I don't have the energy to go into what really happened. Not after going over the whole thing with Pippa earlier.

'Poor you!' Ruby briefly places a hand on my arm.

I shake my head. 'It looks worse than it is. Anyway, Joe and I had a lovely time round at yours last week. We'll arrange an evening at our place next, if you fancy it?'

'Cool. Me and Ian would love to come round yours.'

'Okay, great.' There's a brief awkward silence. 'Did you come in for anything special? Or did you just pop in to say hi?'

'Oh. Yeah. I need a card for Ian's dad. We're going to his retirement party at the weekend. Ian just wanted to get him some booze and chocolates, but we need a card too. Ian told me to get something funny.'

'Sure. Okay. I'll show you what we've got.' I accompany Ruby across to the card section and point out a few that might be suitable.

She picks out quite a rude one and smirks. 'Ian will like this one.'

'Okay, great.' I take the card and ring it through the till. Before she leaves, I promise to sort out a date for our next meal. Through the window, she gives me a short wave before continuing on up the street.

Outside, I notice a youngish guy talking into a mobile phone. But he's holding the handset out in front of him like he's taking photos, or filming. It looks as though he's staring right at me. I tense up. What if he's just pretending to speak to someone as a cover? Could he be filming me? It's warm inside the shop, but suddenly I'm so hot I can barely breathe. I know I'm being irrational, but I can't help myself. Should I go closer? See what he's doing? I step out from behind the counter and move into the centre of the shop. As I do so, the man laughs and turns around. He walks off up the road.

I run to the door, open it and peer out. He's still talking and laughing. If he's been filming me, I have to know. I have to find out, so I stride after him. I have no idea what I'll say when I catch up to the guy, but I hurry after him anyway. I'm so close now, I could tap him on the shoulder. I'm about to pluck up the courage when I see that there's a woman on his phone screen. The man is FaceTiming with someone. He isn't interested in me. He wasn't filming me at all.

My heart is racing; my skin is clammy. I'm an anxiety-ridden mess. I stand where I am for a few seconds more, trying to breathe in some fresh air. But the atmosphere is so close, so moisture-laden, that each breath catches in my throat.

'Lizzy?'

I turn at the sound of a man's voice. I take a step backward when I see who it is.

'Leon,' I croak. 'What are you doing here?'

CHAPTER TWENTY-SEVEN

Dressed in a dark suit, his shirt open at the neck, Leon scowls at me. 'I'm not *here*,' he replies, crossly. 'I mean, I'm just walking up the street. I didn't come to see you, if that's what you think.' His face suddenly creases with concern. 'What happened to you, Lizzy? You look like you've been in an acci…' He breaks off, frowns and raises his hands like he's surrendering. 'Sorry, none of my business.' Leon Whittaker stops talking, walks around me and carries on up the road.

I watch him stride away, relieved I don't have to talk to him, then I realise I've left the shop unattended, so I hurry back down the street and into Georgio's with my head down, making for my safe space behind the counter to await Pippa's return.

The afternoon passes slowly, but I stay tucked away in the stockroom for most of it while Pippa deals with the customers. As a consequence, I'm able to catch up on all the invoicing and ordering, and my desk is totally, satisfyingly clear by the end of the day. So at least that's one good thing. Tomorrow I might even make a start on sorting out the filing cabinets – something I've been meaning to do for months.

After closing time, I take Pippa up on her offer to accompany me to my car. It's not a very Pippa-ish thing to do, so I'm grateful. I decide that tomorrow will be the day I speak to her. It's for her own good as well as mine.

Driving home makes me feel nauseous, the interior of my car still reeks of bananas. Even with the window rolled right down,

I can't get away from the smell. Yesterday, CSI swept my car and the front porch for prints and clues, but I haven't heard whether they found anything or not. Apparently these things take time.

Back home, I hear the water running upstairs. Joe must be in the shower. He was supposed to be out this evening with the lads from the garage. It's Brycie's birthday and they're all going to The Crown after work for drinks and then on for a curry. Joe told me he would give it a miss, that he was happy to stay in with me after everything I've been through. But I told him he should go – despite not really meaning it. I made light of things, saying I'd be quite happy to be in sole charge of the TV remote followed by an early night. But he wouldn't hear of it. Said there was no way he was going to leave me at home alone. Now that I'm home, I'm grateful he's here. Even with him upstairs, I can't relax.

The air inside the cottage has grown stale and warm with no breeze to freshen things up. Frank follows me around while I push open the windows. I'm not reckless enough to open all of them – just the small ventilation ones that are too inaccessible for Frank to get out of, and too tiny for any person to get in through. Poor Frank has been cooped up inside for days, but I daren't let him out, not while there's a psycho on the loose. I've been meaning to buy a fan, but I know that as soon as I get one, the weather will turn cold and the fan will get shoved in the loft.

The creak of the shower screen opening lets me know that Joe has finished showering. My turn next. I'm going to have a cool shower, get into my PJs and then we can curl up on the sofa with dinner on our laps, catching up with our box sets. The thought of it calms me a little.

'Hi, Joe!' I call up the stairs.

There's no reply, so I make my way upstairs and peer round the bathroom door. It's full of steam, but no Joe.

'Joe?' Frank is at my heels and I almost trip over him. 'Bloody hell, Frank, are you trying to kill me, or something?'

'Lizzy? That you?' Joe calls out from the bedroom.

I push open the door to see him pulling on a clean T-shirt. 'Hi. Did you have a good day?'

'Yeah, not bad. You?' He comes over to kiss me.

'I was a bit paranoid. But it was okay. Spent most of the day hiding out the back in the stockroom.'

Joe pulls me into a hug. 'Poor you.'

'I'm all right. Just gonna have a shower, okay?'

'Cool. I'm going downstairs for a beer. See you in a few minutes.'

In the steamed-up bathroom, I stuff Joe's damp, discarded towel into the laundry basket, strip off my work clothes and step into the bath which also doubles up as a shower. Turning the temperature down, I let the water run in a gentle stream so it doesn't sting my grazed skin. I probably shouldn't be getting my scabs wet, but I can't go a second day without a proper shower – not in this heat.

Once I'm nicely cooled down, I step out of the bath and pat myself dry before pulling on a pair of pink-and-white striped cotton PJs. I feel like a new person. Almost like I've washed away some of the terror that's been simmering. I know this is probably a temporary reprieve but I'm enjoying it while it lasts.

Back in the bedroom, I towel-dry my hair, then run a comb through my damp locks. I can't face making a full-on proper dinner tonight. Instead, I'm going to slice up some cheese and pickles and have them with crackers. If Joe wants anything more, he'll have to sort it out himself. Finally, clean and dry, I make my way back downstairs.

Halfway down the staircase, my feeling of well-being is shattered. There, on the doormat below sits a white rectangle. I stop. Grip the banister with my left hand. Taking a breath, I reason that it could be anything. Just a random piece of junk mail. But I know it isn't. I know it's something that will disrupt my evening and ruin my sleep. Something that will get my heart speeding and my guts churning. I wish I could ignore it. Burn it. But the need to see what's written is too strong.

I run back upstairs, go into the bedroom and slide out one of the storage bags from under our bed. I unzip it and root around my carefully folded winter clothes until I find a pair of gloves. They're purple suede, my favourite pair. But as I pull them on, I realise that I'll never enjoy wearing them again.

'Joe!' I hurry back down the stairs, realising that instead of searching for gloves, I should have yanked open the front door to try to catch sight of whoever delivered the letter. It's probably too late now. 'Joe!'

'What is it?' He steps out of the kitchen, a can of lager in his hand.

I point to the envelope on the doormat, my finger shaking.

'Is that…?'

'I think it's another one.' I bend down, pick up the envelope in my gloved hand and yank open the door, stepping barefoot onto the path and staring up and down the road. Joe comes to join me. Frank tries to run past my legs, but I scoop him up and shut him in the lounge before returning to the front path. Joe runs out into the middle of the street and looks one way, then the other. Someone is getting out of their car further down, across the way – a woman and two young kids. But she doesn't look in our direction. She's laughing and the kids are carrying balloons. I doubt she's the person who's threatening me.

'I can't see anyone suspicious,' Joe says.

'Did you see the letter when you came downstairs after your shower?' I ask.

He shakes his head. 'It definitely wasn't there then.'

'So the person must have delivered this only minutes ago.'

'Wait here.' Joe starts jogging up the road. 'I'll see if I can spot anyone,' he calls.

Stepping back inside, I gaze at the letter and turn it over, expecting to see my name emblazoned on the front like all the others. But I frown when I see whose name is actually written in that same blue swirly handwriting:

Emma Beresford

It's addressed to my sister! I blink, trying to clear my vision in case I'm having some kind of weird episode and am reading it wrong. But there's no mistake. This letter is addressed to Emma. Does this mean it really is something to do with her? Is she doing this to confuse me? Or did my stalker make a mistake? Is it someone who knows us both and accidentally wrote down the wrong name?

I open the envelope and pull out two pieces of white paper. It looks like it was originally a single sheet, but it's been torn in two. I hold the pieces together to join two halves of a single word:

Sister

So this stalker knows I have a sister. But why is that important? What is it about my sister that they're interested in? Unless this really is from Emma, and she's playing some twisted game with me.

I set down the envelope and torn letter on the hall table and take my mobile phone out of my bag. I'm going to ring Emma to see if she knows what the hell is going on. I haven't called my sister in years, so I hope she has the same mobile number. I remove one of my gloves, swipe the screen and press contacts. But before I can scroll down to find her name, a call comes through. The caller's name flashes up on the screen.

It's Emma.

CHAPTER TWENTY-EIGHT

'Lizzy? Is that you?' Her words are clipped. She sounds out of breath.

'Emma? How did you… I was just about to…'

'Listen to me,' she says. 'Do you know anything about the letters?'

I sit on the staircase and try to get my breathing under control. 'Are they from you?' I ask. 'Why the hell would you—'

'Shit. So you *are* getting them.'

'What the hell is going on, Emma? If this is about Joe—'

'Shut up a minute, Lizzy.'

It feels weird to be talking to my sister again. I'm transported back to our childhood home where we would argue, snapping at one another about this and that. I'm not sure exactly when we started growing apart. As young kids we were always giggling and mucking around together. I even used to climb into bed with her after having nightmares, and she would tell me funny stories to stop me being scared. We may have had the odd cross word over who was watching what on the telly, or who ate the last biscuit. But actual arguments were few and far between. That is, until we reached adolescence. I think that's when things started to become more… competitive.

'What do you know about the letters?' I ask.

There's a brief silence at the end of the line. Just Emma breathing. 'I've been getting letters too,' she says.

I take a moment for her words to sink in. 'Someone's been sending you weird notes?'

'Yes.' Her voice is small. 'And when I got in from work a few minutes ago, there was another one in our pigeonhole. But it's got *your* name on it.'

'I had the same thing. An envelope with your name on the front. I was just about to call you.'

'And inside the envelope?' Emma asks.

'A piece of paper torn in half.'

'With the word…'

'Sister,' we say at the same time.

'Are you still at Richmond Gardens?' she asks.

'Yes.'

'I'll come over.'

'No,' I say, thinking about Joe. About how awkward it would be to have my sister here.

'Is Joe home?' She says his name with a spit of venom.

'Yes. But he's just run out to see if he can catch whoever left this latest letter.'

'You saw them? The person who delivered it?'

'No. But the letter has only just landed on the doormat, so Joe's gone down the road hoping to catch whoever it is.'

'We need to meet,' she says. 'Talk about what's been going on.'

I don't want to see my sister. I still haven't forgiven her for trying to take my boyfriend. But what choice do I have? If she says she's getting the letters too… 'Okay, but not here.' Bang goes my relaxing evening.

'I know a pub where we can meet,' Emma says. 'Halfway. I'll text you the address.'

'Okay.' I don't know if I'm more disturbed by receiving another letter, or by the thought of meeting my sister to talk.

'Traffic's awful this end,' she says, 'so it'll probably take me over an hour to get there.'

'Fine. See you in a while.' I end the call and wonder what the hell is going on. Why is my sister receiving the same letters as me? Could Joe be something to do with this? No. That doesn't make sense. None of this makes sense. Unless… what if she isn't receiving the letters too? What if she's the one behind the letters, and this is all part of some sick game?

The front door bursts open and I give a squeal of shock before realising that it's only Joe, his face red.

'Nothing,' he pants. 'I went up to the main road, but I couldn't see anyone running away. Whoever delivered that letter is long gone. Probably drove here anyway. Did you open the envelope?'

I nod. Joe comes in and closes the door behind him. 'What does it say?'

'Let's go into the lounge.' I snatch up the letter from the hall table and open the lounge door. Joe follows me in. Neither of us sits down.

'So?' Joe asks.

'It's all a bit weird, Joe. The letter's addressed to Emma.'

'What! So it's not from the stalker?' He wipes a sheen of sweat from his forehead with the back of his hand.

'It is, because it's the same handwriting,' I explain. 'Only, Emma says she's been getting the letters too.'

Joe is staring at me, not comprehending what I'm saying.

'Emma just called me. She just got a letter addressed to me. She says she's been receiving the same kind of harassment.'

'Shit, no way.'

'I'm going to meet her.'

'Who, Emma?'

I nod.

'Not being funny, Lizzy, but what if she's lying? It could be her who's been sending the letters all along.'

'I know. I thought the same thing. But… she sounded just as freaked out on the phone as I am.' I stare out of the window for a moment. 'And anyway, when I thought it was her who pushed me into the traffic, you said I was jumping to conclusions.'

'Show me the letter,' Joe says.

I set it on the coffee table using my gloved hand. 'Don't touch it.'

'I wasn't going to.' He looks at the envelope and the two pieces of paper. '*Sister?* So, let's say it's not Emma, then this person is someone who knows you and Emma are sisters. He's threatening both of you?'

'Looks that way.' My head is whirling so fast that it's a miracle I'm speaking in coherent sentences. 'I'm going to meet her now. Talk about what's going on. Compare notes.'

'I don't think you should go,' Joe says, staring at me. 'Maybe that's what this person wants – to get you both together. And if it is Emma, then you're playing right into her hands.'

'If it is Emma, well, I'll deal with that if it happens. And if not, then the stalker won't know where we are. Emma's texting me the address of a pub halfway.'

'No,' Joe says stubbornly, shaking his head and pursing his lips. 'You can't go.'

'Why not?'

'It's too dodgy.' He begins to count off reasons on his fingers. 'One, it could be Emma behind the letters. Two, it could be someone else who's going to follow you there. Three, I have a bad feeling about this.'

'Well, I am going,' I say, my voice quavering. 'And you can't talk me out of it.'

'Tell Emma to come here instead,' he says. 'I'll go out, if that makes things easier.'

'It'll take too long,' I argue. 'It's rush hour. Quicker if we meet halfway.'

Joe scowls and pulls his phone out of his shorts pocket. I don't know what he's doing, but I haven't got time to hang around and find out. I need to change out of my PJs and get going.

I come back downstairs, dressed in beige linen trousers and a forest-green T-shirt, to find Joe standing at the bottom of the stairs, waving his phone at me.

'I've found a place you can meet,' he says sullenly. 'But I still don't like it. Second thoughts, I'm coming with you. I won't interfere. I can wait in the car.'

'No. I'll be fine. I'll make sure no one's following me.'

'You can't be sure. They might be parked up on the main road waiting for you to leave the house.'

My heart misses a beat. I hadn't thought of that possibility. 'If I see a car behind me, I'll drive to the nearest police station.'

'You should call the police now instead of going to see Emma.' His scowl softens. 'Lizzy, please.'

I know he's just looking out for me, but this is the biggest breakthrough I've had since receiving the first letter. 'I just want to find out what's happening, and then Emma and I can call the police together.' I get a polythene sandwich bag from the kitchen and slide the envelope and torn letter into it, careful not to get any prints on the paper.

My phone buzzes and I look at the screen.

'Who's that?' Joe asks.

'Emma. She's sent the name of the place we're meeting.'

'Well, tell her you're meeting at this place instead.' He holds out his phone and I text Emma the address of a different pub. One that's closer to Malmesbury.

I could argue with Joe, but at least if I take his advice on where to meet, he might be happier about me going alone.

'Call me if you have any worries, or see anyone dodgy,' he says. 'It's six fifteen now. Text me when you get there. If I haven't heard from you by half seven, I'm calling the cops, okay?'

I nod. 'I'll be okay.'

He kisses me, holding my arms a little too tightly. 'Lock your car doors. Don't stop for anyone on the way.' He gives a little growl. 'This is stupid. I'm coming with you. What's the big deal about me coming?'

'You know what the big deal is.' If Joe comes, it will be twice as awkward with Emma. It's bad enough that I have to meet her by myself, but with Joe in the car, it will be awful. Plus, I need time on my own to work out how I'm going to act around her. Whether to mention the kiss that happened with Joe, or to keep things focused on the letters. My mind is a mess.

'This is bloody crazy, Lizzy. If you think I'm going to let you drive off—'

'*Let* me?' I snap. 'This is your problem, Joe. You think you own me. But you don't. We're a couple, we're not joined at the hip!'

'I don't think that,' he splutters. 'I'm just trying to look out for you. What kind of a boyfriend would I be if I let you… if I *stood by* as you drove off into danger?'

'You'd be the kind of boyfriend who respected my wishes.' Yes, I would love to have Joe by my side as support. But this is Emma we're talking about. I can't have the issue of her and Joe clouding whatever's going on here. I won't feel comfortable with him there too. And I can't trust him to stay silently waiting in the car while I speak to her. I know what he's like – he won't be able to help himself. He'll come swaggering into the pub shooting his mouth off.

'Sorry, Joe, but the answer's no. I'll be fine on my own.'

'Lizzy—' His teeth and fists are clenched, but I won't be bullied into changing my mind.

'I said, I'll be fine.'

But as I leave the house and lock myself inside my car, I feel anything but fine.

CHAPTER TWENTY-NINE

The drive is tense. As well as the shock of the letter, and the fact that my sister is somehow connected to all this, I can't get the argument with Joe out of my head. Was I too harsh on him? After all, he was only trying to be supportive. I resolve to make it up to him when I get home.

Despite using Google Maps to set the destination on my phone, my concentration is so poor that I still end up taking several wrong turnings. The fastest route to the pub in Grittleton is along a twisting B-road with very little traffic. I'm making good time, but the emptiness of the road is giving me the serious jitters, especially as there's one car behind me – too far back to see who's driving. All I can tell is that it's red. Every time I press the brakes, they slow down too. When I speed up, so do they.

I check the petrol gauge – half-full, so no worries there. But Google Maps is seriously depleting my phone's battery life. It's on 31 per cent and going down rapidly. I can't lose communication with Joe. Or the police, for that matter. Sod it. I switch off Maps and decide to use good old-fashioned road signs instead.

Finally, I hit the turn-off to Grittleton, relieved to note that the car behind me keeps going straight on by. I pass some kind of walled manor house on my right and then overshoot the pub which sits on the left, its front garden a riot of floral arrangements and customers on picnic benches. There's plenty of street parking, so I pull into the first space I see and unpeel my fingers from the steering wheel. All that bravado in front of Joe about being fine, well, it was a complete load of rubbish. I'm sweating, my left leg is still quivering and my throat feels like there's a snake wrapped around it. That drive was a complete stress-fest. I throw a glance behind me, but there are no cars approaching. No people either. Apart from the laughter and chatter filtering down from the pub, the road is quiet and empty.

Still feeling guilty about yelling at Joe earlier, I send him a text to let him know I've arrived safely, and then I check the time. It's taken me less than twenty minutes to get here. Emma won't be along for at least another half hour. I don't fancy sitting in a strange pub by myself, so I decide to wait in the car.

Turns out I don't have to wait long. Fifteen minutes later, my phone buzzes. It's Emma:

I'm here

I look out the back window but don't see a car coming down the road.

Where?

Inside at the bar

I must have missed her arrival.

See you in a sec

Taking a breath, I get out of the car and stretch out the kinks in my neck. I don't know how I feel about meeting up with Emma. Aside from the fact that I haven't spoken to her in years, I still haven't forgiven her for trying to steal Joe. But I have to put all that out of my head. This whole stalker situation is worse than her betrayal. This could be our lives at stake. But how do I know if I can believe her?

I lock the car and walk back towards the stone inn, up a few steps and past the people sitting in the front garden. The front door has been propped open and I walk straight into a cosy bar area criss-crossed by busy staff carrying trays of food and drinks. I spot Emma straight away. She's standing at the bar talking to a barman, her auburn hair glowing in a shaft of light from the open door. Instantly I think back to that day in Bristol when I saw that girl disappear into the crowd. A girl who looked remarkably like my sister. I stop where I am. This was a mistake. Joe was right. I shouldn't have come. I should never have agreed to meet her. Maybe I should just turn around and leave. Text her some excuse.

But it's too late. She turns at my approach. We stare at one another for a moment. Her chin and forehead are a mass of scabs. She must have noticed that my face is as scratched up as hers.

'Want a drink?' she asks.

'Lime and soda with ice and lemon please,' I reply, my voice not sounding like my own. The implications of Emma's injuries are clear. *Did she get pushed in front of a car, too?* Is she going through the same nightmare as me?

As she gives our order to the barman, I take in the rest of Emma's appearance. Tailored trousers and a fitted white shirt – her work clothes, minus the lab coat. But she still manages to look chic. I feel large, clumsy and over the top next to her.

We take our drinks to a quiet table towards the back of the bar. No one is sitting inside this evening. It's just us and the bar staff.

'Did you bring the letter?' Emma asks as we take our places opposite one another.

I slide out the sandwich bag and lay it on the table. She produces a similar letter in a similar plastic bag and sets it beside mine. I gawp at the name, *Lizzy Beresford.*

'So it really wasn't you?' I ask, unable to help myself.

'What wasn't me?' Then, Emma's mouth drops open. 'You thought *I* sent the letters? Thanks a lot, Lizzy. We might not be close any more, but that doesn't mean… I can't believe you could even ask me that!'

'I'm sorry. But, well, we haven't exactly been the best of friends,' I reply, unable to help myself. If I'm not careful, this meeting is going to degenerate into a shouting match where one or both of us end up storming out. I try to steady my breathing and slow my heart rate. 'Okay, so let's not talk about all that,' I say.

'You were the one who brought it up.' She takes a sip of her drink. 'Anyway, if your face is anything to go by, it looks like whoever's responsible attacked you too.'

'Fine. Let's talk about the letters,' I say.

'That's what we're here for,' she says.

I decide to play along and act as though I believe she's telling the truth. 'Do you think they mixed up the letters? Or that they sent us the wrong ones on purpose?'

'I can't imagine they would make a mistake like that,' Emma replies. 'Pretty sure they wanted us to know they're targeting both of us. Especially as it said the word *sister*.'

I nod slowly, thinking that what she's saying makes sense.

'When did you receive your very first letter?' Emma asks.

I take a few gulps of my lime and soda and then tell her about how it all started.

'What did the letter say?' she asks.

'*You're my only obsession.*'

'I got mine a couple of days after that,' she says. 'Nothing as creepy as yours, though. Just a letter left in our mailbox. It was addressed to me and said exactly the same thing: *You're my only obsession*. Which is obviously not true, because it looks like they're obsessed with both of us.'

Something occurs to me. 'Do you think other people might be getting the letters?'

'Besides me and you?' Emma asks. 'I don't know. No, I don't think so. The *sister* thing makes me think it's just us.'

'Maybe it's someone we went to school with,' I say, stirring the crushed ice in my drink with my straw. 'Someone from our past.'

'Did they do *that*?' she asks, pointing to my face.

My skin crawls as I remember the two hands at my back. Bile stings the back of my throat and I push the glass of lime and soda away, slide my hands between my thighs to stop them shaking. 'They pushed me off the pavement onto the road.' I take a breath. 'Luckily, the guy in the oncoming car had fast reactions and braked before… before hitting me.'

'Shit. Lizzy, that's terrible.' Emma looks genuinely appalled.

'What about you?' I ask. 'Looks like you've got yourself a scabby beard.'

'Thanks.'

'Sorry, I was just trying to…' I tail off and give a shrug. 'Anyway, what happened?'

She stares at the table, making marks in the condensation with her forefinger. 'I was out with some friends last Friday evening, people from work. I didn't stay out late. Didn't even drink any alcohol. But it was getting dark when I walked back to my car. I was only parked five minutes away from the bar. Stupid of me. I even turned down the offer of a couple of friends to accompany me. Don't know why I did that – pride or something? Not wanting to put them out? The truth was, as I walked to my car I was terrified. I'd been getting the letters and I knew someone had been watching me. But I told myself I'd be okay. I walked quickly, had my keys out ready.

'Anyway, I was just outside the multistorey car park when someone came up behind me and shoved me really hard. Knocked me to the ground. And then they ran off. I didn't even get a look at them. Just saw they were wearing black trainers and grey joggers. That's it. I knew it was *them* immediately.' Her voice wavers. 'They didn't take my purse or my phone. They wanted to scare me. *Hurt* me. It worked.'

Emma's hardness has evaporated, her eyes fill with tears and her face is properly white like the two sheets of paper on the table. If this was anybody else, I would stand up and walk around the table to give her a hug. But this is Emma, the sister I haven't spoken to in years. And I can't ignore what she did. I don't know why we've never talked about it properly. Never had a blazing row where she apologised. Hardly even mentioned it.

'Sorry that happened to you, Emma,' I say. 'You must have been terrified.'

'There's other stuff that's happened,' she says. 'Other letters. They also wrote a message in lipstick on the windscreen of my car.'

'What did it say?'

She shakes her head. 'I… can't repeat it. It's too vile.'

'Did you tell the police?' I ask, wondering what could be so awful that she can't tell me.

'Of course I told them. Did you?'

I nod. 'I wonder why they haven't put two and two together? Surely our cases are so similar that they would have matched them up?'

'Different policing departments?' she suggests. 'Bristol comes under Somerset. You're in Wiltshire. Could be something like that.'

'I thought they shared databases these days.'

'We should call them,' Emma says.

I'm pulling my phone out of my bag when a familiar voice behind me makes me start.

'Lizzy? What are you doing here?'

CHAPTER THIRTY

Emma looks up at whoever is behind me, and I turn to see Pippa's bemused face staring down at me.

'Pippa?' I cry. 'What are *you* doing here?' I realise I don't sound very friendly, but it's quite a coincidence to see her here at the same time as me. Especially after what's just happened.

'I was about to ask you the same thing,' she replies. 'And is this… is that you, Emma?'

Emma frowns and then smiles as recognition dawns. 'Pippa Hargreaves? From dance classes?'

'How *are* you?' Pippa comes around the table to give Emma a hug. 'Haven't seen you for yonks. Not since we were teenagers.'

'Must be at least… fifteen years,' Emma says.

'I work with Lizzy now. Or rather *for* Lizzy.' Pippa raises an eyebrow and squeezes my shoulder.

'How come you're here, Pippa?' I ask again.

'I've come for a drink with Sebbie. He's brought me here to cheer me up after Toby dumped me. I've been a right old misery guts.'

'Seb's here?' My palms begin to sweat.

'At the bar.'

I glance over, see his broad back as he waits to order. This is beyond strange. He was in Bristol at the same time I was pushed into the road, and now he's here, in this out-of-the-way pub at the same time as me and Emma.

'Don't suppose you girlies fancy some company?' Pippa asks, gesturing to the two free chairs at our table.

'Any other time would've been lovely, Pip, but Emma and I are here to discuss some important family stuff.'

Pippa raises her hands. 'Say no more. We'll keep out of your hair. Lovely to see you, Emma. We'll have to catch up another time.'

'Sure,' Emma replies. 'That would be great.'

Pippa walks back to the bar, leaving me shaken.

'We should leave,' I hiss across the table to Emma.

'Leave? Why? We've only just got here.' She scratches her cheek. 'Is it because Pippa's here? Does she know what's been going on?'

'Some of it.' I lean forward. 'But it's not her I'm worried about. I don't trust her brother.'

'Why not?'

'He "just happened" to be in Bristol at the same time I was pushed into the road, and now he "just happens" to show up here…'

'Shit.' Emma leans back in her chair, inhaling deeply. 'But why would he do it? What's the reason?'

'I don't know. A misplaced crush?'

'What? On both of us? I doubt it. I've never even met the guy.'

'You have,' I correct her. 'He used to be there every week, waiting with his mum while we were at the dance studio.'

'He was just a kid back then.'

'Yeah, but he's not a kid any more,' I say through clenched teeth. 'I can't stay here, not while he's here too.'

'You really want to leave?' Emma asks. 'We haven't even talked properly.'

My mind is racing. I'm glad I convinced Joe to stay at home, because if he was here, he would have confronted Seb by now and I know how that conversation would have ended up. 'I'm not staying.'

'Fine,' Emma says. 'Let's go. We need to report today's letters to the police anyway.'

'Why don't you follow me to Malmesbury?' I suggest. 'We can go to the police station together. Tell them about the letters… and about Seb.'

Emma downs the rest of her drink and nods. 'Okay.' She gets to her feet.

'Hang on,' I say, motioning her to sit back down. 'I don't want Seb or Pippa to see us leaving.' I angle my chair round so I can see the siblings out of the corner of my eye. They're still waiting at the bar, their backs to us. 'Okay, quickly, while they're getting their drinks, let's go.'

Swiftly and silently, Emma and I gather our things and walk out of the pub. Once outside, we pick up our pace and almost race across the front patio and down onto the pavement.

'Where are you parked?' I gasp, jamming my hands into my armpits, hugging myself tight.

'Car park,' she whispers, glancing behind us. She looks as scared as I feel. Either she's as nervous about Seb as I am, or she's a bloody good actor.

'I'm parked on the road. I'll turn round and you can follow me back. My car's a red Polo.'

'I'm in a grey Prius.'

Of course she is. Even her car is perfect. But that doesn't matter any more. Not now I've got my sister back after all these years. I never thought it would ever happen and it's only now I'm realising just how much I've missed her. It looks like I'm going to have to keep us both from harm. I jog back to my car, casting constant glances behind me. I fumble with my car keys, eventually falling into the driver's seat and slamming the door, my heart racing, skin prickling. I bang down the lock and take a breath. I'd better get going, in case Emma's already in her car waiting for me. I pull out into the road and immediately stall the engine. With shaking fingers, I restart the car. If I don't want to have a road accident, I'd better calm down. I take a breath and tell myself it's just a coincidence that Seb and Pippa are here. I tell myself that everything is going to be okay. I'm going to drive calmly to the police station, and once I'm there, I'll tell them all my suspicions. Hopefully they'll be able to help me work out just what the hell is going on.

My sister and I park up outside the front of Malmesbury Police Station, a long, low, Cotswold stone building on the outskirts of town. The drive back from the pub went by in a blur of adrenalin. Could Sebastian Hargreaves really be our stalker? But then why would he have brought Pippa with him to the pub? And why let Emma and I see him there in plain view? I can't seem to think straight any more.

The station smells faintly of mould and antiseptic, and the air inside is cool, drying the faint layer of perspiration on my body. I shiver, rubbing at my goose-bumped arms, wishing I'd brought a cardigan. The lobby is empty – must be a slow crime day in Malmesbury.

We walk up to the front counter together and I ask for Sergeant Llewellyn. The officer behind the desk tells me Llewellyn is due to start her shift in about ten minutes, so Emma and I take a seat, turning down his offer to speak to another officer. The seconds drag as we wait. The lobby is too quiet and exposed to have a conversation, so Emma and I sit in silence. She's texting, and I'm alternating between staring at the wall clock and watching the front door.

Fifteen minutes later, Llewellyn emerges, not through the front door, but down a corridor at the far end of the lobby.

'Lizzy,' she says, coming closer. 'I heard you were here. How are you? Has something else happened? Hope you haven't been waiting too long.' She runs a hand through her short hair.

'Hi.' I get to my feet along with Emma, who slides her phone into her bag. 'This is my sister, Emma. Emma, this is Sergeant Jenny Llewellyn, who's been dealing with my case.'

'Hello.' Emma and Llewellyn nod at one another.

'Did you want to come and have a chat?' Llewellyn asks us. 'I'm afraid we haven't any further news at this end.'

'We've got news,' I say. 'More letters. And another development.'

'Oh, yes?' Llewellyn raises an eyebrow.

'I found out today that Emma's been receiving the letters too.'

The sergeant transfers her gaze to Emma, who nods. 'I've been reporting the letters to my local station in Bristol,' she says.

'You've *both* been receiving threatening letters?' Llewellyn asks. 'From the same person, as far as you're aware?'

'Yes,' Emma replies. 'And, like Lizzy, I was also pushed over.' She points to her scratched-up face.

Llewellyn shakes her head in sympathy. 'I see. Okay, let's go and talk in one of the interview rooms and I can take statements from each of you. Then I'll speak to Bristol and we can compare notes. Hopefully sharing our info will move us closer to catching whoever's behind all this.'

Knowing that Emma has been reporting all this activity to the police at the same time as me makes me realise the extent to which the stalker has planned all this. But I still can't for the life of me figure out why. It's strange to think that something as awful as this, could be the thing to reconcile me and my sister.

Emma and I follow Llewellyn down the corridor, our shoes squeaking against the linoleum floor. She stops at one of the doors and uses a key to open it. Inside, the room is small and basic, characterless, the air warm and stale. She gestures for us to take a seat. There are two plastic coffee cups on the table in front of us. One with a lipstick ring; the other still full, but the coffee is cold, the milk congealing. Llewellyn mutters something under her breath, picks up the cups and takes them away. 'Back in a sec.' She returns a minute later minus the cups. 'Mind if I record this?' she asks. 'Save me scribbling in my pad.'

'Yes, that's fine,' I reply. Emma nods. Somehow, being here at the station makes everything seem more real. More serious. I rub at my arms as though to warm them up, even though I'm not cold any more. Emma glances at me, but I still can't quite think of her as my ally in all this.

Llewellyn sits opposite us and presses a switch on what I presume must be the recording equipment. She states the date and time and we all say our names for the record. Emma and I spend the next few minutes telling Llewellyn about today's letters that were addressed wrongly. We show them to her in their sealed polythene bags. Llewellyn then asks Emma for a rundown of the letters she's been receiving. My sister tells her about the letters, as well as the lipstick-scrawled message on her car windscreen and the incident where she was pushed to the ground.

'We'll get the full statements from Bristol,' Llewellyn says. 'But it's helpful to have this information now. Do either of you want to add anything further?'

I go on to tell her my suspicions about Sebastian Hargreaves, explaining that I recently discovered he was in Bristol at the time of the assault, and that he arrived at the Grittleton pub moments after Emma and I arrived.

Llewellyn nods. 'We'll interview him,' she says. 'Is that it for now? Anything else to add?'

I shake my head, suddenly exhausted.

'Nothing else,' Emma says.

'Do you have any mutual enemies?' Llewellyn asks. 'Family feuds? A disgruntled cousin? Anything like that?'

But neither Emma nor I can think of any relation or mutual friend who might want to scare us or threaten us in this way. Apart from each other.

Llewellyn drums her fingernails on the table. 'The fact that these letters are targeting the *pair* of you is leading me to believe that this might not be a random stranger. It seems more personal. Maybe an old school friend? A boyfriend you might have had in common?'

My mind immediately jumps to Joe. Emma and I both catch one another's eye.

Llewellyn picks up on this. 'Something you want to share?' she prods.

But I know it's not him. It's not Joe. Why would he do this? The kiss with Emma happened years ago. 'No one I can think of,' I say quickly, before Emma opens her mouth.

Emma shrugs and shakes her head at Llewellyn, but her lips are pursed and her whole body has gone rigid.

Llewellyn gives us each a hard stare. 'Okay, well, it might be an idea for the two of you to get together and make a list of all your mutual acquaintances, and think seriously about who might hold a grudge. May not even be a recent thing. Might be something that's been festering over weeks, or months. Even years.'

As Llewellyn ends the interview, the blood is whooshing in my ears. It seems like Emma and I have an awful lot more talking to do. And this is one conversation I would rather not have. But we can't put it off. Our unwelcome past is tapping on the window. And there's no hiding from it. Not any longer.

CHAPTER THIRTY-ONE

'I should go home,' Emma says as we leave the police station and walk out into the floodlit car park. 'Mike will be worried about me.'

Night has fallen while we've been inside talking about unpleasant things. Joe will want me home, too, but now that my sister and I are finally speaking, I feel like we need to finish off a long-overdue conversation. 'We should go for a drink. There are a few things I need to talk to you about.'

Emma stops walking. 'Do you think that's a good idea? Maybe things are better left as they are.'

'Maybe for you,' I snap. But getting angry isn't going to persuade her to stay. I take a slow breath and try to stay calm. 'I just mean, I would really like it if we could… clear the air. If we could talk about what happened with Joe. If I could find out why you…' I pause. 'If I could find out what really happened between you two. Maybe, maybe it's got something to do with the letters. Or maybe not. But either way, I think we need to have that conversation.' Even as I say the words, I know it's probably a mistake. Far easier to leave everything buried. To go back to ignoring one another. But outside influences are forcing my hand. If it weren't for these damned letters, I could go back to pretending my sister doesn't exist. But maybe the past is influencing the present. Maybe what happened between her and Joe is something to do with these threats. Like it or not, Emma's life is intertwined with mine, our history woven together like twisted vines around a tree.

Emma puts her fingertips to her temples and stares down at the ground for a moment before facing me again. 'Fine. May as well get all the shit out into the open.'

Emma isn't the sweary type, so her words shake me a little. Does she have more to tell me? Things she wants to confess? 'Where do you want to go? A restaurant? A bar?'

'Let's just sit in the car,' she says. 'This conversation isn't really one for a public place, and we can't exactly go back to *your* house.'

'Fine. But not here. I don't feel like talking in a police station car park.'

We get into her car and she drives us two minutes up the road, parking up by the river, the Victorian-style street lamp throwing a pool of yellow light across the dark, rippling water. We each stare out of the windscreen for a few minutes. Neither of us willing to start the conversation.

'Do you remember when you fell in?' Emma asks.

'Yeah.' I smile grimly. 'I remember. But we're not here to reminisce about our childhood.'

'You went in head first,' Emma says. 'I was terrified.'

I'd been about seven years old and Emma was ten. We'd raced ahead of Dad, who had stopped at the pub to buy some cigarettes. He was in charge of us that morning, giving Mum a break. It was a grey, drizzly day. No one else around. We stopped by the river to feed the ducks and to wait for Dad to catch us up. There was a duckling behind all the others who wasn't managing to reach any of the bread. I squashed up my pieces into doughy balls so I could throw them further in the hope that it would reach the tiny creature. But I must have been a bit too enthusiastic, because I lost my balance and toppled into the river. I remember the thick, brown water surging up my nose and down the back of my throat. I'd been too startled to be scared. I was more worried that Mum was going to tell me off for getting soaked. And then I remember a sharp pain in my legs. Emma had reached down and grabbed my feet, tugging me out, sliding me up the muddy bank and out of the freezing water.

'You pulled me out,' I reply. 'You saved me… what happened to us, Emma? I mean, I know we were never exactly best friends when we were teenagers, but we're sisters. We're supposed to look out for one another, like you did for me that day.'

Emma sighs and tips her head back to lean on the headrest.

'Are you going to tell me why you made a play for Joe that night?' I ask. 'And why you never apologised? Why you've been so cold to me over the past few years?'

'Are you sure you want to hear this?' she asks.

'I'm asking, aren't I?' It's like picking at a scab. I'm asking the questions but I'm beginning to get the feeling that I won't like the answers.

She turns to look at me and I stare back at her face illuminated by the street light. Even with the scratches marring her porcelain skin, there's no denying that my sister is a beautiful woman.

'I didn't try to kiss Joe that night,' Emma says.

'How did I know you were going to say that?' I turn my face away in disgust. This is just going to be a repeat conversation of the one we had five years ago. Stupidly, I thought that with all this crap going on, Emma might think it was a good time to come clean. To admit what she did and finally apologise. Obviously not.

'Look, Lizzy. I know that's not what you want to hear. I know you want me to say it was all my fault and I'm a terrible person. So if that's what you want, then I'll say those things. I'll say yes, I kissed Joe, I was in love with him, I've hated you ever since. But that's not what happened. So do you want to hear the truth or not?'

'Your version of the truth?'

'Of course. My version. Who else's version would it be? But Lizzy, this is the God's honest truth as I remember it.'

'Go on, then. Tell me your *version*.' I can't keep the sarcasm out of my voice. My nails are digging into my palms and my body is rigid. Part of me wants to get out of the car and run home.

'I didn't kiss Joe,' Emma says calmly. 'I never even fancied him. He came on to *me* that night. Not the other way round.'

'So nothing's changed,' I say. 'You're still denying it.'

'Joe cornered me as I was coming out of the loos and trapped me against the wall, between his arms. He told me… he told me I was prettier than you and that he would drop you in a heartbeat if I gave him the word.'

Her words come at me like blows to my abdomen. If she's telling the truth, then my boyfriend is a two-faced monster. If she's lying, then she's the monster. To my shame, the second option is more appealing. But I have this awful feeling she's not lying. The way she's telling it this time, it's like she doesn't want to hurt me. It's like she pities me.

'I told him that even if I did like him – which I didn't – I would never betray you like that. I said that he didn't deserve you but that if he left me alone, I would forget the conversation ever happened.'

I picture the scene unfolding as Emma tells it. Picture her leaning against the wall with Joe leaning into her, wanting her. Did it really happen like that? Is my sister telling the truth?

'Joe was annoyed by my rejection,' Emma continues, staring straight ahead through the windscreen. Is she picturing the scene in her head, too? Or is she conjuring up more lies from her twisted imagination?

'He was embarrassed,' Emma says. 'He let me go and said he was only joking. That of course he loved you and would never hurt you. I was relieved. I thought that was the last I'd hear of it. I thought he'd simply had too much to drink and that he'd come on to me in a moment of drunken lunacy. I knew how much you loved him, Lizzy. I thought if I brushed it off and pretended it had never happened that it would all be forgotten and no one would ever get hurt. He was young and idiotic. But I didn't realise the stupid bastard would go straight to your house, make up some insane story about me trying to kiss him. That's why I never rang you to apologise – because I hadn't done anything to apologise for.'

'So why didn't you tell me all this back then when I came to see you?' I ask through gritted teeth. It's so hot in here. I open the car door and suck in a lungful of soupy air.

'I did try to tell you. But you wouldn't listen to me, Lizzy. You were furious. I'd never seen you so mad in all your life. And I was angry with you for taking Joe's side over mine. I thought you were more loyal than that. I thought blood was thicker than a pretty boyfriend. So I thought, okay, I'm not going to break my neck trying to convince you of the truth, you're welcome to him. And I assumed he would let you down eventually, that he would stray and have his head turned by other girls. To be quite honest, every year at Mum's birthday I'm always stunned that the two of you are still together.'

I unclick my seatbelt and step out of the car, taking in deep breaths of the river-scented night. Do I believe my sister? If it's true, then the past five years with Joe have been a lie... I can't even think about it.

'Lizzy.' Emma gets out of the car and comes around the back towards me, but I hold out a hand, warding her off. She stays where she is, keeping her distance.

'Can you drop me back at my car?' I ask, swatting away a cloud of midges that have gathered nearby.

'I'm sorry,' she says. 'I should have made more of an effort to make you listen to me back then. To make you hear the truth. I kept quiet because I was angry with you for taking his side over mine. Despite that, I never wanted to upset you. You always had self-esteem issues, and I thought that harping on about what had happened would make things even worse. I thought you'd blame me and I'd end up losing you. Funny thing is, I lost you anyway.'

Her voices cracks. 'But you've been happy with Joe, right? He loves you? You love him?'

I ignore Emma's questions and get back into the car, slamming the door. Why is she being so reasonable? So nice? I was expecting her to be cold. To be a bitch. Question is, do I believe her? I don't want to believe her. If I do, it means my life with Joe is a sham.

My sister gets back in the car and starts up the engine. 'Are you okay?' she asks.

I can't even respond. My thoughts are flying all over the place.

'I'll drive you back to your car. But we should keep in touch over the letters. Whoever's doing this, I don't think they're about to stop any time soon.'

'How would you know that?' I ask. And then under my breath I mumble, 'Unless you're the one sending them.' Luckily she doesn't hear me, and I don't really believe it anyway. I'm simply clinging onto the shred of hope that it isn't Joe. That he didn't betray me.

'I don't know anything for sure,' she replies, reversing onto the quiet road. 'I'm just saying, it doesn't seem likely whoever it is will stop.'

A wave of anger bubbles up from my core, like a volcano about to erupt. But I tamp it down, swallow the bile. Is my sister a liar? Is she manipulating the truth, trying to get me to forgive her? Maybe she's still trying to break up my relationship with Joe. So why, then, if I don't believe her, am I still picturing Joe coming on to Emma? Why is my heart twisting and my stomach hollow? Why am I scared to confront Joe about what Emma has just told me?

Maybe because I know that when I look into his eyes I'll see the truth.

CHAPTER THIRTY-TWO

I step into the hallway and stare around at the familiar space, at the mirror on the wall, the ceiling pendant. It seems like weeks since I was last here.

'Lizzy! That you?' The lounge door flies open and Joe comes out, his hair messy, T-shirt creased. 'How'd it go? What did she say?' He stares at me for a long moment. 'Are you okay? You look a bit… odd.'

I walk past him into the lounge. Frank is asleep on the armchair. He opens one eye and then closes it again. The TV is paused – a freeze-frame of some cop drama where a guy is yelling at a police officer, his mouth twisted in anger.

'Do you want a cuppa?' Joe asks.

'No.' My stomach feels empty and my throat is dry. I feel as though I'm on the precipice of the rest of my life and it's about to go into free fall.

'Are you going to sit down, or are you just going to stand there in the middle of the room?' Joe gives a short laugh, but it dies in his throat when I don't respond. 'Are you still annoyed because I wanted to come with you? Because I was only trying to be—'

'I don't care about that,' I say, scratching at the back of my neck.

'Good, okay. But I was thinking about it, and you're right, Lizzy. I do get overprotective sometimes, and maybe it's a bit much. But it's only because I love you. And I'm worried about you, what with all this stuff that's been going on.'

'Yes.' I nod slowly. 'You say that a lot. You're always telling me that you love me and you're worried about me.'

'That's because it's true.'

'Is it?'

'What do you mean, *is it*? Of course it is.' Joe's cheeks flush. He takes a step closer. 'Lizzy…'

'I had an interesting chat with Emma this evening.' I tilt my head and stare at my boyfriend, studying his face for clues to the truth.

'About the letters?' he asks. 'What did she say?'

'About the letters, and about… other things.'

Joe licks his lips. 'Let's sit down.' He tries to herd me over to the sofa, but I stay where I am.

'I'd rather stand.'

'Okay.' He raises his hands in surrender. 'Just feels a bit weird, standing in the middle of the room like this.' He gives another nervous laugh.

My face remains stony, the muscles in my jaw tense and stiff. 'Did it feel weird when you were propositioning my sister?'

Joe's face drains of colour. He splutters. 'What! What the hell are you talking about? I never propositioned Emma. Is this why you're acting so weird? Has she been spouting off more lies about me? What's she said this time?'

'She said she never tried to kiss you. She said it was you who came on to her.'

'For fuck's sake, Lizzy. Not this again. We've been over it all before, years ago. I thought we'd put all this crap behind us. *What?* You're telling me you believe her lies now, that it, hmm?'

'Save it, Joe. I know the truth. Emma has no reason to lie to me. We don't even have a relationship any more, thanks to you.'

'This is bollocks. I'm going out.'

'Yeah, well if you leave now, don't bother coming back.'

He strides over to the lounge door and then stops. His body sags. He turns. 'I can't go over it all again, Lizzy. Your sister, she's a liar. She's a flirt.'

'What, a flirt like me, you mean?'

He tuts. 'Don't be daft.'

'You called me a flirt the other day.'

'Yeah, but I was wrong. I was angry.'

'Joe,' I say, my voice calmer. 'Can you do me a favour?'

'Anything.' His eyes widen. He's the picture of blue-eyed innocence.

I fix him with a stare. 'Can you please just tell me the truth about what happened that night? Did you try it on with Emma? Just a simple yes or no. Tell me the truth and I promise I won't get mad.' That last part is a promise I may not be able to keep.

Joe takes a breath and chews his lip. I see his brain working behind his eyes. Weighing it up. His hesitation is enough to tell me that Emma's version of events is the real one.

I shake my head. 'Fuck, Joe. Why?'

He freezes, and then: 'Look, Lizzy, it's the only time I've ever done anything like that. I was drunk. I'm an idiot. I… I don't know what I was thinking. But I love you, Lizzy. I can't lose you over something that happened years ago. Over something that meant nothing.'

The thing that keeps playing over and over in my mind is when Emma told me that Joe thought she was prettier than me. That Joe would drop me for her if she gave him the word. Was that true? Would he have let me go if she had crooked her finger? I can't bring myself to ask him. It's too demeaning, too humiliating. But it makes no difference anyway, because after his betrayal and his lies, this is the end of our relationship. How could I ever trust Joe again? Nausea rises from my gut, the acrid, taste of betrayal in my throat. I can hardly bear to look at my so-called boyfriend.

'Why don't you ask Brycie if he has room on his couch,' I say. 'Because you're not staying here.'

'Lizzy, please.' His eyes are bright with tears. 'I get that you're angry, but we need to talk about this properly.'

All this time I was worrying about Joe's jealousy. About the fact that he didn't trust me. But it should have been me worrying about him. 'How many other women have you chatted up while we've been together?' I ask. 'How many times have you LIED TO ME?'

'None! Nobody! I swear, Lizzy. I love you, I love you.'

'She's my sister! All those years… you let me believe that she'd betrayed me, when it was YOU!' I pick up a cushion and throw it at his head. *Good job there aren't any rocks lying around, or I'd smash his cheating head in*. 'Would you ever have told me the truth?' I pant. 'You're a total and utter bastard for lying to me. For putting me and Emma through all that crap!' I collapse onto the sofa. Joe takes a tentative step towards me. But I glare at him, daring him to come any closer. He stays where he is, by the window. The TV is still frozen on the yelling man. He looks like I feel.

'Lizzy, I'm so, so sorry. I made a terrible mistake. Please don't punish me for one mistake.'

'One mistake?' I snarl. '*One mistake!*'

'It's because I love you. I didn't want to lose you. I'd do anything to keep you, you must know that.'

Now that Joe has confessed to trying it on with Emma, now I know for certain that my sister is innocent, I realise it can't be her who sent the letters. She doesn't want to split Joe and I up. She never did. Was Joe the one behind it all along? What if he was trying to set me up somehow? Or to make me believe it was her? My brain is spinning. All I know is that I can't trust him. I need him gone.

'You need to leave,' I say, my anger mixing with a swirl of darker thoughts.

'Please, Lizzy.'

'Now. Just get your things and get out.' I pick up the remote and switch off the TV. But the actor's glaring face is tangled up with my own fury. My own hurt. My own devastation. And it's not only Joe I'm angry with. I'm angry at myself. At my stubbornness. I should have spoken to my sister years ago, but I was too scared of the truth. I was too scared that believing her would mean breaking up with Joe. But the truth has a way of worming its way out. Of wriggling free. And what should have come to light back then is coming to light now instead. Only this time the crust of lies has grown thicker. It has distorted everything. I don't think Joe and I will ever recover from this. And the look in his eyes tells me he knows it.

CHAPTER THIRTY-THREE

The heat inside the shop wraps itself around me like a shroud. My stomach is hollow, my throat tight and scratchy. As I go through the morning ritual of opening up, it's like I'm moving through lava.

'Are you sure you're okay, Lizzy?' Pippa asks, opening the front door and setting out the A-board. 'You really do look very peaky. And I'm not being funny, but if you are coming down with something then you should be at home, in quarantine, not breathing your flu all over the customers, or me.'

'I'm fine.' My voice is thick, echoing inside my head as though my ears are blocked. I do actually feel like I might have the flu, but I know it's not a virus that's making me feel like hell. It's my life disintegrating around me, pulling my defences down. I kicked Joe out last night, and, quite honestly, I never want to set eyes on him again. But that doesn't stop me grieving for the man I thought he was. True, he had his flaws. He was overprotective, jealous and maybe even a little bit controlling. But I never thought of him as a liar, or a cheat. He let me believe my sister betrayed me. All those wasted years I spent loving him and hating her…

'You're clearly not fine,' Pippa continues. 'Are you hung-over? Where did you and Emma disappear off to last night? One minute you were there, the next minute, poof! Off you'd popped in a puff of smoke. Sebbie was disappointed. He wanted to come and say hi. You know he does have a bit of a mini-crush on you, Lizzy. And before you start, no, he's not your stalker. And you could do worse. I mean, I know you're with Joe, but Sebbie's handsome and kind. Plus, he's got a pretty nice pad, even if it is a bit dilapidated.' She laughs.

As I switch on the shop lights, Pippa's words float over me like butterflies over a lilac tree. Hovering, but never settling. Always moving, drifting. I hear them, but their meaning doesn't seem to register. It's all just meaningless chatter.

'Your phone,' Pippa says.

I try to think what I'm supposed to be doing next. I need to put the float in the till.

'Lizzy, Liz! Your phone's ringing!'

I glance over at Pippa, who's by the front door looking at me like I'm deranged. 'My phone?'

'It's ringing. In case, you know, you wanted to answer it.'

'Oh, yes. Okay.' I walk into the stockroom in a daze and take my phone out of my bag, but of course it's stopped ringing now. I wonder if it was Joe. But a quick glance tells me that it's George. Thank goodness I missed the call. He's going to ask me if I've spoken to Pippa. He doesn't realise that I have more terrifying things to worry about than a few missing dresses. But that's not fair. Theft is theft. George comes back from holiday today, and if he finds out I haven't spoken to Pippa, he won't hesitate – he'll call the police. He may even fire me. I can't let that happen.

'Pippa!' I call out down the shop to her. I don't have the strength to do this now, but I have no choice. Everything is rising to the surface – the secrets, the lies, the betrayals. This is just one more uncovering of the truth. 'Pippa! Can you lock the front door again?'

'Lock it? I've only just opened it.' She checks her watch. 'It's past opening time.'

'I know. But I need to talk to you. It's urgent.'

Pippa does as she's asked and turns over the closed sign once more. She smooths her blonde hair and walks the length of the shop to reach me in the stockroom. I feel strangely calm, but at the same time I'm aware that I might be about to lose Pippa's friendship. And Pippa is quite possibly the closest thing I have to a proper friend right now.

'You do know George is back from his hols today,' Pippa says. 'If he comes to the shop and sees it's closed, he won't be a happy bunny.'

'Don't worry about that,' I say.

'Who are you, and what have you done with Lizzy Beresford?' Pippa laughs, but stops when she sees I'm not joining in. 'What's the problem, Liz?'

'It's awkward,' I say, my veneer of calm peeling away. I pull at my shirt collar. 'Is it just me, or is it really hot in here?'

'Spit it out, Lizzy.'

The stockroom feels too small, too enclosed for this conversation, but we can't stand out there in the shop where anyone can see us through the window. I pull the stockroom door closed with a firm click. 'I firstly need to say, this isn't my doing. This is George's decision.'

'Now you're making me worried.' She gives a nervous laugh. 'You're not giving me the sack, I hope?'

I clear my throat and take a step back so we're not standing so close to one another. 'George thinks you've been taking things from the shop without paying. Goods and cash.'

Pippa's face blanches. She swallows and then her expression quickly turns neutral. 'I see. And what do *you* think, Lizzy?'

'I honestly don't know, Pippa. There have been some… discrepancies.' I give a small shrug.

'And you told George about them. About these… discrepancies?' Her nostrils flare.

'No. No, I ignored them, if you must know. Thought I must be mistaken. It was George who came to me. He told me he wanted to catch you in the act, then call the police.'

Pippa's face flushes, her expression tightens.

'I begged him not to get the police involved. I told him I would ask you to return what's been taken. And he agreed.'

'So you believe George? You think I've been stealing!' Pippa folds her arms across her chest, a look of outrage settling across her face.

Have I made a mistake? Is she innocent? But my mind catalogues all the incidents and discrepancies, and I know I'm not wrong. She's guilty, she's just not owning up to it. 'Pippa, listen to me, I'm not taking sides. All I'm saying is that if you don't bring back what you've taken, George has said he'll get the police involved. And I know you don't want that. I'm trying to look out for you.'

'Bloody funny way of showing it.' She strides over to the shelf and grabs her handbag. 'You can tell George to stick his job up his arse.' A tear slides down her cheek and she swipes it away. 'And as for you… well, I thought you were my friend. Obviously I was mistaken.'

'Pippa! I *am* your friend. That's why—'

'Oh, just piss off, Lizzy.'

Pippa stalks out of the stockroom and I follow her, my heart pounding, wondering how I can make things right between us. But I'm in an impossible situation. 'George was going to call the police! What else was I supposed to do?'

She stops and turns to face me. 'You could have stuck up for me! Or spoken to me. We could have figured it out together.'

'I'm speaking to you now.'

'Yes, but now it's too late. You've already been gossiping about me to George.'

'I wasn't gossiping, I was trying to protect you after he came to see me.'

'He came to see you? When was this? It must have been before he went on holiday. So you've known about this for over a week and you didn't think it was worth mentioning until *now*? Until the day he gets back?'

'I didn't know what to say, Pip. I was trying to work out the best way of telling you.'

'So, when you were "sticking up for me", did you tell George that there's no way I'd been taking any goods? Did you tell him I was innocent?'

'I…'

'That'll be a "no" then.'

'Pippa! Someone's been helping themselves to stock and cash and it isn't me. What was I supposed to tell George?'

'Goodbye, Lizzy. Doesn't look like I'll be coming back.' Pippa opens the side door and slams it behind her so violently that one of the jewellery boards becomes dislodged from the wall and crashes down, scattering silver necklaces, earrings and beads across the floor.

'Pippa!' A few seconds later, the outer door slams and I see my friend march past the window and off down the road. My hands tremble. My heart races. I knew this conversation was going to be tricky, but I hadn't anticipated just how angry Pippa would be. I naively supposed she might cry, or even admit to what she'd done. I didn't expect this defensive rage.

Is she right? Should I have spoken to her when I first had my suspicions? If Pippa has serious money worries, maybe I could have helped in some way. A wave of nausea hits me; everything seems to be going wrong. But I get the feeling that there would never have been a right time to bring this up. I exhale. *No*. She's done something wrong and she's been found out. Let's face it, nobody likes to get caught.

I feel like I've been alone all my life. Like there will never be a place for me in this world. I can be surrounded by people at work or at home, but nothing ever fills the void inside.

Will I always be drifting? Empty?

Only rage blots it out. Temporarily makes me forget. Channels the emptiness into something more. Something white hot. It's been simmering for years, like a caged creature that is finally getting its chance to escape.

Soon they'll realise what they've created.

And they'll be sorry.

CHAPTER THIRTY-FOUR

The rest of the day is a blur. In between serving customers, I clean the shop from top to bottom. I dust shelves, polish the glass units, replenish stock and freshen up the displays. I'm sweating, crumpled, frazzled. Anxiety gnaws at my chest and stomach. Exhaustion tugs at my shoulders and eyelids. But I can't stop working. If I stop, I'll collapse into a sticky puddle on the shop floor and I might never get up again.

I've set my phone to silent, but when I last checked, I had eight missed calls from Joe and three from my sister. Plus numerous texts. The only one I read was from George, who said his flight doesn't land until this evening, but he'll drop by Georgio's first thing tomorrow. Another confrontation I can do without. I'm going to have to explain to him that Pippa is denying everything and it's probably too late to call the police as she'll have dumped the evidence by now. George will go mad. He quite rightly wanted the stolen goods and cash returned to him, but now it looks like he'll be out of pocket. And it's my fault for talking him out of calling the police. *Don't think about that now*. Don't think about anything. Especially don't think about Joe. About the lies.

It's almost closing time. Almost time to go home. But is it still a home if the person you loved is no longer there? The last customer comes to the till to pay for her items. I ring them up without paying attention to what they are, what they cost. My mouth issues pleasantries without my brain's involvement. A smile.

A thank you. A goodbye. The shop bell jangles and closes. My knees buckle and I grip the counter to steady myself. Although my body is upright, I feel as though I'm in free fall. When you dream that you're falling, you always wake up before you hit the ground. But what happens if you're already awake?

I need to lock up, but the door opens again. One more customer. I welcome them. I would stay open all night if it meant I didn't have to go home and face my life. I decide that I won't shut the shop just yet. I take a breath and prepare to ask whoever it is if they're happy browsing, or whether they need any help. But I tense up when I see who it is – Pippa's brother.

'Hi, Seb. Are you here to pick Pippa up? She's not here. She's…' My words die on my lips. I don't know how to explain why she's not here.

He's striding through the shop towards me, a scowl on his face. Maybe he already knows. Maybe he hasn't come here to collect her from work. Seb comes up to the counter and places both his hands on the glass top, like two pink hams. His face is red, a tuft of light brown hair sticking up on one side. 'I used to like you, Lizzy,' he booms.

'Seb, I—'

'No. You listen to me.' He jabs a forefinger in my direction. 'I used to like you, but that was before I found out that you're an utter, utter bitch!'

I take a step back from the counter and place a hand on the stool to steady myself. This is not the Seb I'm familiar with.

'Pippa came home this morning in tears,' he cries. 'She's been in bed all day. Wouldn't speak to any of us. She actually told Mummy to fuck off and leave her alone. Pip would never normally say anything like that. Anyway, I finally got it out of her that you – her supposed friend.' He bangs on the counter with his fist to emphasise his point. 'You accused her of shoplifting and now she's lost her job!'

'Seb, if you'd just listen for a second—'

'I told her she must be mistaken. I said, Lizzy Beresford would never do anything like that. But she insisted that's what you said. So here I am asking you, face to face, did you accuse my sister of shoplifting?'

Seb is a huge man, intimidating. I'm worried that if I admit to it, he might do something… violent. The other thing that's spinning around my head is that he could be my stalker. I haven't forgotten that he was at the pub in Grittleton last night. Or that Pippa admitted he has a crush on me. Although, now, it's a pretty good bet that his crush has evaporated.

'Seb, look, maybe you could calm down a bit.'

'Calm down?' he roars. 'This is not acceptable and I will not calm down until you explain why Pippa is crying in her bedroom. Pippa doesn't cry!' He moves around the counter and takes a step towards me.

Okay, this is getting scary. His eyes are glittering with rage and now there's nothing between us; no counter blocking him any more. I glance at the front door, willing another customer to come in. But the street beyond is quiet. Maybe I should run and barricade myself inside the stockroom.

'Seb, you need to leave.' My voice is quavering. 'Whatever happened between me and Pippa, you have no right to come barging in here, threatening me.'

'Don't tell me what I can and can't do.'

'Seb, if you don't leave right now, I'm calling the police.' I reach for the shop phone on the counter.

'The police?' His mouth drops open. 'Why would you call the police?'

'Because you're scaring the shit out of me.'

'Am I?' Seb takes a step back. He runs a hand over his hair and exhales.

'If you lay one finger on me, you'll be arrested.'

'Arrested? I'm not going to… but I haven't…'

I pick up the phone and stand a little taller.

He swallows and finally looks like he's coming to his senses. 'Don't call the police, Lizzy. I'm sorry… I didn't mean to frighten you.' His voice is a little softer now. He takes another step back, bashing into a clothes rail. 'I only came here to stick up for Pips. This job, it's the only thing she has in her life that she really loves. She respects you. You're her best friend.'

'Her best friend?' I frown. 'What about Fenella and all those other girls she went to school with?'

'Oh, that lot? They're all a bunch of snobs. No, you're her only true friend – or so she thought. Pippa's always rabbiting on about how down to earth you are, and how you never judge. How you're so this and so that.' Seb waves his hands around, and it would be almost comical if he weren't so upset. 'She even…' He flushes. 'She even keeps suggesting that you and I should… never mind. Anyway, that's why this… this *business* is so damned awful. I just don't know what to do.' His body sags.

'I'm sorry, Seb. I really am,' I say, replacing the phone back in its cradle, realising that Seb isn't about to attack me. 'Look, Pippa's my friend too. But I had no choice. George was going to call the police. He wanted to have her arrested for theft. I managed to persuade him not to, and he agreed not to make things official on the condition that I spoke to Pippa and made her return everything she's taken.'

'Do you believe she's guilty?' he asks.

'I'm sorry, but yes. It really does look that way.'

Seb shakes his head and looks down at his shoes. 'What am I supposed to do, Lizzy?' he asks. 'How can I fix this?'

I give my head a little shake. 'Sometimes we can't fix things. Sometimes we have to let them mend on their own. And sometimes things get broken and they stay broken.' I give a bitter laugh.

'I'm sorry.' Seb bows his head. 'I apologise for coming in here and shouting like that. For calling you a bitch. For the record, I don't think you are. Not for one minute. I always wondered what it would be like to have a proper conversation with you – something other than a "hello, how are you?". I never imagined it would be like this.' He turns away. Walks back towards the door.

'Seb, wait!' I know I probably shouldn't trust him, but now that we're being honest with one another, I want to talk further. I want to get a sense of him. To see if there's any possibility whatsoever that he could be the person behind the messages. I can't let him leave not knowing for sure. And maybe he could be the link to fixing things between me and Pippa.

Seb stops and turns, his shoulders stooped.

'Want to go for a drink?' I ask, feeling reckless, like I have nothing left to lose. 'My shout?'

'What, now?'

'Yes.'

He straightens up a little. 'I'd like that, Lizzy. Yes. I'd like that very much.'

'Okay, hang on, let me get my stuff.' I ignore the drumming of my heart and the warning voices in my head. I'm sick of being scared. Of putting things off. From now on, I'm going to face my doubts and fears head-on.

CHAPTER THIRTY-FIVE

We settle ourselves into a corner booth of The Pig and Whistle, the best pub in which to have a drink without being disturbed by anyone we know, as the average age of the clientele in here is around eighty-five. Seb sips his pint while I take a gulp of the house white, and grimace.

I'm not fooling myself. This drink with Seb is my way of delaying going home. Of putting off facing my life. 'I really am sorry, you know. About Pippa. If there had been any other way…'

He holds up a hand. 'I know you are. The whole thing is just a bloody great mess.'

'Do you believe me?' I ask. 'Do you accept that she's been taking things from Georgio's?'

He sighs. 'I don't know. Possibly.' He shakes his head. 'Possibly. Yes. Probably.' He blows air out of his mouth and stares up at a spot on the ceiling behind me. 'In fact, it's all starting to add up.'

'What is?'

'Well, you know. She'll often come home with extravagant gifts for one or other of us. Sometimes she'll give Mum an extra twenty pounds towards the housekeeping. She has no end of new outfits, and tells us they're samples, or faulty stock. Damn it! What was she thinking?'

'Oh, Seb. Why do you think she's been doing it?'

'God knows. Keeping up appearances? Wanting to treat us? She's a good person, you know. She's not a criminal. I mean, you know her, Pippa's not a bad person. She just… she strayed. Gave in to temptation or some such thing. She mixes in such wealthy circles – it must have made her feel inadequate. Oh, I don't know. There's no excuse.' He takes two long gulps from his pint.

'How long do you think it's been going on?' I ask. 'The stealing?'

'You tell me. I've only just realised it's been happening. If this gets out, it's going to destroy Mum and Dad. They'll be thoroughly humiliated. Please, Lizzy, can you tell George to drop it? Make him believe she's innocent?'

'I can't, Seb. It's gone past all that. He knows it's her.'

'But if you talked to him…'

'Believe me, I already have. Just get her to return everything and George will let it go.'

Seb pulls at his lower lip. 'She's already given most of the stuff away as gifts. The money is long gone, and the clothes have all been worn. How will she be able to return it all?'

'She'll have to total it all up and give George the cash. I wonder how much it all comes to.'

'No bloody idea. She probably doesn't even know herself. And we have no spare cash whatsoever. Not a single bean. The land is all gone, bar a few acres. The house is all we have left.'

'What about the artwork? Pippa said you visited an auction house the other day. Maybe that will bring in something.' Mentioning his trip to Bristol reminds me that I thought Seb was my stalker. Talking to him now, I'm convinced it's not him. He's too worried about his sister. His face is an open book. Guileless. I remember that Llewellyn said she was going to bring him in for questioning. I'll have to let her know that I don't suspect Seb any longer. Being hauled into the police station and accused of being a stalker would be the last straw for him. The poor guy already seems at the end of his rope.

'I'm not holding out too much hope for the auction,' he says, 'but yes, I suppose that could yield a bit of income. The money was supposed to pay off a couple of loans, though, not pay George back for stolen goods. This is a nightmare!' He drops his head in his hands. 'One step forward, ten steps back.'

The last thing I thought I'd be doing this evening is consoling Pippa's brother. Although I know I'm delaying the inevitable. I can't hide out in the pub all night.

'Are these dead?' A middle-aged barmaid comes and scoops up our glasses without waiting for a reply. Despite the fact that there are still a good few sips left, she takes our glasses and makes her way across to the next table, where the three men all wrap their hands around their pints.

'Hands off, Joanne.'

'In yer dreams, fellas.'

They all laugh.

But neither Seb nor I are laughing.

'Do you want another?' he asks, inclining his head towards the bar.

'I'll get them.'

'No, no, it's fine. I can—'

'Seb, please. Let me.'

'Okay, thanks. Another pint would be welcome.'

I nod and get us another couple of drinks – this time I opt for a gin and tonic to wash away the taste of the dodgy wine. When I return, I ask him the obvious question. 'Seb, why don't you sell the Manor House? You could sort out all your money worries and enjoy life. Sorry if that's too personal a question, but if things are really that bad…'

'It's okay. You're only saying what everyone else is thinking. But Dad just won't do it. He's adamant that it should be passed down to me. Even though I don't want it. Bloody place is a millstone. But the estate's been in our family for generations, since the fourteenth century.'

'Blimey. That's some inheritance.'

'Yeah. I'll be Lord Hargreaves one day, without two pennies to rub together.' He gives me a sad smile. 'Look, I'll sort something out with Pippa. I'll get the money to give to George somehow. And you'll… you'll make sure he doesn't press charges?'

'He's already said he'll forget the whole thing if he's compensated.'

'Thank you, Lizzy.'

'That's okay.'

'I mean it. Thank you.'

I glance at my watch. 'I think I'd better get back. I need to feed Frank.'

'I thought your boyfriend's name was Joe?'

'Frank's my cat. And Joe… well, he's not my boyfriend any more.' It's hard to say the words out loud, but I'd better get used to it, because there's no way I'll be taking my lying boyfriend back.

'Oh, I'm sorry.'

I get to my feet. 'Say hello to Pippa from me. Tell her I'm sorry things turned out like this.'

'Can I give you a lift home?' Seb asks, draining his pint and standing up.

I pause for a moment. Although I truly don't think Seb is a threat, the thought of getting into a vehicle with him is more than a little disconcerting. But I'm too drunk to drive, the journey is too short to warrant a taxi and I'm too nervous to walk home alone, so his offer is tempting.

'It's fine if you'd rather walk,' he adds, noticing my hesitation. 'Just thought I'd offer. You seem a little… tired.'

I am tired. I'm exhausted. Everything seems to be catching up with me. 'Actually, that would be great, if you don't mind. That G&T has gone straight to my head. I'd better leave the car where it is.' I realise I haven't eaten anything all day, and I feel a bit sozzled.

'No problem. I'm parked around the corner.'

Seb and I leave the dingy pub and I squint into the evening sunshine, suddenly longing to be home in bed. To blot out the awfulness of the past twenty-four hours. We walk up the High Street and turn into a side lane, where Seb's battered blue Land

Rover is parked with two wheels up on the kerb. He unlocks it and I climb up into the passenger seat.

As he starts the engine and pulls away, Seb glances across at me. 'Lizzy, I really am sorry I yelled at you earlier. Don't know what came over me.'

'You were sticking up for your family, weren't you?'

'Yes, but this whole thing isn't your fault. It was unforgivable of me to shout at you like that. I apologise.'

'Apology accepted.' Pippa was right, he's a nice guy. He glances across at me once more and smiles. I wish I had a big brother who stuck up for me like that. Pippa may be going through a tricky time, but at least she's lucky to have Seb by her side. How could I ever have thought Sebastian Hargreaves was out to get me?

CHAPTER THIRTY-SIX

As I step through the front door, the cottage is silent. No Joe upstairs in the shower or watching TV. And it hits me – he will never be here again. I'll never forgive him for what he did. It's just occurred to me that without Joe, I won't be able to afford the rent on this place. I'll have to hand my notice in to George. I run a hand down the wall, stroking it. This was my home. Joe and I were saving for a deposit to buy something similar to this. We were even going to ask George if he'd consider selling his rental to us. But now… Well. Now everything has changed.

'Frank!' My gorgeous cat comes strolling down the stairs, purring loudly. 'At least someone's here to greet me.' I bend down to scratch behind his ears. 'Let's get your supper, Mr Frankie.' He trots into the kitchen ahead of me, tail in the air, and I get him his food.

What a day. I never knew Seb had such a terrifying temper. For a moment back there at the shop, I really did think he was going to physically attack me. But now I realise he was simply sticking up for Pippa. He had thought I had unfairly sacked her. I hope she'll be okay. I wonder if she will ever forgive me. Maybe Seb can talk her round. Or maybe it's best that we take a break for a while. After all, I can't lose sight of the fact that she was stealing from the shop. No matter how much of a friend I consider her to be, what she did was wrong. It could have cost me my job as well.

'There you go, Frank. Food.' I set his bowl down on his mat and he starts eating. I should eat too. My stomach is hollow and I'm more than a little light-headed. But my throat is too constricted to eat a proper meal. I take a cream cracker out of the biscuit tin and nibble at the corner. It tastes of sawdust, and even the smallest mouthful is like swallowing rocks. But I persevere.

Should I go to bed? My mind is numb. I should surely be crying or angry or something, but I've been suppressing my emotions all day at work, and now that I'm finally free to let them out, they want to stay locked down tight. I should speak to Emma. I owe her a huge apology. I wonder if we'll ever regain the bond we once had, or if it's shattered for good. I can't speak to her now, though, I'm no good for anything.

I finish chewing my cracker and run myself a glass of water from the tap. The whoosh of water is loud, echoing. I drink down the whole glass and it revives me a little. It's so quiet. I'm beginning to wish I'd stayed out a little longer. But I would still have had to come home at some point.

The doorbell sounds and I freeze. Who could it be? Seb again? Emma? Not Joe – I'm pretty sure he would use his key, unless he's trying to be thoughtful. I can't face talking to him. Not this evening. Everything is still too raw. I don't have the energy for another screaming match. What if it's my stalker? The doorbell rings once more. I tiptoe along the hall and sidle into the sitting room, where I peer out of the window. Exhaling in relief, I see it's only Ruby from next door. I suppose I could ignore the bell, pretend I'm out. But maybe she saw me coming home earlier. I give myself a shake. I should just answer the flipping door. I stretch out my arms and then rub at my cheeks, hoping I don't look too much of a mess.

'Hi, Ruby!' I cry, pulling open the door. I was aiming for a normal-slash-friendly tone, but my voice sounds manic and too high-pitched.

She's standing on the doorstep wearing baby-pink tracksuit bottoms with her regulation crop top, showing off an incredible figure. 'Hi, Lizzy,' she says. 'Tell me to piss off and mind my own business, but are you okay?'

'Okay?' I smile brightly. 'Yes, I'm fine.'

Ruby bites her lip. 'You sure? Only Ian bumped into Joe today, and he said you two had had a fight. I'm not being nosy or anything, I just wondered if you might want some company?' Her blue eyes are huge and filled with concern.

'Oh.' Annoyingly, my emotions seem to have chosen this particular moment to surface. A tear slips down my face.

'Lizzy! Are you okay? Stupid question, 'course you're not.' She steps into the hallway and gives me an awkward hug.

'I'm fine, honestly. I know I don't look like it.' I give a strangled laugh. 'But I'll be okay in a sec.'

'You don't have to put a brave face on for me,' Ruby says. 'I know what it's like when your boyfriend acts like a dickhead. Not Ian! No, Ian's good as gold. My last boyfriend, though, he was a total knob. Used to cheat on me all the time, till I kicked him to the kerb. You and Joe will get back together though, won't you? You look rock solid, you two.'

I shake my head slowly. 'No, Ruby. We're finished.'

'Did he break up with you? Sorry, ignore me. Just being a nosy cow. You don't have to talk about it. I just wanted to see if you were okay, and if there's anything I can do.'

'You're really sweet,' I say, sniffing back more tears.

'Ha! Never been called sweet before.'

Despite my tears, I manage a small smile. 'Why don't you come in for a bit? If you're not too busy. Have a cuppa with me, or… hang on, I think there's a bottle of Sauvignon Blanc in the fridge.' I go into the kitchen and pull open the fridge door. Ruby follows me down the hallway. 'Yep, three quarters of a bottle. Want to help me finish it off?'

'Not really a wine drinker, but yeah, okay, why not. Thanks.'

'Hey, Frank.' I reach down to stroke him, but now he's had his food, he's not too interested and he scoots past Ruby and scampers back upstairs.

'Cute cat,' Ruby says. 'He used to hang out in our garden, but I haven't seen him for a while.'

'He had an injury, so I've had to keep him indoors.'

'Poor thing,' Ruby says. 'Sounds like you're both having a crap time.'

I pour us each a glass of wine and open a packet of Kettle Chips that Joe was saving for the weekend. I pass Ruby a glass and shake the crisps into a bowl. 'Let's go into the lounge.'

I sit in my usual spot on the sofa while Ruby sits on one of the armchairs. I take a sip of the cool, crisp wine and try to think of something to say. It seemed like a good idea, inviting her in for a drink. But now she's here, the atmosphere is a little awkward.

'So, how come you and Joe split up?' Ruby asks.

I don't know if I have the energy to recount the whole story with her. She seems lovely, but we hardly know one another. I'll keep it vague. 'I found out he lied to me.'

'About another girl?'

I nod. 'My sister, actually.' I hadn't meant to say that.

Ruby's eyes widen. 'That's harsh.'

'She didn't do anything with him. But he tried it on with her.'

Ruby shakes her head. 'I would never have put Joe as the cheating type. I mean, he's fit as anything – good-looking, ripped. But I could tell he was really into you when you came round to ours. Didn't look like he wanted anyone else. Not being funny, but most blokes flirt with me *a lot*. Joe? Not so much.'

'Yeah, well. The thing with my sister was five years ago, so maybe he's not like that any more.'

'Five years ago? So why are you getting mad now?'

'I only just found out. And the thing is, I blamed Emma – my sister. And he let me blame her. He let me think she was the one who'd chased him, not the other way around.' I realise my glass is empty. 'Want another?'

Ruby nods. 'What a wanker. Yeah, I guess I'd have kicked him out too.'

I get up and weave my way unsteadily into the kitchen, bring back the bottle of wine and distribute the rest between us. I take a handful of crisps and stuff them into my mouth. I need something to soak up the alcohol. They're sharp and salty, scraping the back of my throat. I offer the bowl to Ruby, but she shakes her head.

'You ever catch that stalker?' she asks.

'No.' The crisps feel hard and undigested in my throat, so I gulp down more wine. 'It's all gone wrong, Ruby.' I set my glass down on the coffee table and try to bite back my tears.

She comes and sits by my side. 'Hey, it's bad now, but it'll be okay. My mum always used to say that sometimes things have to fall apart to make way for better things.'

'Your mum sounds like a wise woman.' I sniff.

'Have the police got any closer to catching him, whoever it is?'

I shake my head. 'The police are supportive, but they haven't come up with any evidence or DNA or anything.'

'Bummer. Look, if you ever feel down, or nervous or anything, you know you can always come next door. Ian and me, we don't have that many friends – losers, I know! But we love having people round. And I already feel like we're friends. So, just saying.'

'Thanks, Ruby. I really appreciate that. And I also appreciate you coming round like this. It was really thoughtful. Makes me feel like I'm not so alone.'

''Course.' She nudges me with her elbow and I manage a smile. Even though I have a hollow feeling inside that's not due to lack of food. 'Look,' she says, 'I've just thought of something.' She kicks off her flip-flops, wriggles back into the sofa and brings her feet up under her.

'What?'

'Well, you know I clean for CCR.'

'Who?'

'Cotswold Country Retreats.'

'Oh, yeah, the holiday let company.'

'Yeah. Well, at the end of each quarter, all the staff's names are put into a sweepstake to win a minibreak, and I won the last one.'

'Nice. When are you going?'

'Well, that's the thing. I booked it for this coming Friday and Saturday night. Me and Ian were going to have a dirty weekend away.' She winks.

I wish she hadn't put that image in my head.

'Anyway, long story short, remember I came into Georgio's for that retirement card? Well, the party's this Saturday night. I got the dates of the holiday mixed up. Bloody annoying. But we have to go to Ian's dad's thing – he's renting next door to us really cheap, and he's Ian's dad, so we kind of have to show our support. But it's too late to change the booking for the minibreak. So bang goes our weekend in a posh place.'

'Oh no, that's a shame. Surely your company will let you change the booking?'

'Nope, too short notice. It's my own fault for cocking up the dates.' She pulls a face. 'Anyway, what I'm getting at is that *you* should go.'

'Go? I don't understand.'

'On the posh minibreak!' She beams. 'You'd love it, Lizzy. It's not naff. It's proper premium. Honestly, like something out of a magazine. It's got a swimming pool and everything.'

'Sounds amazing,' I say, thinking that the last thing I need to be doing is going to a posh holiday home on my own. I'm just not in the mood.

'Look.' Ruby pulls her phone out of her pocket and starts tapping and swiping. She scooches up next to me again and shows me some pictures of a place that looks like it's straight out of *Ideal Home* magazine.

'It's beautiful,' I agree.

'So you'll go? You deserve a weekend to pamper yourself, after all the crap you've been going through.'

'I'd love to, but I've got to work tomorrow and Saturday.'

'Call in sick.'

'Ruby!'

'What?'

'I love my job. I can't call in sick. Especially now that… well, let's just say that I'm short-staffed at the moment. And with Joe gone, the last thing I need is to lose my job.'

'Okay, then. Go for one night. Saturday night after work. It's only up the road, about fifteen minutes' drive away. One night of *serious* luxury.'

I stare at the aqua swimming pool on the screen. At the teak sunloungers and the striped hammock. I think of easing myself into the hammock. Letting the sun warm my bones as I pretend to live a life of luxury. Of gliding beneath the surface of the pool like you see in the holiday adverts. 'I can't,' I reply. 'But thanks so much for offering. It was really generous of you.'

'Well, the offer's still there if you change your mind,' Ruby says, getting to her feet. 'Better get back. Ian will be wondering where I've got to.'

'Thank you, Ruby.'

I see my neighbour out and close the door behind her. The house feels emptier than ever. But I'm not going to wallow. I'm not going to think about it. I'm going to crawl into bed and try to sleep.

I climb the stairs, run a toothbrush around my mouth, peel off my clothes and slide beneath the sheets. The space next to me is as wide as a mile and as empty as a canyon. Even Frank has deserted me, taking himself back downstairs. Lying huddled on 'my side' of the bed, I feel like a failure. Like I've done something wrong, when I know I haven't. I close my eyes and attempt to empty my mind. To slip between the silences of my ticking bedside clock. But it's impossible to stop thinking about everything.

Defiantly, I stretch my legs across the mattress, kicking angrily at the covers as they try to impede my movement. And now I'm lying diagonally across the bed, proving to myself that I don't miss him. That it's better this way, with my toes meeting no resistance. I'm free to sprawl whichever way I like. But the truth is, it's strange. And my heart is heavy.

My eyes remain closed, but my brain doesn't want to shut down. Maybe I should give up on the idea of sleep; read or get up and go downstairs. However, at some point during the night, I must have dozed off eventually because now I'm being dragged awake by a furious banging sound. I gasp and sit upright, trying to reorientate myself. I'm in my bed. Joe's gone. I'm alone. My heart is pounding. The landing light throws a narrow strip of light into the bedroom. I glance at the bedside clock. It reads 2.15 a.m. Now the doorbell is ringing, too, accompanied by further heavy banging.

Someone is at the front door.

CHAPTER THIRTY-SEVEN

I pull the sheet up around my neck, half asleep and sick with fear. Who is it? Who could be banging on my door in the dead of night? *Joe?* Could it be Joe? No. He'd use a key, surely. In the gloom, I hear a soft swishing noise as the door to my bedroom opens. Light from the landing spills into the room. I squeal, squashing myself back against the headboard, bracing myself for the intruder to show themselves. *Is this it?* Is this when my stalker finally reveals their identity? Am I in danger?

I feel a soft pressure on the bed. I see a dark shape. It's Frank! He has leapt up onto the bed. It was my cat who pushed open the bedroom door. I relax my shoulders and put a hand to my chest, feeling the staccato beats of my heart through my fingertips. Frank's fur is standing on end, his ears flattened.

'You scared me, Frankie!' I chide. Then I stroke his head, as much to soothe myself as to soothe him. The air is close, thick with our stress and anxiety.

The banging finally stops and I exhale. Even with the sound ringing in my ears, I wonder if I imagined it. I'm still half asleep; could it have been the remnants of a realistic dream? Am I dreaming right now? I swallow and press my fingers to my warm face. I feel awake. I don't think it was a dream.

Pushing away the sheet, I slide out of bed, pull on my dressing gown and tiptoe onto the landing, Frank at my feet. We make our way down the stairs, his fur velveteen on my ankles. I wonder who it was banging at the door. If they're still there. Do I dare open up to see?

As I reach the bottom of the stairs, the banging starts up again. So loud that I almost cry out in shock. What should I do? I could run back up the stairs and hide under the covers, or I could see who it is. Be brave, Lizzy. Be brave.

I creep into the lounge and peer out through the window. A large blue van is parked in the middle of the street. Beneath the street lamps, I make out the logo on the side – British Gas. A man in a boiler suit stands on the pathway outside the cottage. He's swiping at the screen of a mobile phone. I exhale and rub my eyes. This is who was banging on the door. Not Joe. Not some psycho. My shoulders relax. But then I experience a stab of annoyance. What the hell is British Gas doing knocking on my door at two fifteen in the morning?

Lifting Frank up into my arms, I march out of the lounge and fling open the front door. 'Hello? Can I help you?' I snap.

The man glances up from his phone. He's an older guy. Maybe in his fifties or sixties. 'Miss Beresford?' His voice is deep and drawling.

'Yes?' I pull my dressing gown tighter around my body.

'I'm here about the gas leak.'

I frown. 'What gas leak?'

'You called us twenty minutes ago reporting the smell of gas. I've been knocking and ringing for ages. Thought you might have passed out from the fumes. I was just about to call an ambulance.'

I have no idea what this man is talking about. 'I wasn't passed out, I was asleep! There's no leak here. No fumes.' My voice is slow, still thick with sleep.

'Better let me in to check the readings.'

'You're not coming into my house!'

'I'll need to come in. I'll have to do a safety ch—'

'*I said*, you're not coming into my house. And I never called you about any sort of gas leak.'

He slides a clipboard out from under his arm. 'You're a Miss Elizabeth Beresford? And this is seven, Richmond Gardens?'

'Yes,' I reply grudgingly.

'Well, like I said, you called us to report a—'

'And like *I* said, I made no such phone call to you.'

The man uses the corner of his phone to scratch his head. 'You didn't call?'

'No. I didn't. What number was it that called you?' I ask.

The man frowns.

'The phone number,' I clarify. 'Someone called you to report the leak. What number did they call from?'

'I looked it up on the log details when you didn't answer the door. But it shows a withheld number. It also says the person terminated the call before we could get all the details from them. It's why we rushed round so quickly.'

'Damn.'

'So you're telling me there's no leak?' He presses his lips together in a thin line.

'No, there's no leak,' I confirm. Although I realise I was probably far too sleepy to notice if there actually was a smell of gas in the house. What if this is something to do with my stalker, and they've done something to the boiler? What if they came into the house while I was asleep and tampered with the pipes? But we changed the locks, so they can't have got in. Unless… Joe still has a set of keys… could it have been him? I have no idea what to think. 'Do you have any ID?' I ask the man, noting once more the recognisable logo on his van and his British Gas boiler suit.

The man slips his phone into his pocket and shows me his laminated ID card. His name is Bob Packham, and his identification appears legitimate, but how would I know what a genuine British Gas ID card looks like?

'Can you wait here a sec?' I ask.

He nods.

I close the front door and go back into the house, sniffing the air. I pad into the kitchen and open the boiler cupboard. It all looks and smells normal. I set Frank down and shut him in the kitchen before returning to Bob.

'Well?' he asks.

'No smell of gas,' I reply.

'I really should come inside and take some readings.'

'I think it must have been a hoax call,' I say. 'I've been getting a few of them.'

The man shakes his head. 'Some right sickos out there. I should check, though, just to be on the safe side. The bosses won't like it if I—'

'Look, I understand that this is your job. But there's no way I'm letting you inside my house. Sorry you've had a wasted journey.'

'Suit yourself, love, but gas leaks are dangerous. We've had people pass out from the fumes before. They can kill you. Anyway, sorry if I scared you before, knocking on the door like that. I was worried, that's all.'

'It's okay. Not your fault.'

'You wanna call the police about this. If it really was a hoax call then it's time-wasting and harassment.'

'Thanks.'

Bob nods and turns to leave.

I sigh and close the front door, fully awake now. What the hell was all that about? Did someone really report a gas leak on my behalf? This is all getting too much. And with Joe gone, I'm dealing with it all on my own.

I let my cat out of the kitchen and sit on the stairs, unable to contemplate going back to bed right now. Frank lies on his side on the hall floor, pretending to be relaxed. One eye open, his striped tail flicks periodically back and forth. 'I know how you feel, Frank.'

I need to tell the police what's happened, but it almost seems pointless. They won't be able to trace the call; they won't be able to find out who's behind it. It will just get logged as yet another incident. And meanwhile, I'm having yet another interrupted night's sleep. Which means I'll feel like crap tomorrow at work. Whoever's doing this is becoming more and more creative with their methods of harassment. And the thing is, I have no way of knowing how far they're prepared to go…

CHAPTER THIRTY-EIGHT

In theory, getting ready for work this morning shouldn't have felt too different to normal. Joe was always out of the house before me anyway, so I generally have the house to myself. But, after last night's scare, the house feels anything but normal. I'm alone. I have no one to talk to. And someone is trying to scare the daylights out of me. Trying to make me feel terrified in my own home. But *why?* Why can't they simply tell me what it is they want?

I reported the supposed gas leak to the police last night and, as I predicted, they logged the incident but couldn't trace the call. So it's just another incident in a long line of incidents.

I check my phone, finally feeling brave enough to read my messages. I scroll through Joe's texts. They all say variations of the same thing:

I'm so sorry

I love you

Please don't ignore me

When can we talk?

These texts don't look like they were written by someone who's trying to scare me. But maybe that's part of some twisted plan. Pretend to be in love with me while playing with my mind. It makes no difference either way – whether he's behind everything that's happened or not, I'm still not going to reply to any of his messages. I'm going to put all this crap on the back burner and I'm going to go to work.

True to his word, George is already inside the shop when I arrive, wandering around, checking the place out. At least I managed to speak to Pippa while he was away, although the outcome of that conversation isn't likely to impress my boss.

'Hello, Lizzy, love.' We kiss on both cheeks.

'Still in holiday mode?' I ask, staring pointedly at his shorts and polo shirt, rather than one of his usual suits.

'The missus has booked us in for some wakeboarding thing over at Cerney Lakes. Says our holiday isn't over yet. I told her, Sophie, love, I've got work to do. I can't be mucking about doing water sports. Got to earn the money to pay for all these holidays she's been booking. But she's not having any of it.'

'Wakeboarding sounds fun, though,' I reply.

He throws his hands in the air. 'Not at my age. Not sure the old knees will take it. But I can't deny it'll be good to cool down on the water. Warm in here, isn't it? You got that fan switched on?'

I nod and point to the little machine that's next to useless in this sweltering heat.

George makes a non-committal noise in his throat. 'Anyway, shop's looking great. Which is more than can be said for you. You all right? Looking a bit pale and peaky. You need to get out in the sunshine more, Lizzy.'

I nod, not about to get into all my personal issues with George.

'You speak to Pippa yet? She's not here, so I take it you've given her the old heave-ho.' He jingles the keys in his shorts pocket.

'I spoke to her, yes.'

'And? She gonna bring back all the stuff she's nicked?'

I decide to tell a little white lie and repeat what Seb and I agreed. 'She's going to add it all up and give you the cash. She just needs a little while longer to get it together.'

'Fine.' He nods. 'I'll have to hire someone ASAP, but in the meantime, you okay to look after the place on your own? I can cancel today's wakeboarding if you need me to stay today. Just say the word. To be honest, I need an excuse to get out of it.'

I manage a small laugh. 'No, you go, George. I'll be fine.'

'Damn. Well, okay, but it's your fault if I break my neck! Only joking. You're a little diamond, you are.' He gives my arm a squeeze and turns to go.

'There's something else, George.'

'Oh yeah?' He turns back to me.

'I'm going to have to hand in my notice at the cottage.'

'What? Oh, that's a shame. Fed up of renting? You and Joe gonna buy somewhere instead?'

'I doubt it. Joe and I broke up.' I tense up against the threatening tears.

'Oh, Lizzy. I'm sorry… no chance of you two getting back together?'

I shake my head. 'He's moved out.'

'Oh.' He chews his lip for a moment. 'Well, if you're having trouble coming up with the rent, I can help out.'

'What do you mean?'

'Have a couple of months half price. See how you get on.'

'George! Thank you!' I can't believe I'm actually having a bit of good luck for a change.

'My pleasure, Lizzy. You've always been a good tenant. Be sorry to lose you. Must be getting soft in my old age. Right, I'm off. Wish me luck with this wakeboarding malarkey.'

The rest of the day passes quickly enough. I'm rushed off my feet with absolutely no time to think about anything, thank goodness. Despite my brain being occupied with customers, my stomach is constantly queasy and my eyes are scratchy and tired. At least I have a couple of months' financial breathing space while I figure out where I'm going to live. George certainly surprised me with his generous offer to halve the rent. It's totally out of character. But I'm not about to complain.

Back home after work, I decide that even though I'm shattered, I'm going to make a start on packing up Joe's things. I can't bear to look at them, and the sooner he collects his stuff, the sooner I can put his lies behind me and move on with my life. But move on *where* and *how*, I have no idea.

I make my way upstairs and heave the largest suitcase down from the loft, dragging it into our bedroom. I open the wardrobe and stare at Joe's clothes, which have been chucked in any which way. I'll throw all his clothes and toiletries into the case and then he can pick them up while I'm out tomorrow. He'll have to bring some boxes for the rest of his things. I try not to remember the two of us moving in here. How excited we were to have our own place. This cottage represented the beginning of my adult life. Of being exactly where I wanted to be. *So now what?*

My biggest worry about moving is Frank. Most rental places don't allow pets, especially flats, which is probably what I'm looking at being able to afford, if I'm lucky. I push away images of tiny bedsits, of having to give Frank away. But it surely won't come to that. Will it? I pull out my first armful of his clothes, a waft of his scent making me catch my breath. Why didn't Joe come clean at the time? If he'd admitted what he'd done, we could have argued about it and moved on one way or another. But the fact he lied and ruined my relationship with Emma for so many years… it means there's no way back.

The only upside to all this heartache is that it's taking my mind off my stalker. I clench my fists and square my shoulders. In fact, if he showed his face right now, far from being scared, I'd probably give him a piece of my mind. But the reality is that I now live alone. I'll have no one here to turn to when the next letter arrives. And it will arrive, of that I'm sure. My heady moment of bravado is rapidly disappearing.

I spend the next half hour clearing out Joe's clothes. *At least I'll have more space in the wardrobe*, I think, trying to tease out a silver lining. By the time the case is bulging with my ex-boyfriend's belongings, I'm hot and sweaty and thirsty. I jump in the shower, change into a thin cotton dress and sit on the end of the bed, my eyes closed for a moment, trying not to give in to the sadness. I don't want to cry. I don't want to think about any of this. I just want to live a normal life, with a nice boyfriend, a decent job and no stalker. Is that too much to ask?

My stomach lurches as the doorbell rings. Maybe it's Ruby again. I stand up, smooth back my damp hair and walk down the stairs. Yesterday's hesitancy to answer the door has gone. I pull open the door. 'Emma!'

She's in her work clothes, smart but stressed-looking, several creases lining her brow. 'Are you okay? I came as soon as I could,' she says, glancing up and down the road. 'Is it the stalker again? Or Joe? Why didn't you return my calls?'

'Sorry, am I missing something?' I ask. 'Come in.' I step back and she follows me into the hall.'

'Is Joe…?'

'Moved out,' I reply. 'I was going to call you. I was going to apologise. You were right, about everything. And I was wrong. I'm so sorry, Ems. I'm so, so sorry.'

'Is this what your message was about?' she asks, a puzzled look on her face.

'Message?'

'Your text message.'

My heart begins to pound. 'I never sent you a message.'

'Yes, you did, look.' Emma pulls her phone out of her bag, pulls up the message and shows me:

Emma, can you come over. It's urgent. I need to see you ASAP, Lizzy.

'I never sent that!'

'You didn't?' Emma stares at me intently.

'No.' A low bellow of thunder rumbles in the distance, but we're too caught up in our conversation to remark upon it. 'So if the message wasn't from me…'

Emma's face hardens. We stare at one another, realising at the same time that this is another message from our stalker. The question is, what does it mean? And what do they want?

CHAPTER THIRTY-NINE

'Was it sent from my phone?' I scan the message details on her mobile and see that there's a number attached to the text. But it's not mine.

'I tried calling the number,' Emma says, 'but it wouldn't connect. So I called your other number, but that one just went straight through to voicemail.'

'Sorry about that. I put my phone on silent so I could ignore all Joe's messages and calls.'

'And you're absolutely sure this text isn't from you?'

'Nope, definitely not.'

'So…' She grimaces.

'Yeah. It must be from the same person who's sending the letters. I can't think of anyone else who would do it.'

'Check your phone,' Emma says. 'See if they've sent you anything.'

She follows me into the kitchen where I pull my phone out of my bag and start scrolling past all Joe's texts, dreading spotting an anonymous number. But there are no unusual texts. 'Nothing that I can see,' I say, my heart rate slowing. 'Why would they send you that message?'

'To mess with us?' Emma replies. 'To make me worried about you? Who knows? It's bloody annoying. I was looking forward to a relaxing night in front of the telly, not a mad dash down the motorway in Friday-night traffic.'

'Sorry,' I say.

'You don't need to say sorry. It wasn't you who sent the message… was it?'

'No! I already said it wasn't.'

Emma gives a grim smile. 'Just double-checking.' She slips her phone back in her bag and drums her nails on the kitchen counter. 'So, you and Joe… he finally admitted it, then?'

I nod, hardly daring to speak about it.

'How did you get him to own up?'

'I asked him outright. I knew straight away from the expression on his face. And he knew I knew. So there was no point him denying it any more.'

She sits down heavily on the kitchen stool, rests her elbows on the counter top.

'Oh, Emma,' I cry, 'I am so sorry. I'm the worst sister in the world. I don't know what I was thinking back then, and for all these years. Do you hate me? You must do.'

Emma fixes me with an unreadable stare. 'Of course I don't hate you. You're my little sister. You're bloody annoying, and stubborn, but even after all this time I still love you, Lizzy. Even if you have massively pissed me off.'

Her words warm me, but also fill me with shame. 'How can you even look at me after I took Joe's side against you? I basically cut you out of my life for no good reason.'

She shrugs. 'He's charming. You loved him. I guess he was easy to believe.'

I shake my head and stare at my feet.

'Don't get me wrong,' Emma says, 'for the first couple of years I hated your guts. I was furious with you and with Joe. Those bloody birthday lunches of Mum's were torture. But then I met Mike, and one day I told him about everything that had happened between us, and he explained how we all make errors in judgement. How, if you truly believed Joe was telling the truth, then of course you would take his side. He made me see that this was Joe's fault, not yours. You were just caught up in his lie. He told me that the truth would eventually come out.' She gives a brittle laugh. 'I didn't believe him, but it turns out he was right.'

I'm now seeing Emma's fiancé in a whole new light. 'Sounds like you've got the perfect man there, Emma. What is he, a Christian, a Buddhist?'

Emma smiles. 'No, he's just kind. I actually tried to set up a meeting with Joe a couple of years ago, to try to talk him into owning up to what he'd done. To tell him I would forgive him. But he wouldn't even meet with me. Wouldn't return my calls. So I gave up, and just carried on living my life, without you in it.'

How could I have got things so wrong? Mum's right about me, I'm not half the person Emma is. I need to sit down, to digest everything. But there's only one stool in the kitchen and Emma is sitting on it. I lean back against the counter instead, trying to take it all in.

'What are we going to do about this message?' Emma asks.

'What *can* we do?' I say, crossing my arms. 'Nothing. I guess we need to let the police know about it. But there's no traceable number. We don't know why they left the message in the first place. To get you here?'

'Maybe.'

'There's something else…'

Emma raises an eyebrow and I tell her about the hoax call to British Gas.

'Bloody hell,' she says, her eyes filling with concern. 'Are you okay?'

I shrug. 'I guess I should be thankful there wasn't an actual gas leak. But it makes me worried that it was some kind of threat. That they might actually act on it next time. Maybe even do something to the boiler.'

'You should get an alarm system.'

'I'll probably be moving out soon, so there's no point.'

'Why don't I stay and keep you company?' she says.

'That's okay. You should probably just go back home and enjoy your evening.' But I realise I don't want her to go.

'I can't leave you here on your own. Not while there's a crazy person out there. You could come back to Bristol with me. Our flat's pretty big, and we've got a lovely spare room that hardly ever gets used. Come on, pack a bag, let's go.' She springs to her feet.

'I can't, Emma. I've got work tomorrow.'

'You can still go to work. Plenty of people commute that distance. Traffic won't be too bad on a Saturday morning.'

'Honestly, Emma, thank you, but I can't.'

'You can.'

'I'd feel weird with Mike there. He knows everything about us, about me not believing you, my own sister. I feel crap about it. Ashamed.'

'Mike's not like that. He's a good guy. You'll see once you get to know him properly.'

'I'm sure I will. Just… just not yet, okay?'

'Fine. I'll stay here with you then. Have you got a spare room? Or I can sleep on the sofa.'

'I can't ask you to do that.'

'You're not asking, I'm offering. And anyway, we've got a lot of catching up to do.' Emma takes my hand in both of hers and squeezes it. 'I've got you back in my life again, Lizzy. I'm not letting you stay here on your own where some psycho stalker can get to you. We can order in a takeaway and talk about old times, before our misunderstanding.'

But even with my sister in the cottage with me, I realise I don't want to stay here. Not with the memories of Joe all around me and the distinct possibility of him turning up unannounced. Plus, it will be awful if Emma's here when Joe shows up – and I know he will, it's only a matter of time. Joe turning up is almost as bad as the threat of our stalker leaving another letter… or worse.

Something suddenly occurs to me. Something that would be perfect. 'Emma, I've got an idea. Wait here a minute.' Infused with a sudden burst of energy, I leave the kitchen.

'Where are you going?' my sister calls after me.

'I'll be two minutes!' I snatch up my keys and leave the house, heading next door to Ian and Ruby's. While I'm outside a streak of lightning flashes above me, splitting the sky in two.

Ian answers the door. 'All right, Lizzy,' he says, scratching the side of his groin and staring up at the sky. 'Looks like it's about to piss down.'

'Ian, hi. Yes, must be a summer shower on its way. Is Ruby in?'

'Hang on, I'll get her.' He disappears into the lounge and Ruby comes out.

'Hiya.' Her hair is pulled up in a high ponytail, and her shorts are so short I'm almost embarrassed to look at her. 'You okay?' she asks. 'Wanna come in for a drink?'

'No, I won't stop, but thank you. I was wondering… is that offer of the minibreak still available? No worries if not, I just thought—'

'Yeah, 'course it is. You wanna go?'

'If that's okay?'

She gives me a huge grin. 'Honestly, Lizzy, you're gonna love it. I am well jel. Although it looks like there's a massive storm on the way…'

'Doesn't bother me. We could do with a storm to cool things down a bit.'

We both give a start as a crack of thunder shakes the air.

'Fuck!' Ruby cries. ''Scuse my French.'

I laugh at her expression. 'There's just one other thing…'

'Oh yeah?'

'Would you mind if my sister came with me on the minibreak?'

'Your sister? I thought you two weren't speaking. What about that thing with Joe?'

'Long story, but we've sort of made up. So I thought the holiday home thing could be a nice break, a chance to reconnect.'

'Sounds good,' she says with a smile.

I'm actually starting to get excited about this trip. It could be a really good way to spend time with my sister. A really positive start to the rest of my life. 'Thank you, Ruby.' I kiss her cheek and she turns bright red.

'No worries,' she chirps. 'I'll text you the details and the key code, okay?'

'Brilliant. Thank you so much. Have a good time at Ian's dad's do. I bet it will be great.'

Ruby rolls her eyes.

I head home, looking forward to telling my sister the news that we're about to have a night away in a five-star holiday home. Away from bad boyfriends. Away from untrustworthy friends. Away from scary stalkers. I can't wait.

CHAPTER-FORTY

'A holiday home?' Emma replies.

'Hang on a minute.' I've finally taken my phone off silent and all my messages are buzzing and pinging like the damn thing is about to explode. 'Here.' I show her the text that Ruby has just sent across. It's the details for the rental property, along with a link to the website page. I click on it and start scrolling through the photos.

Emma's eyes widen as she sees the images. 'And this neighbour of yours has said we can stay there?'

'Yep. She said we can have it for two nights.'

'I wish I had your neighbours!'

'I've still got to go to work tomorrow, but that doesn't mean you can't enjoy it while I'm gone during the day.'

'Really?' she turns and wrinkles her nose at me.

'Yes, sorry. But I'll be back by five thirty. You can relax by the pool while I'm gone.'

'Okay. I suppose a day by the pool doesn't sound too bad.' She gives me a rueful smile.

'I'm sure you'll cope. It'll just sit empty if we don't go. I really didn't fancy staying there on my own, so I'm glad you're up for it.'

'Totally! I'll need to borrow some clothes, though.' She chews her bottom lip and I know what she's thinking – that my clothes will swamp her slender frame.

'No problem,' I reply. 'I've got a whole load of "skinny" clothes from back when I was on a diet in 2014. It lasted all of six months and I almost made it down to a size ten. It was possibly the only time Mum ever smiled at me.'

'She's not that bad, Lizzy.'

I give Emma a look.

'Okay, maybe she is, but it's only because she loves you and she thinks she's helping.'

'Tell you what, Ems, let's agree not to talk about Mum this evening.'

'Agreed. I'll just call Mike and let him know what's going on.'

'Okay, and while you're doing that, I'm going to nip next door.'

Emma holds a finger up as Mike has already answered the phone.

I leave her talking to her fiancé and head back out. This time I go to Mrs P's house. It's after 8 p.m., so I hope she hasn't turned in early. I needn't have worried; she answers the door almost immediately.

'Lizzy, hello.'

'Hi.'

'Looks like we're about to have a storm.' She eyes up the darkening sky. 'Everything okay?'

'Sort of. Yes. But I was wondering. Is there any chance you could look after Frank for the next couple of days?'

'You going away, dear? Want me to pop in and feed him? No problem.'

'Are you sure that's all right? Sorry it's a bit short notice. The thing is, you can't let him out at all, because…' Even though Mrs P knows about the letters, I don't want to freak her out by explaining the rest of it. 'Because Frank's hurt his paw and has to stay inside until it's healed properly.'

'Not a problem at all. I'll make sure he stays in.'

'Thank you so much. I should be back by Sunday at the latest, so it's just tomorrow and Sunday morning. I'll leave his food out in the kitchen on the side. Here's the spare key.'

'That's absolutely fine, dear. Any news on who wrote those awful letters? I've been thinking about you.' She pats my shoulder. 'Wondering about it, you know. About who would do such a thing.'

'The police don't know anything yet.'

She tuts. 'But you're okay, yes?'

I pause. I don't have time to get into the saga of my life right now. 'Yes, I'm fine, thanks. Just going away with my sister for a few days.'

She frowns and then her eyes light up. 'Ah, yes, Emma Beresford. Haven't seen her since school. One of the brightest pupils we ever had. Not that you weren't bright, dear,' she adds. 'It's just that Emma had an extremely scientific brain. What's she up to these days?'

'Cancer research scientist.'

'Is she, by golly? Well, isn't that something. Do pass on my best wishes.'

'Of course, and thanks so much again for looking after Frank.'

'My pleasure. Where is it you're off to?'

'Only up the road – a holiday home just outside Rodmarton.'

'Lovely. And what about Joe? Is he going with you?'

My breath catches in my throat. 'No. Just me and Emma. Joe… he's not here at the moment.'

'Well, do have a wonderful time. I hope this storm doesn't ruin your stay.'

'I don't mind a bit of rain. Hoping it'll clear up by tomorrow. Thanks, Mrs P.'

She gives me one of her twinkly smiles and we wave goodbye to one another. As I head back home, my stomach flutters with nerves and anticipation. I can't believe my sister and I are back on speaking terms. I never thought it would happen. I thought she had crossed a line over which there was no coming back. And while my heart is happy to have her in my life again, it's also aching from Joe's betrayal.

Emma and I spend the next half hour packing. 'We can take my car if you like?' she says, carrying a small case down the stairs.

I follow her down with a holdall full of swimming gear and towels. 'We'd better go in separate cars. I still have work tomorrow.'

'Oh, yeah. Okay.'

Finally, with a last cuddle for Frank, I lock up the house, and Emma and I step out into the dusky gloom, the first heavy spots of rain beginning to fall. Now that we're actually going, I'm panicking about leaving Frank on his own in the storm. Thunder doesn't normally bother him, but I still feel guilty. *Don't be ridiculous, he'll be fine*. Mrs P will look out for him. And anyway, I need this break.

Emma follows my battered Polo in her grown-up Prius, its headlights a steady glare in my rear-view mirror as I crawl along, squinting through the windscreen. The rain is hammering down now and my wipers are almost ineffective, even though they're on full blast. The sky is black as thunder, and lightning growls and flashes in unison, a violent concerto accompanying our journey. Of all the times for the weather to break, why did it have to choose now, when we're heading to a beautiful house and garden with a swimming pool? Never mind. Think positive. Might be fun to have a midnight swim in the rain.

We turn off the main road onto a narrow country lane with no road markings, bordered by high hedgerows. The lane twists and turns and I'm glad I didn't decide to come here alone. It already feels a long way from civilisation. Up ahead I spy a pale wooden signpost, so I slow down even further until I'm right up close to it. The sign says *The Elms* and then underneath *Private lane, no turning*. This is the place.

The signpost points left, so I switch on my indicator and turn down the lane, which soon opens up into an impressive tree-lined driveway with open fields to my left and right. I flick my headlights on to full beam and gasp as a building is illuminated up ahead. Even in the torrential rain, it is beautiful – a honey-coloured, stone country house with a slate roof topped off with several clusters of chimney pots. Two bright yellow urns of conical clipped box hedge sit sentry-like outside a wooden front door and swaying wisteria clings to the exterior, determined that the storm won't shake it free.

I come to a stop on the vast gravel drive and Emma pulls up alongside me as the ultra-bright security lights flick on. After I switch off the engine, the sound and scale of the storm becomes even more apparent. The whine of the wind and the hammering rain outside seem even more ferocious this far from town. I push open the car door and make a run for the front entrance, which luckily has a wooden porch to shelter me somewhat. Emma joins me, panting and laughing. We're already soaked from the short run from car to porch.

'This is unbelievable!' she cries.

'What, the house or the weather?'

'Both!'

I locate the metal box on the wall and punch in the code. After a couple of failed attempts, the front of the box finally drops open and I take out the bunch of keys and unlock the door.

Emma and I step into the wide hallway, but before I can take in my new surroundings, I have to deal with the alarm. It's beeping on the wall to my right and I fumble with my phone to find the code Ruby sent. Finally I locate her message and key in the four digits. The beeping stops.

Emma is walking in a slow circle, staring wide-eyed around the massive entrance hall. The interior is more gorgeous in real life than we could have imagined, with limestone floors and twinkling chandeliers. There's a warm, homely smell of herbs and vanilla, and of lilies from the fresh flowers, which sit in crystal vases on the polished antique console table. We walk through glass doors to a massive kitchen with dove-grey units and marble counter tops. A cream Aga sits in the corner, and there's a silver American-style fridge-freezer as well as a breakfast bar lined with Heritage-coloured stools.

'Can we live here permanently?' Emma asks.

I nod. 'I vote we stay here forever and never leave.'

The kitchen leads on to a more formal dining area which, in turn, leads into a spacious but cosy lounge furnished with velvet sofas and scatter cushions, and a marble fireplace framing a wood-burning stove. But the real joy of this place has to be the vaulted-ceilinged, wooden-framed garden room, which looks out on to what must be a thirty-foot, floodlit outdoor swimming pool, its aqua surface churning and frothing beneath the relentless rain. Emma and I gaze in wonder at the pool, unable to tear our eyes away.

'I know it's peeing down out there, but we have to go in, right?' Emma asks.

I grin.

We get our stuff from the cars, get changed and run, squealing, across the dark slate patio and into the pool. As I dive beneath the surface, the stress and anxiety of the past few days recede along with the noise of the storm. All I hear is a dull whooshing in my ears as the warm water ripples over my skin. Before too long, my lungs cry out for air and I surface with a gasp, treading water. Emma is lying on her back with her eyes closed, letting the rainwater batter her skin.

Although it's only up the road from Malmesbury, this place feels like a million miles away from home, from reality, from all my problems. I swim to the edge and rest my arms on the side. Night stretches away into darkness beyond the pool, until a flash of lightning illuminates the countryside – swathes of dark green velvet rolling on into infinity. As the landscape is plunged back into darkness, I give a shiver as though someone has walked over my grave. I'm reminded that somewhere out there in the storm-lashed darkness, our stalker could be planning their next move. But at least here in this secret spot we're safe for a while.

At least, I hope so.

With just one small step, I can change everything.

I can walk away and take the 'sane' route. Or I can carry on and see what happens. See if I can even things up a little. Make them feel how I feel. Make them know that their safe, secure, cosy little life is balanced on the edge of a razor-sharp blade. I could push them off into an abyss or I could push down hard and slice their life in two.

No. It's too late to walk away.

CHAPTER FORTY-ONE

Dried off from our swim, and wearing the fluffy grey robes we found in our rooms, Emma and I open a bottle of complimentary wine and curl up on squashy sofas in the garden room. We sit in companionable silence for a few moments while I drink in my surroundings: the dark rain bouncing off the indigo pool, the liquid gold of my wine.

'What a place,' Emma says with a yawn. 'When I got that fake text message, I never for one second thought it would lead to us relaxing in a five-star holiday home. What a mad evening.'

I take a sip of wine, enjoying the burn at the back of my throat. 'Here's to my lovely neighbour,' I say, lifting my glass in a toast.

'Yeah, massive cheers to your neighbour.' Emma raises her glass too and then gives me a long look. 'How are you doing, Lizzy?'

'How am I doing?'

'Yeah, you know, after Joe…'

I purse my lips and remember the leaden feeling in my guts. 'I don't know how I'm doing, to be honest. It's all a bit surreal. I wish I could erase Joe from my mind. I wish I'd never met him.' My voice cracks. 'And it's even weirder because of all this other stuff going on.'

Emma nods. 'I know.'

'Who do you think it could be?'

She stares out at the floodlit pool for a moment. 'I know I might be way off base, but you don't think it could be *Joe*, do you?'

I give a grim laugh. 'Believe me, I've thought about it. But you didn't see his reaction when I told him about getting the letters. He went all protective and macho. Whoever it is, he wanted to beat them up. I really don't think it is him. Although, to be honest, I have no real idea.'

'Okay. I just thought, because of our history, and the fact that he lied to you for so long. Maybe he's…' She tails off.

'Got a screw loose?' I inhale deeply. 'Do you know what, Ems? I'm sick of the whole bloody thing. Shall we make a pact not to talk about Joe or the "S" word while we're here? Treat this place like it's a real holiday from our lives out there.' I use my glass to point to the dark fields beyond the pool.

'Okay, yes. Good idea. Agreed.'

Emma and I spend the next couple of hours reminiscing about our shared past and catching up on our careers, on funny incidents at work and other non-threatening topics of conversation. We polish off the wine and demolish the complimentary bread, cheese and olives.

'I wish you didn't have to go into work tomorrow,' she says.

'I know, but I'll come straight back here afterwards and we can have another fab evening. I'll pick up some groceries on the way over so we can have something proper to eat.'

'No, that's okay. You're working. I'll nip out and get some stuff during the day.'

'Thanks, Ems. I'm so happy we're friends again. It's weird, but it feels like we were never not friends. Almost like it never happened.'

She shrugs, and I see a shadow flit across her features.

'Sorry. That was a stupid thing to say. Of course it happened. And it was my fault for letting it happen.'

'Let's not rake over it all again,' Emma says. 'I'm just nipping to the loo.' She gets to her feet and leaves the garden room. The rain has eased a little, the thunder now a distant rumble from another village. I'm tired and a little drunk and I think I need to go to bed, especially as I have to get up early tomorrow. I close my eyes, but I mustn't fall asleep here. I need to brush my teeth and take my make-up off. I need to take advantage of that lovely big bed upstairs.

I wake to a strange, dull, clanking sound. Like metal on concrete. It's pitch-black and everything feels strange. Then I remember, I'm in the holiday house. I fell asleep on the sofa. Emma woke me up, and helped me stagger into my beautiful bedroom with its French-style furniture and floral bedspread.

What *is* that noise? My head thumps along with the weird banging from outside. I drank far too much wine last night; I'm not used to it. I reach out to the side, hoping my fingers will alight upon a bedside light. After a few seconds of finding nothing, *bingo*. I locate the switch, turn it on and blink my eyes open in the soft light.

My phone says it's 2.45 a.m. What the hell is going on out there? Maybe the house is next to a farm and it's some weird machinery making that noise. But come *on*, at this time of the morning? And anyway, the clanking sounds closer than that. Like it's emanating from the back of the house… by the pool. My skin tightens and the hairs stand up on my bare arms. I sit up, suddenly wide awake, my senses on high alert. Could it be Emma out there? No. What would she be doing at this time of night? I slide out of bed and scrabble about in my case for something to wear. I throw a cotton dress over my head and pad out onto the landing. The noise is definitely louder out here.

Emma's room is next to mine, but her door is closed. I wonder, should I knock? Or should I just tiptoe in? Maybe I should leave her sleeping and go to investigate the noise myself. But I'm scared. It's dark outside. I don't even remember locking up last night. Did we leave any of the doors open?

The clanking noise stops. I freeze and cock my ear.

What if that means whoever was making the noise is already inside the house?

With a dry mouth and shaking knees, I open my sister's door and creep into her room. I daren't turn on her light in case we have an intruder and they see the sudden brightness.

'Emma!' I hiss. 'Emma, wake up!' Is she even in here? Maybe it *is* her downstairs. But goodness knows what she's doing if it is. Maybe she's sleepwalking. I bash my shin into the end of the bed and swear under my breath.

A moan comes from the bed.

'Emma?' I say, a little louder this time.

Another unintelligible mumble. And then, 'Lizzy? Is that you? What's the matter?' Her voice is thick with sleep and confusion.

'I think there's someone outside.'

'What? Are you sure?'

'No, but I heard a weird noise out there, and now it's gone quiet.' I make out the dark shape of my sister sitting up in bed.

'Probably foxes.'

'I don't think so. It was loud. It sounded… metallic.'

'Okay, give me a sec to wake up.' She stretches noisily and I shush her.

'There might be someone inside the house,' I warn.

'Shit. Really? Do you think so?' Now she sounds properly wide awake. The bed creaks as she gets out and takes my hand. I grip it tightly.

Out on the landing, I notice she's wearing the nightshirt I lent her, but it swamps her slender frame. The lamp from my bedroom gives us just enough light to see by as we make our way cautiously down the carpeted stairs. We stop and I stifle a squeal at a sudden noise from outside. It sounds like a piece of patio furniture being dragged across the ground.

'Okay, there's definitely someone out there,' I whisper.

'Ya think?' Emma replies, her sarcasm trying to cover up her fear.

We head across the hall through the dark kitchen and over to the garden room, our tiptoes as light as dandelion seeds. The house no longer feels like a safe hideaway or a sanctuary. It's too big, too strange and unfamiliar. I realise too late – it's too remote. I want to be at home in my little cottage.

The garden room doors are wide open, creaking back and forth in the breeze. The rain has stopped, but the air is cool and damp. The pool area beyond is in darkness.

'Did you close those doors before we went to bed?' I whisper to Emma.

'Yes, I bloody did. Someone's opened them.'

'Shall we just run?' I suggest. 'Go back to our cars and get the hell out of here?'

'Good idea,' Emma says, pulling me back. 'Have you got your phone?'

I grimace. 'No. Left it upstairs.'

'Leave it. Let's just go.'

'My car keys are upstairs too.'

'Fuck, so are mine.'

My eyes are becoming accustomed to the gloom, and out through the doors, I spy a dark shape moving beyond the pool. 'Emma,' I hiss.

'I see,' she says.

We're frozen in place, rooted to the spot in the garden room, staring outside. I think about running into the kitchen and grabbing a knife. But my legs won't move, and I can't leave Emma.

Around the side of the pool, a shadowy figure is walking towards us.

Slowly, deliberately, someone is heading our way.

CHAPTER FORTY-TWO

The security lights click on as the person draws closer to the house. When I see who it is, I relax and let go of my sister's hand.

'It's fine,' I say to Emma with a smile. 'I know her.'

'Well, I don't! Who is she?' Emma hisses.

'You scared us to death!' I call out with a laugh. 'What are you doing here? I thought you were away this weekend. Did you decide not to go? Emma and I can leave if you want to stay here instead.' I'm smiling, but it's a bit much, showing up at this hour. She could surely have waited until the morning.

'Who *is* that?' Emma hisses.

'My neighbour, Ruby,' I explain in a low whisper. 'The one who said we can stay here. Maybe she changed her mind. Or maybe there's some kind of problem.'

Ruby has an odd smile on her face. She stops where she is and stares strangely at me and Emma. I notice her appearance is quite different to normal. Her face is make-up free and she's wearing jeans and a T-shirt instead of one of her usual skimpy outfits. She seems somehow older.

Emma is nudging me in the ribs and pointing to the far side of the pool. 'Is that...' And then she cries, 'Dad? Is that you?'

I whip my gaze over to where Emma is staring, shocked to see our father sitting on the edge of the pool with his legs dangling in the water. But stranger than that – he's got something tied around his mouth. Some kind of... gag! And then my eyes drop to his lap, which seems to be covered in some dark, amorphous shape. It looks like a coiled iron chain.

'Dad!' I cry, and start to move towards him, Emma by my side.

'Stay where you are!' Ruby says firmly, walking quickly back towards him.

Emma and I hesitate, automatically heeding her words. Just as I decide to ignore Ruby's instruction, she speaks again:

'He's chained to a concrete parasol base,' she says. Even her voice sounds older. Her Bristol accent has completely disappeared and she sounds less scatty, less bubbly, less… *Ruby*. 'His wrists and ankles are zip-tied. If either of you takes a step closer, I'll wheel the base into the pool and poor old Daddy will be pulled in and dragged to the bottom. The chain's locked around his waist. It's shorter than the depth of the pool. So even if you do reach him before his lungs fill with water, you won't be able to pull him out.'

Emma squeals.

I go rigid. Am I having a nightmare? The air is damp, and the faint scent of chlorine catches in the back of my throat. I don't understand what's going on. Why is Ruby here? Why does she have Dad chained up? Why is she threatening to hurt him? None of this makes any sense. Dad is staring at us, his eyes wide. He's trying to speak, but the gag is doing its job of silencing him.

'Emma,' I whisper. 'I think we've found our stalker.'

'Who *is* she?'

'Ruby. My neighbour.'

'Yeah, but—'

'Can you both please shut up!' Ruby cries. 'I can hear you. Your pathetic attempts to whisper aren't working.'

I rack my brains to think what I could have done to offend my neighbour. Did I say something out of line? Did I snub her? Was I rude? Were Joe and I bad neighbours? I can't think of a single thing. And why would any of that involve Emma? Or Dad?

'Don't worry,' she drawls, tossing her hair back with a flick of her hand. 'I'll explain what's going on. You don't think I'd go to all this trouble without telling you what Daddy dearest has been up to.'

'Was it you who sent us all those letters?' Emma cries.

'I'll get to that. Didn't I just tell you to shut your mouth?'

I gasp at Ruby's vicious tone. Emma stiffens beside me but she does as Ruby asks and stops talking. The night air is cool after the storm. A few spatters of rain fall on my face, droplets from a nearby tree, blown down by the gusting wind. I wipe them away with my fingers and wrap my arms around my body to try to keep from shivering.

'So,' Ruby says. 'Here's what you need to know. My name is Ruby Davies and I'm from Bristol. I'm twenty-three years old.'

This isn't new information to me. But I guess she might be saying this stuff for Emma's benefit, and maybe Dad's. Does Ruby really mean to harm him? Will she harm me and Emma? But there's only one of her, and there are three of us. She's not holding any kind of weapon, unless she has a knife or gun concealed in her waistband. If she makes a move to hurt Dad, I reckon I can dive in and try to save him. But how heavy is that chain? Would I be strong enough to pull him out of the water with the concrete parasol base and the chain? Maybe if both Emma and I dive in together. But what if Ruby tries to stop us? All these scenarios whirl around my brain as I try to concentrate on what she's saying. How can this be real?

'My mum, Sue, brought me up on her own.' Ruby is speaking directly to me and Emma. She isn't paying any attention to our father at this point. 'She was a single mum and she had a hard time. We were always skint. She was always stressed about money and where we were going to live – one grotty flat after another. Always in dodgy areas with dodgy neighbours, blah, blah, blah. But who cares, right? There's plenty of single mums out there with no support and no money. Anyway, me and Mum, we got on all right. We argued, you know, like families do, but I loved her, my mum. She was everything to me.

'So, when she got cancer last year, I was gutted. She only took two months to die. Bam. That was it. Suddenly, no more Mum. I was on my own. No siblings, no aunts or uncles, no grandparents, cousins, whatever. Just me. Fine. That's fine. I miss my mum, but I've always been tough. I can cope on my own. It helps that I look good. That men are drawn to me.' She flicks her eyes across to Dad, licks her lips.

I'm getting a queasy feeling in my throat. I hope she isn't implying that my dad has done anything inappropriate. He wouldn't. He's not like that. Not with a girl young enough to be his daughter.

'So, you can imagine,' Ruby continues, 'that it came as a bit of a shock when I was going through Mum's things and I found a letter from my dad – who I'd never met, by the way. Mum told me he died just before I was born.' Ruby reaches into the back pocket of her jeans and pulls out what looks like a piece of folded paper. 'Do you want me to read it to you?'

Nobody answers her. I think we're too mesmerised by her story. Too stunned. But she doesn't seem to need a response. Ruby unfolds the paper and clears her throat.

Dear Sue,

I got your note, and I'm sorry to hear your news. In another lifetime, I'd want us to be together. But you already know my situation. You know I have a wife and two young girls. I can't leave them. So I'm really sorry, but I think it's best if we don't see each other any more. You shouldn't let your predicament hold you back, so I really think you should have an abortion. It's the best thing. Then you can forget me and make a new start. Find someone who deserves you. I'm enclosing some money in case there are any expenses, or in case you have to stop working while you have the procedure. I'm leaving Bristol, but I'll never forget you and our time together.

Wishing you all the best.

Yours,

Tony

CHAPTER FORTY-THREE

I gasp. Emma clutches my arm so tightly it hurts.

Ruby stops talking, refolds the letter and slots it back in her pocket. Her voice was shaking near the end of the letter, yet she remains dry-eyed, her face colourless and unreadable under the security lighting.

I shift my gaze to look at Dad. He's staring at Ruby, shaking his head, tears streaming down his face. I can hardly believe what Ruby has just read us. But it must be true to elicit such a reaction from Dad.

'In case you didn't "get it",' Ruby says, making air quotes, 'Tony here is my biological father. Which means…'

'… we're your sisters,' Emma finishes.

'Surprise!' Ruby says without enthusiasm. 'I did some family history research and tracked him down on Facebook. I found you two first. Only I wasn't sure you were related as you weren't Facebook friends. But you both looked similar to each other, and to me. And the name fit. And you were both the daughters of Tony Beresford, who was originally from Bristol, but who moved with his family to Malmesbury just before I was born.

'So, from having no family at all, I found out I had this whole other family. Only, you didn't want me. You would rather I was dead and buried. You would rather I had never existed at all.'

'That's not true!' I cry. 'If we'd known you existed we would've—'

'You would've *what*!' she spits, putting her hands on her hips. 'You would have welcomed me with open arms? I don't think so. You're both as bad as he is. You two had each other. You had everything. But you let some stupid fuckwit get between you. How can you let an idiot boyfriend ruin your family bond? You're sisters. But you ignored each another for years. Neither of you deserves to have a sister. You don't deserve your family. And Daddy doesn't deserve you, either.'

She begins pacing up and down by the side of the pool. If only she were on this side, I could charge and push her in, buy us some time to free Dad and get out of here. Call the police.

'So, yeah, I sent you the letters,' she continues. 'I thought, if a letter is good enough for dear old Tony Beresford to send to my mum, then letters will be good enough for his daughters. Letters, and a few other little additions to spice things up,' she says with a smirk.

I shudder when I think back to my day in Bristol. Being pushed into the road. Seeing a flash of auburn hair – hair exactly like Emma's. But it wasn't Emma. It was Ruby. 'You pushed me!' I cry.

'I did. I pushed you both. And you fell, and you cried and you whined and you were scared. And I was glad. Because I had years of being scared and pushed around. And Mum couldn't protect me all the time. I wanted you to have a taste of what it was like. Of what your dad let me and Mum live through. He could have helped us out. He could have checked up to see how we were doing. But instead, he wrote his little letter and he ran away and left us to it.' She stops pacing and turns to look at my dad. 'Out of sight, out of mind, hey, Tones?

'I was just a dirty little secret. Something to be ashamed of, while you two were Daddy's pride and joy. His two precious little girls. Yeah, well, thanks a lot, Dad. Thanks for nothing.'

I don't even know what to say to her revelation. Part of me can understand her anger. But the things she did… they're not the actions of a sane person. And I have no idea what she intends to do right now. Is she capable of hurting Dad? Of carrying out her threat to try to drown him?

'You know what gave me the most satisfaction out of all of this?' she says. 'Hurling the ashtray through Georgio's window. That ashtray was the only thing of Dad's that Mum owned. I treasured that piece of marble all my life. When I was a kid I used to stroke it. And I would think, my dad may be dead, but he touched this same piece of marble that I'm touching right now. And I thought by doing that I would be closer to him in heaven. How pathetic is that! Especially as he wasn't in heaven, he was a few miles up the road in Malmesbury. And instead of a little kid stroking a filthy ashtray, I could have been stroking his cheek. So, yeah, it felt good to smash that sucker through the shop window.'

Her story is heartbreaking, and terrifying. She is a wild, unpredictable, angry creature. She's been wronged, of that there's no doubt. But this has to stop now.

'Ruby,' I say carefully, 'I'm truly sorry. I honestly had no idea. And I wish you had been part of our lives. Dad made a terrible, terrible mistake. But now that we know… now that we know we have a sister… surely this can be a good thing. We can get to know one another. You can be part of our family.'

She looks down at the ground for a moment and then snaps her head back up. 'I've seen enough of your family to know that I don't want any part of it. You're both a couple of stuck-up bitches. Your mum's a clueless snob, and your dad is spineless. So thanks, but no thanks. I think I'm best off on my own.' Her face is flushed now and she wipes away a loose lock of hair with a hand that's shaking violently.

Her words are harsh, but she's angry. And maybe I would be angry, too, if I'd had her upbringing. But whatever happened in her life, it doesn't justify what she's done to us, and what she's doing to Dad. Yet I can't deny that I'm shocked by my father's history. He cheated on Mum. He has another daughter! But right now, I can't dwell on that. He's still my dad – and I need to help him.

'What about Ian?' I ask, trying to change the subject a little, trying to buy some more time so I can figure out what to do. 'I take it you used our neighbour to get to me?'

'Yeah,' she says disinterestedly. 'He was a small price to pay to be able to keep an eye on you. And you were oblivious, Lizzy. You bought my ditzy act, behaving like you were so much better than me. Patronising me and Ian like we were a couple of idiots.'

I shake my head. That's not how I remember it. I didn't patronise them, did I?

Emma takes a couple of tiny steps forward, and I shuffle up next to her. I get the feeling she's about to do something, but I'm nervous. If she makes a sudden move, Ruby could hurt Dad, and I'm not convinced we could save him in time.

'How did you know we'd come here?' Emma asks.

Ruby gives a dry laugh. 'You two were so easy to manipulate. First, I sent you the "wrongly addressed" letters to get you together. Then, once Joe was out of the picture, I sent Emma the fake text message to get you over to Lizzy's house. I'd already sowed the seed of the holiday home in your mind, Lizzy, so I was ninety per cent sure you'd go for it.'

'Did you really win a minibreak here?' I ask.

'You're joking, aren't you?' She laughs. 'I clean the place, that's all. They don't give away posh breaks to the likes of me. But I'm friends with the receptionist, and she let it slip that this house had a cancellation, so I thought it would be perfect for what I was planning.'

So we're trespassing. We've been enjoying this house without anyone's permission. And now I'm wondering what it is that Ruby's actually got planned. Did she bring us here purely for dramatic effect, or does she really mean to hurt Dad? I know what he did was very wrong. Was *awful*. And she has every right to be furious. But I can't let her harm him.

Emma and I inch forward a little further.

'Anyway,' Ruby says, walking over to the grey concrete parasol base next to Dad, 'we can talk all night about this crap, but that's not why we're here.'

I break out into a sweat. My whole body tenses. I get the feeling I'm going to have to dive into that pool any minute.

'No,' Ruby says. 'We're here to watch Daddy dear get what he deserves.'

Dad's eyes widen and he begins to struggle, but it's no good. He's tied too tightly and he's weighed down by the enormous, thick chain across his lap.

Ruby bends down and pushes the parasol base, which rumbles and slides into the pool with a heavy plop. Mine and Emma's screams drown out the hideous, slithering splashes as the chain unravels, pulled into the pool at an alarming speed.

'Dad!' Emma cries out.

I stagger to the edge of the pool, willing myself to stay strong, to not panic. I suck in a huge breath, preparing to dive. Preparing to pull my father out as soon as he's yanked into the water by the slithering chain. Emma is by my side.

Any second now…

CHAPTER FORTY-FOUR

Emma dives beneath the surface of the pool, and I'm just about to follow her when I hear Ruby cackling with laughter. The chain has disappeared into the pool but my father is still seated on the side, his legs dangling in the water, his face red, his eyes bright with shock.

What the hell?

Ruby mustn't have chained him up properly. But she is still laughing, doubled over with her hands on her hips. 'Oh my God! Your faces!' she cries. 'That was fucking hilarious.'

I step back from the edge as Emma surfaces, treading water, and spins around to face me, a look of confusion on her face. All I know is that Dad is safe. He's not about to drown. And then I march around the pool towards Ruby. Any pity I felt for her has now been suffocated by a white-hot fury. My heart pounds and my face burns.

'That was priceless!' she says, still laughing. 'You actually though I was going to kill him. Oh, I wish I'd videoed it.'

'You mental bitch!' I cry.

As I approach her, Ruby's laughter peters out. 'Come on. He deserved it. You all did. What's one moment of fear compared to the lifetime of crap I've had to put up with? I'd say we're not even close to being even.'

As I close in on Ruby, Emma is pulling herself up out of the pool by Dad's side. With dripping fingers, she starts working his gag loose.

'You're mad,' I say to Ruby through gritted teeth. 'You need help. Serious help.' I can't bear to look at her smug face. Memories of the past few weeks' stresses and fears scroll through my mind – a catalogue of terror. How could she have put me and Emma through all that? We had no clue about my father, or about who she really is, so why did she feel it necessary to punish us? But she doesn't seem in the least bit remorseful. She actually believes that Emma and I deserved what she put us through.

All the anxiety, terror and anger rush to the surface and I charge the final few feet towards my half-sister. With all the force I can muster, I push her into the swimming pool. She topples sideways, her hands flailing out to try and stop herself falling, but it's too late. A shove into a warm pool might not be much of a punishment, but it feels good. The water splashes up and over me, but I don't care about that. I have to check on Dad, see if he's okay. I'm mad at him, too, but I'm also worried about what this ordeal has done to him. Whether he might need medical help.

'We need some scissors or a knife to cut him loose,' Emma says, finally pulling down his gag so it hangs around his neck. She hugs our shivering father who's breathing really heavily, his eyes wild and staring. His ankles are tied, his hands still bound behind his back.

'Ruby,' he gasps.

'I know, Dad,' I say, stroking his arm. 'It's okay. She can't hurt you now.'

'No,' he cries, jerking his head forward. 'Ruby!'

Emma and I turn to see her flailing in the centre of the pool. Her hands rising up and clawing at the air while her head keeps disappearing beneath the water. When she resurfaces briefly, her eyes are panicked.

I realise she can't swim! She's drowning, gasping for air, and she can't get enough into her lungs to cry for help so her struggle is silent, aside from a few pathetic splashes.

'Get her!' Dad cries. 'Pull her out!'

'We should bloody well leave her there,' I snap.

But now she's just a dark shape. Sinking.

'Lizzy! Emma!' Dad roars. 'You pull her out of there. Right now!' He's struggling against his restraints, but he's tied up tight.

Much as I want to throttle Ruby right now, I know Dad's right. I jump into the pool, push myself down and open my eyes to see a mass of red hair floating around Ruby's white, terrified face. Bubbles stream upwards from her mouth and nostrils. I kick over towards her and try to hook my arm around her body, but she's thrashing too wildly and I can't get close enough to establish a firm grip. I suddenly realise she truly is in danger of drowning. And I don't want that. I really don't. Despite what she did.

Emma is in the water now, and she manages to grab hold of one of Ruby's arms. She pulls it down around her shoulders. I swim up close and yank Ruby's other arm down around my own shoulders. Together, Emma and I kick up to the surface, hard. As we hit the air, Ruby splutters, still kicking and flailing. But Emma and I grip her tightly. Between us, we tow her to the edge and hoist her out of the water.

'Is she all right?' Dad asks, his eyes filled with concern as Ruby lies on her side, wheezing and retching.

Emma and I are too exhausted to reply. We pull ourselves out of the pool and sit on the side, gasping to get our breath back. My arms are aching and my legs are going to be bruised to hell where Ruby was thrashing about so much. We're going to have to get both Dad and Ruby checked out by a doctor. But right this second, I need to just sit here. Relieved to be alive. For the nightmare to be over.

CHAPTER FORTY-FIVE

Six months later

Checking the satnav in Emma's Prius, I see we're only ten minutes away from our destination. I pick at the skin around my nails, wondering for the millionth time whether or not this is a good idea.

'Remind me why we're doing this again?' I ask.

'It'll be fine,' Emma replies, weaving in and out of the lanes like a Formula One driver. This is Emma's route to work, so she knows the roads like the back of her hand. But her rally driving is making me nervous. The roads are icy and it's beginning to sleet.

I lean back and take a deep breath. It was Emma who persuaded me to come today. She stressed the fact that Ruby is mentally ill and needs our support. Part of me knows Emma is right. *She's always right.* But the other part of me wants to forget Ruby exists. Sister or no sister, the girl tried to kill me. She assaulted Emma and she threatened to kill Dad, but she actually pushed me into a stream of traffic. I get the feeling she hated me the most. I give a shiver.

'Want me switch on the heated seats?' Emma asks.

'Thanks, but no. Last time I got into a car with heated seats, it felt like I was coming down with flu. You know, that slow warm feeling spreading over your back – it's freaky.'

'Suit yourself. I *love* them.'

'Weirdo,' I tease.

Anyway, whatever Ruby's done, I've agreed to go with Emma today to visit her. She's in Bristol Hospital's psychiatric care unit where she's been receiving treatment – in the secure wing, thankfully. After being taken into police custody, Ruby was eventually given a hospital order by the court. This will stay in effect until she's no longer deemed a risk to the public. Her doctors think she'll need to remain there for a long time to come. Maybe even years.

'So, she's expecting us?' I ask.

'Yeah. Apparently, she's making good progress. She specifically asked to see us both.'

Dad already visits Ruby on a weekly basis. He's trying to make amends for abandoning her and her mum all those years ago. Ultimately, he's a good man who's made some terrible decisions. But he's sorry for the past. Sorry for all the hurt he's caused. Hurt which has rippled through all of our lives.

With regard to my own mother, my parents are no longer together. She threw him out when she heard about his affair with Sue Davies. And she was absolutely beside herself when she discovered that he has another child. Funnily enough, it's brought me and Mum closer together. Maybe because we're both newly single. Maybe because she's no longer living what she sees as 'the perfect life'. She now phones me to moan about Dad and all his shortcomings. We've even taken to meeting up for a coffee every month or so, and she's learnt to bite her tongue if I decide to have *cake* with my coffee.

Dad is bunking down in his arch-enemy Ray's house. Ray is a widower and lives alone, so Dad rents out one of his spare rooms. They've joined forces in their shared microbrewery hobby, and I actually think Dad has never been happier; which is tough on Mum. I still love him, but I'm realising that my perfect dad isn't quite so perfect after all.

Over the past six months, my life has changed beyond all recognition. Joe and I split up for good. He begged and wheedled and apologised, but there was nothing he could say to change my mind. He crossed the line, and I let myself be blinded to the truth. When Joe betrayed me, he made sure Emma and I were separated for good, like he did with all my relationships, gradually cutting me off from my friends and family until he was the only person in my life. How did I let myself get sucked into *that* situation? I'll never make that mistake again.

I've given up the cottage – I even turned down George's generous offer of a couple of months' half-price rent. I also left my beloved job at Georgio's, and now have a new position managing an upmarket boutique in Bristol.

I'm staying in Emma and Mike's spare room until I can get myself sorted with a flat-share. Unfortunately their apartment block doesn't allow pets, so Mrs P is looking after my beloved Frank until I'm settled somewhere cat-friendly. But my long-term plan is to go to uni to study fashion. They have a few interesting degree courses here in Bristol, so I'm going to apply next year. I couldn't have done any of this without Emma. She's been my lifeline. My rock. I still carry enormous guilt for not speaking to her sooner – I pushed her away, instead of listening to her. Instead of believing her.

Sadly, Pippa and I never made up. I'm still in touch with Seb, though. Unexpectedly, he's proved to be a good friend over the past few months. Seb said Pippa was too embarrassed and humiliated to see me again. I can't really blame her, but it's a shame because I really did consider her to be a good friend. I know I was too stubborn to reach out to Emma for all those years, but I didn't want to make the same mistake twice. So I tried to reach out to Pippa, to be the first to hold out an olive branch, but she never returned my calls. Maybe she'll change her mind and give me a call. But I won't hold my breath.

Her family have had a bit of good luck, though – a television production company has started filming a historical drama at the

Manor House. As well as paying for a lot of the house repairs, their fees are really generous and they think it could be a long-term thing, as the drama is based on a series of twelve books, which means twelve seasons. It also means that the Hargreaves could open the house up to tourists who will probably come flocking after the show airs next spring.

Emma turns into the hospital car park and follows the signs to the psychiatric wing. My heart is thumping a little harder than usual. I haven't seen my half-sister since that terrible night. I wonder if she will still be hostile towards me. I don't think I can take any more confrontation. Not now that I'm finally getting my life back on an even keel.

'Maybe this isn't such a good idea,' I begin.

'It's one hour out of your life, Lizzy.'

'Yes, but what if—'

'We need to do this. It's closure. It's healthy.'

I rub my forehead, knowing she's right but wishing she wasn't. 'Fine, okay, let's do it. But don't leave me alone with her.'

'Don't worry, I won't.'

'Promise?'

'Promise.'

It's warm inside the hospital unit, and the air smells of medicine, sterilised floors and general mustiness. Ruby is sitting at a wooden table in a large, depressing-looking lounge with blue carpet tiles on the floor and an assortment of mismatched furniture dotted about the room. A couple of other people are sitting chatting in low voices, and two orderlies in uniform are standing by the door, but I don't pay them much attention. All my focus is now on Ruby. With her hair tied back in a simple ponytail and her skin free of make-up, she looks so young. And vulnerable.

I glance at Emma, but her gaze, too, is focused on our half-sister.

'Hi,' Emma says.

Ruby nods and gives a small smile.

We both sit opposite her and I immediately feel like this was the wrong thing to do. It now feels like it's us versus her. But it's too late to get up and move without it appearing strange, so I stay seated where I am.

'Thanks for coming,' Ruby says, her eyes darting from me to Emma. 'I appreciate it.'

I still can't get over how different she is from 'Ruby, my neighbour'. Her voice is lower, quieter, less hyper. But I don't know if that's down to her being in here, or if it's down to the act she'd been putting on for my benefit.

'How are you?' Emma asks.

Ruby shrugs. 'You know… I'm in a psych ward, doped up to the eyeballs.'

'Sorry.' Emma flushes.

'No, I'm sorry, that was flippant. I'm much better, thanks,' Ruby says. 'I want to apologise to both of you, for everything. I put you through hell. I know that.'

'You had a rough time. You were angry.' Emma is being far more forgiving than I feel. Now that I know Ruby is my sister, rather than just a neighbour, I can't seem to take my eyes off her. I notice things I never noticed before, like how she wrinkles her nose just like Emma. And how her cheeks dimple just like mine. It's uncanny.

'And what about you?' Ruby's gaze lands on me, but I can't quite catch her eye. My gaze slides away to a point beyond her shoulder. I wipe my clammy hands on my jeans and try to get my breathing under control.

'I'm fine,' I reply.

She nods. 'I really am sorry for what I did. I wasn't in my right mind. I'm still not… I'm unwell. But my doctor thinks I'll get better in time. It helps that our dad wants to have a relationship with me. I was mad at him, but he says he loves me, so…' She scratches hard at a flaky patch of skin on the back of her hand, then self-consciously moves both hands beneath the table.

'How did you get into my house?' I ask.

She flushes. 'Your back door was unlocked while you and Joe were cleaning your cars out the front. I crept in, and stole a set of your house, car and shop keys. Had them copied. It was easy.' She tells me this in a matter-of-fact way, like she's talking about a day out at the park. 'I guess I just wanted you to know that I was there. That I *existed.* But I didn't know how to tell you properly. I went about it all the wrong way.'

That's one way of putting it. 'Ruby,' I say, 'you tried to kill me. You pushed me into the path of an oncoming car.'

Ruby exhales through her mouth, making an 'o' shape. 'I never meant to try to kill you.' She bows her head. 'I was going to push you, the same way I pushed Emma. Just a shove to get you to take me seriously. But then I saw you standing there on the edge of the pavement, and I just thought… well, I didn't think. I let the rage take over. I have no excuse. I did a despicable thing…' She starts scratching at the patch on her hand once more. 'I don't expect your forgiveness. I just want you to know I truly am sorry. And I know talk is cheap, but it's all I have right now.'

'There's one more thing…' I say.

She gives a nod and I clench my fists. My nails dig into the palms of my hands.

'Frank…' I begin. 'My cat. Did you cut his paw? Was it *his* blood on the letter?' Strangely, out of everything that happened, this was the incident that upset me the most.

'No,' she says instantly.

'But the police confirmed that it was feline blood. They said—'

'I found Frank in our garden,' she explains in a matter-of-fact way, like she's telling me about something mundane. 'He was limping. I saw the blood and it gave me an idea. I admit, I did wipe his paw on the letter. But then I cleaned his cut and made sure he was okay. I know I've done some awful things, which I fully admit to, but I didn't do that. I didn't hurt Frank. I just… I used the situation to freak you out. I'm sorry,' she adds. 'But I'm not a monster.'

That's up for debate, I think.

What a mess. This girl is truly damaged. I don't know if she's always been this way, or if discovering the news about our dad tipped her over the edge. But whatever the reason, I realise that I'm glad she's getting help now. Sadness grips my chest. *I had a sister I never knew about*. Maybe if we'd known about Ruby when she was born, she wouldn't have ended up in this situation. Maybe we would have been close. The three of us. Too late for wishes. It is what it is. But at least something good has come out of all this: I have my older sister back in my life. I take Emma's hand under the table and give it a squeeze. Emma glances at me and smiles.

There's a phone vibrating somewhere. I reach down to my handbag, but it's not mine. Emma draws her mobile out of her purse, looks at the screen and frowns. 'It's Mike, I'd better take this. Back in a mo, okay?'

I nod and watch her leave the room, slightly uneasy that Emma is leaving me on my own with Ruby. She promised she wouldn't. But Ruby gives me a nervous smile. I realise this isn't easy for either of us. I guess we'll have to adjust to one another. Slowly.

'Of course,' Ruby says, 'you know they've got me all doped up in here, Lizzy.'

I nod, wary of speaking to her without Emma to back me up. 'I know. Does it feel strange?' I ask. 'Do you feel different on the medication? *Better?*'

'I don't know about *better*,' Ruby replies. 'At least I'm all nice and friendly in here. Not likely to do anything… unexpected.' She smiles and then fixes me with a strange look that sets my teeth on edge. 'But then again, I won't be in here forever.'

My stomach lurches. *Was that a threat?* Where the hell is Emma? She promised she wouldn't leave me alone with Ruby. I glance back towards the door, but there's still no sign of my older sister.

Ruby doesn't seem quite as stable now Emma's disappeared from the room. Is her whole apologetic vibe simply an act? It better not be. I hope she's not still a danger to me and Emma. I give a small shiver and wonder… am I safe? She's in a secure place now, but what happens once she's discharged? I'm sure someone as complex and devious as Ruby could fake sanity. Maybe not now, or next year, but some day she'll find a way to get out of here. And when that time comes, will I be looking over my shoulder for the rest of my life?

EPILOGUE

I march out of the lounge, past the orderlies, my heart pumping, my breathing erratic. I can't have this conversation anywhere near Lizzy. I keep walking until I reach the end of the corridor.

'What the hell are you doing, calling me here? I told you I was coming with Lizzy to the hospital this morning.'

'I know, I know. I'm sorry. I just… it's hard, being here while you're living over there with Lizzy, and with Mike. I need to see you. I need to see you right now.'

I give an exasperated sigh. Not this again. 'Look, I told you that I wasn't going to give Mike up. You knew the score and you agreed to it.'

'Yes, but that was back when I had Lizzy.' His voice turns petulant. 'Now it's just me on my own in a grotty bedsit…'

'Stop it.' I need to nip this in the bud right now. 'You listen to me. If you can't handle it, then we'll have to end things. I like having Lizzy around again. I'm not jeopardising that.'

'But we could—'

'No. You and I, we both agreed that you would tell her it was all your doing. You were happy to give her up so that I could have my sister back in my life. You don't have her any more. And you never will. You'll just have to accept it.' I realise I need to get him onside again so I take a breath and try to calm down. 'Look, I promise, you'll have me forever. But Mike stays in my life, and so does Lizzy.'

'Fine,' he growls. 'Okay, have it your way.' He pauses for a moment and I hear his breathing, ragged and desperate. Then his voice softens. 'You know I'd do anything for you, Emma. I love you.'

'I love you too.' My shoulders relax. I needn't have worried about him. I know he'll do anything for me. Ever since I cornered him in that seedy pub five years ago, he's been mine. True, he was reluctant to betray Lizzy at first, but after I kissed him that night – and the rest – I knew he'd do anything I asked. 'Joe, you know what we have is special, so don't spoil things, okay? I'll call you when it's safe.'

'Okay, I'm sorry.' His voice turns husky. 'You know, even your voice drives me crazy, Ems.'

I smile. 'Goodbye, Joe. I'll see you soon, and when I do my voice won't be the only thing driving you crazy.'

I end the call, pat my face and smooth my hair. I need to compose myself before I go back in there.

Back to my sisters.

A LETTER FROM SHALINI

Thank you for reading my sixth psychological thriller *The Silent Sister*. I hope you enjoyed reading Lizzy's story as much as I enjoyed writing it. The story is set in Malmesbury where my mum used to own a lovely little clothes and gift shop, and where I had a Saturday job and worked during the holidays. Luckily, I didn't have a psycho stalker or a shop-lifting co-worker!

If you would like to keep up to date with my latest releases, just sign up here www.bookouture.com/shalini-boland and I'll let you know when I have a new book coming out.

I'm always grateful to get feedback about my books, so if you enjoyed my novel, I'd love it if you could post a short review online or tell your friends about it. Your reviews can also help new readers to discover one of my books for the first time.

When I'm not busy making up conversations with fictional characters, I adore chatting to my real-life readers, so please feel free to get in touch via my Facebook page, through Twitter, Goodreads or my website.

Thanks so much!
Shalini Boland x

ShaliniBolandAuthor

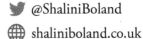

@ShaliniBoland

shaliniboland.co.uk

ACKNOWLEDGEMENTS

Thank you to everyone at Bookouture for publishing my books with such style and expertise. I feel extremely lucky to have your support. Special thanks to my incredibly talented publisher Natasha Harding for being so fantastic to work with. Your ideas are always the best!

Thanks also to the wonderful Ellen Gleeson, Lauren Finger, Peta Nightingale, Natalie Butlin and Alex Crow for everything you do. Thank you doesn't quite seem to cover it, but I really do appreciate you all.

A huge, great, squishy thank you to Publicity team Kim Nash and Noelle Holten who always ensure that my books get plenty of release-day love and more. You are truly awesome!

Thanks to my copy editor Donna Hillyer for your insightful comments. And to Jenny Page for such a great and thorough proofread. Also thank you to fabulous designer Emma Graves for yet another eye-catching cover.

Thank you Sammy H.K. Smith for advising on all the police-procedural aspects of my book. As always, any mistakes and embellishments in procedure are my own.

Thank you to Terry Harden, Deanna Finn, Julie Carey and Amara Gillo for being the best beta readers in the universe. I'm lucky to have your eagle eyes on my books.

Thank you to all the fabulous book bloggers out there who are so supportive and enthusiastic, giving up their time to read, review, blog and share on social media. You guys all rock. I'm also grateful to my readers who take the time to read, review or recommend my books. I appreciate your tremendous support and it's been great getting to know a lot of you.

Pete Boland, you're always there to help iron out plot wrinkles or make me a cuppa when I forget to come up for air. Couldn't do it without you.

Lightning Source UK Ltd.
Milton Keynes UK
UKHW021806010319
338299UK00014B/326/P

9 781786 815569